THE GROOTE PARK MURDER

'THE DETECTIVE STORY CLUB is a clearing house for the best detective and mystery stories chosen for you by a select committee of experts. Only the most ingenious crime stories will be published under the THE DETECTIVE STORY CLUB imprint. A special distinguishing stamp appears on the wrapper and title page of every THE DETECTIVE STORY CLUB book—the Man with the Gun. Always look for the Man with the Gun when buying a Crime book.'

Wm. Collins Sons & Co. Ltd., 1929

Now the Man with the Gun is back in this series of COLLINS CRIME CLUB reprints, and with him the chance to experience the classic books that influenced the Golden Age of crime fiction.

THE DETECTIVE STORY CLUB

FURTHER TITLES IN PREPARATION

THE
GROOTE PARK
MURDER

A STORY OF CRIME
BY

FREEMAN WILLS CROFTS

WITH AN INTRODUCTION BY
FREEMAN WILLS CROFTS

COLLINS
CRIME
CLUB

COLLINS CRIME CLUB
An imprint of HarperCollins*Publishers*
1 London Bridge Street
London SE1 9GF
www.harpercollins.co.uk

This edition 2017

First published in Great Britain by
W. Collins Sons & Co. Ltd 1923

A catalogue record for this book is available from the British Library

ISBN 978-0-00-815933-7

Typeset in Bulmer MT Std by
Palimpsest Book Production Ltd, Falkirk, Stirlingshire
Printed and bound in Great Britain by Clays Ltd, St Ives plc

MIX
Paper from
responsible sources
FSC™ C007454

INTRODUCTION

THE WRITING OF A DETECTIVE NOVEL

WE are going, you and I, to write a detective novel, or so I am informed. Let us see, then, how we would set about it and what we would find ourselves up against.

Necessarily we must follow a hypothetical method, for if we asked a hundred detective-novelists how they worked, we should probably get a hundred quite different replies. And we are going to write a *detective* story, which we are doubtless agreed deals with detection and in which the problem is supreme: not a thriller, which depends on conflict and thrills, nor yet a crime novel, which is the history of some particular crime, usually from the criminal's point of view.

Before we begin we must settle one or two points about our detective. Is he to be a gifted amateur, a professional private detective, or a man from the C.I.D.? Is he to be a 'character' or an ordinary humdrum citizen? Is he to work alone or to have a Watson? Suppose *you* settle these points? You have? Then let's get down to it.

If we're lucky we shall begin with a really good idea. This may be one of five kinds. Firstly, it may be an idea for the opening of our book: some dramatic situation or happening to excite and hold the reader's interest. The standard way of finding a body in the first chapter, if hackneyed, is hard to beat.

Secondly, our idea may be for the closing or climax of our book. This must also be dramatic. As an example I suggest the well-known situation in which Tom, who thinks Jack is dead and has impersonated him, is unexpectedly confronted with Jack in a police office or court of law.

Our idea, thirdly, may be for a good way of committing a crime, probably a murder. It should be novel and ingenious— but not too ingenious—and if possible concerned with things with which the man in the street is familiar. This is probably the most usual way of starting work on a book. Every detective fan will think of dozens of examples.

A fourth kind of idea on which to build a book is that we shall write about some definite crime, such as smuggling, gun-running, coining, arson, or frauds in high finance.

Lastly, our idea may be simply to place the action in a definite setting, such as a mining setting, or a golf or fishing setting, or to lay our scenes in a certain place: a bus or an office, an opium den or Canterbury Cathedral.

We may of course build our book on some idea which does not fall under one of these heads. For instance, Dr Austin Freeman's book, *The Red Thumb Mark*, was probably built on the idea that a fingerprint is not necessarily convincing evidence.

This then is the first stage in our work: getting the idea to start on. Our second stage is more difficult: we have to build up the plot on our idea.

We do this in a very simple, but very tedious way: we ask ourselves innumerable questions and think out the answers. One question invariably leads to another, and as we go on our plot gradually takes shape.

Suppose we have decided on a murder by antimony poisoning. We shall ask ourselves questions such as: Where does the murderer get the antimony? How does he administer it? What is his motive?

Suppose in answering this last question we choose greed: that he inherits money from the man he kills. At once new questions suggest themselves. What was the relationship between the two men? Why had the deceased left money to the other? And so on.

As we continue propounding and answering these questions,

we shall have the happiness of finding a story gradually growing out of nothing. We continue the good work 'til the whole happening is built up, from the first thought of the crime right down to its completion, together with the subterfuges the criminal adopts to secure his safety. A rough synopsis is then made, together with sketch maps of the important localities, short biographies of the principal characters, and a chronology of the main events.

It should be clearly understood that this synopsis is of the actual facts which are supposed to have happened: It is not a synopsis of the book. We don't get to the book 'til the third stage, for which, however, we are now ready.

In this third stage we reconsider the whole circumstances from a new viewpoint, the viewpoint of the person or persons through whom we are going to tell the story. What is the first thing that would have become known? Would it have been the finding of the body? If so, begin with that. What would then be done? The police would be sent for. What would they do? They would make certain enquiries, they would look for motives, they would find out who was in the neighbourhood when the crime was committed.

We continue working in this way 'til we have completed a second synopsis of the case, this time describing the gradual revealing of the details to the detective. As we do so, we find that we have to supply a good deal of fresh material. That means of course a new set of questions to be answered. There is, for instance, the very important problem of how the detective discovers the truth. He could if possible do so through some flaw inherent in the criminal's plans, unperceived 'til now by the reader. If, however, this can't be arranged, the necessary clues must be planted for the detective to find.

This second synopsis which, let us suppose, we have now completed, gives us the sequence of events right from the discovery of the crime up to the arrest and conviction of the criminal. It is, in other words, a *précis* of our book. We probably have to make another chronology giving the movements of the detective, as well possibly as more sketch maps. Then, having estimated the length of our various scenes and satisfied ourselves that our book is going to run to the required 80,000 words, we can proceed to our next stage.

The fourth stage is the actual writing, and there is nothing to be said about it except that we take the advice of the King in *Alice in Wonderland* and begin at the beginning, go on 'til we come to the end, and then stop.

When writing we invent the minor episodes. For instance, our synopsis may read: 'Detective finds paper in X's room.' We have now to think out how the detective obtains access to X's room, whereabouts the paper is hidden, and how the detective comes to look in that place.

The writing of the passages which give the necessary clues to the reader requires a lot of thought. *All* the clues must be given which he needs to enable him, by the use of his intelligence, to reach the truth. At the same time they must not be easy to pick up.

There are many tricks for concealing clues. The chief is perhaps to invert the sequence of events or to alter their connection. Suppose we want to tell the reader that the murderer is a good shot. If his skill be mentioned in connection with the shooting of the victim, the story is given away. But if it be brought out in relation to a shooting competition in another part of the book, the reader will probably miss its significance.

Let us now pause for a moment to consider our climax. In this we shall try to clear up as suddenly as possible what has been up to now a complete mystery. If on reaching the climax the reader says: 'Of course! Why didn't I think of that?' we shall have done our job well.

Well, we go over our manuscript, checking and cutting and patching and re-writing. Then having typed a fair copy, we try it on the dog: we get as many of our friends to read it as we can. We incorporate the more useful of their suggestions, and at last our book goes off, carefully registered, and with a magic name on the cover. Whereupon we settle down to wait.

FREEMAN WILLS CROFTS
1937

CONTENTS

PART I

SOUTH AFRICA

CHAPTER I

JOSEPH ASHE, signalman in the employment of the Union of South Africa Government Railways, stood in his box at the west end of Middeldorp station, gazing meditatively down the yard to the platforms beyond.

It was his week on night duty, which he took in rotation with two other men. Not by any stretch of the imagination could the night shift in this particular box be called sweated labour. For the best part of an hour—indeed, since he had wearied reading and re-reading yesterday's Middeldorp *Record*—Ashe had paced his cabin, or stood looking ruminatively out of its windows. For the slackest period of the twenty-four hours was just then drawing to a close. It was nearly six a.m., and since the north express had passed through shortly before four, no train had arrived or left. Except to let the engine of an early goods pass from the locomotive sheds opposite the cabin to the marshalling yards at the far end of the station, Ashe had not put his hand to a lever during the whole two hours.

He was now watching the platforms for the appearance of his mate, who was due to relieve him at six a.m. Every morning, when the hands of his clock drew to five minutes before the hour, the squat figure of the man next in the cycle would emerge from behind the Permanent Way Inspector's hut at the end of No. 1 Platform, as though operated by the timepiece on some extension of the cuckoo principle. Can in hand, the man would come down the ramp, pass along the side of the line, and, crossing the neck of a group of carriage sidings, would reach the box in time to take over at the hour.

Suddenly a bell rang sharply, a single, clear, imperious stroke.

Obedient, Ashe turned to an instrument placed at the back of the box, and marked with a brass label, 'Gunter's Kloof,' and pressed a plunger. Again and again the bell sounded, and Ashe, having replied in the same code, pushed in the plunger and held it steady. With a slight click, a little card bearing the word 'IN' in black letters on a white ground shot from behind a tiny window in the instrument, and another card bearing in white letters on a red ground the word 'OUT' took its place. Ashe released the plunger, and, glancing at the clock, turned to a book lying open on the desk, and laboriously entered in spidery figures the time—5.57 a.m. At the same moment the door opened, and the relief man appeared.

'That No. 17?' queried the newcomer, as he placed his can beside the little stove and hung up his coat.

'Ay, she's running twelve minutes late,' Ashe answered. 'Warned at fifty-seven.'

'No specials?'

'Not so far.'

Some further conversation passed between the two men, then Ashe, having signed off, took his can and stepped out of the box.

It was a brilliant morning in late November. The sun, still low in the sky, was pleasantly warm after the chill which always obtains at night in South African uplands. Not a cloud was visible, and the air was extraordinarily clear and thin. Objects stood out, sharply defined, and throwing deep black shadows. Except for the faint rumble of an engine creeping out of the round-house, everything was very still.

Ashe descended the cabin steps and took his way along the railway in the opposite direction to that in which his mate had approached. He lived in a western suburb, and the railway was his most direct way home. The tracks, which were eight wide opposite the cabin, gradually converged towards the west, 'til at the Ballat Road overbridge, a quarter of a mile away, they had shrunk to the single main line which, after wandering interminably across the country, ended at Cape Town, nearly one thousand miles distant.

Beyond the Ballat Road bridge, the line curved sharply to the left, and in a cutting some twenty feet deep ran for a couple of hundred yards to a short tunnel, which carried one of the main streets of the town, Dartie Avenue, at a skew angle across the railway. To be in the centre of a city, the stretch of line between these bridges was extraordinarily secluded. Busy though both the streets in question were, all view from them was cut off by tall boardings carried up from the parapet of each bridge, and placed there originally to prevent the steam of passing trains from startling horses. At the top of the cutting at each side of the line the boundary was marked by a five-foot stone wall. Behind that, on the left side—the inside of the curve—were the houses of the town. The right-hand wall divided the railway from the Groote Park, a botanical gardens of exceptional size and luxuriance.

Ashe trudged slowly along the four foot, his eyes on the ground and his thoughts dwelling with satisfaction on the hot rashers and the clean, white sheets he was so soon to enjoy. He had almost reached the Dartie Avenue Tunnel when, looking up suddenly at the dark opening in the grey stonework, he saw something which made him halt abruptly.

Lying in the right-hand offset, close against the masonry of the side, and about twenty yards inside the mouth, was a body, apparently a man's. Something in the attitude, even with the vague outline which was all that the gloom of the archway revealed, suggested disaster, and Ashe, after his first instinctive pause, hurried forward, half expecting what he would find.

His worst fears were confirmed as he reached the place and stood looking down with horror-stricken eyes at the battered and disfigured remains of what had once been a tall, strongly-built man. It was evident at a glance that he had been struck by a passing train, and there could be no doubt that death had been instantaneous. The injuries were terrible. The body seemed to have been dragged along the ground by the engine cow-catcher, rather than to have been struck and thrown cleanly aside. It looked even as if the head had got under the cow-catcher, for the back of the skull was crushed in like an eggshell, while the features were torn and unrecognisable as if from contact with the rough ballast. The back was similarly crushed and the chest scraped open. Three of the limbs were broken, and, what seemed to Ashe the most appalling spectacle of all, the fourth, the right arm, was entirely parted from the trunk and lay by itself between the rails some yards farther back along the line.

For some moments Ashe stood transfixed, overcome by the revolting sight. Then, pulling himself together, he turned and hurried back along the railway to report his discovery. 'No. 17,' the goods train he had accepted before going off duty, clattered past him near the Ballat Road bridge, and when he reached the station he found that its driver had seen the body and already given the alarm. The stationmaster, hastily summoned, had just arrived, and Ashe was able to let him have some additional details of the tragedy.

'Police job,' the stationmaster curtly decided. 'You say the body is thrown clear of the trains?'

'Up against the tunnel wall,' Ashe agreed.

'I'll go and 'phone police headquarters now,' went on the stationmaster. 'You tell that man that's just come off No. 17 that his engine will be wanted to run out to the place, and see Deane and get a passenger van shunted out. Then 'phone the west cabin what we're going to do.'

The stationmaster hurried off, and Ashe turned to carry out his orders. Ten minutes later the special pulled out, having on board the stationmaster, Ashe, Sergeant Clarke of the City Police, as well as Dr Bakker, a police surgeon, and two constables. It stopped a few yards short of the mouth of the tunnel, and the men, clambering down from the van, went forward on foot. Even the hardened nerves of the police were not proof against the horrible sight which met their eyes on reaching the body, and all six men stood for some moments, shocked into silence. Then, with a muttered oath, Sergeant Clarke took charge.

'We'll not touch anything for a minute until we have a look round,' he said, and, suiting the action to the word, he began to take stock of his surroundings.

The dead man was lying parallel to the rails in the offset, or flat track at the side of the line. He was dressed in a suit of light brown tweed, with brown tie and soft collar. On his feet were tan shoes, and his soft brown felt hat, cut nearly in two, lay between the rails some yards nearer to the station. The gleam of a gold watch chain showed beneath his partly open coat.

The manner of the happening was writ only too clearly on the ground. The first mark, some thirty yards farther into the tunnel, was a small stain of blood on the rail, and from there to where the body lay, the traces of the disaster were sadly apparent. Save as to the man's identity, there was no mystery here. Each one of the little group standing round could reconstruct for himself how the tragedy had occurred.

Sergeant Clarke, having observed these details, turned slowly to his companions.

'Who found the body?' he asked, producing a well-thumbed notebook.

Both Ashe and the driver claiming the distinction, Clarke took statements from each.

'It's clear from the marks,' he went on, 'that the man was killed by an incoming train?' The stationmaster at whom he glanced, nodded decisively. 'Now, what trains pass through during the night?'

'Down trains?' the stationmaster answered. 'There are four. First there's a local passenger from Harrisonville; gets here at 8.50 in the evening. The next is the mail, the through express for the north. It passes here at 11.10 p.m. Then there's a goods gets in about midnight, and another goods about 2.30 a.m. These are not very regular, but we can get you the time they arrived last night.'

The sergeant nodded as he laboriously noted these details.

'What about the engines of those trains?' he asked. 'No marks found on any of them?'

'None reported so far. All the engines come off here—this is a locomotive depot, you understand—and they're all examined by the shed staff before stabling. But we can have them looked over again if you think necessary.'

'It might be as well.' The sergeant wrote for some seconds, then resumed with a slightly consequential air: 'Now tell me, who would be the last person to walk along the line, I mean the last person before this'—he looked at his notes—'this Signalman Ashe?'

'I could hardly answer that question offhand,' the station-master said slowly. 'The last I know of would be the permanent way men leaving work about six last night. But some of the station staff or the locomotive men might have been by later.' He turned to the signalman. 'What about you, Ashe? Don't you come to work by the railway?'

'Sometimes,' the man admitted, 'but there weren't no body here when I passed last night.' The sergeant fixed him with a cold eye.

'What time was that?' he demanded.

'About 8.48. My shift doesn't begin 'til 10.00 p.m., but last night I came in earlier because I wanted to make a call up town first. But I know the time it was because No. 43—that's the passenger from Harrisonville he was speaking of'—Ashe jerked his head towards the stationmaster—'she passed me just a few yards on the other side of the tunnel. If she had put this man down I should have seen him.'

'But it was dark at that time.'

'Ay, it was dark, but it weren't here for all that.' Ashe expectorated skilfully. 'Why, if it had been, I'd have fallen over it, for I was walking down the offset.'

Again Clarke wrote laboriously.

'Well, Stationmaster,' he said at length, 'I think we'll get the body moved, and then I should like to have those engines looked at again. I suppose, Doctor, there's nothing you can do here?'

Dr Bakker having signified his approval, the remains were lifted on to a stretcher and placed on the floor of the van, the melancholy little party climbed on board, and the train set back to Middeldorp station. There the body was carried to a disused office, where it would remain until arrangements could be made to remove it to the morgue. The railwaymen were dismissed, and Dr Bakker and the sergeant set themselves to make the necessary examination.

The clothes were soon stripped off, and Clarke took them to the table in an adjoining room, while his colleague busied himself with the remains. First the sergeant emptied the pockets, making a list of the articles found. With one exception, these were of the kind usually carried by a well-to-do man of the middle class. There was a gold watch and chain, a knife, a bunch of keys, a half-filled cigarette case, some fifteen shillings in loose money, a pocketbook and three folded papers. But in addition to these, there was an object which at once excited the sergeant's curiosity—a small automatic pistol, quite clean and apparently new. Clarke drew out the magazine and found it full of shells. There was no trace in the barrel of a shot having been fired.

But, interesting as was this find, it offered no aid to identification, and Clarke turned with some eagerness to the pocketbook and papers.

The latter turned out to be letters. Two were addressed to Mr Albert Smith, c/o Messrs. Hope Bros., 120-130 Mees Street, Middeldorp, and the third to the same gentleman at 25 Rotterdam Road. Sergeant Clarke knew Hope Bros. establishment, a large provision store in the centre of the town, and he assumed that Mr Smith must have been an employee, the Rotterdam Road address being his residence. If so, his problem, or part of it at all events, seemed to be solved.

As a matter of routine he glanced through the letters. The two addressed to the store were about provision business matters, the other was a memorandum containing a number of figures apparently relating to betting transactions.

Though Sergeant Clarke was satisfied he already had sufficient information to lead to the deceased's identification, he went on in his stolid, routine way to complete his inquiry. Laying aside the letters, he picked up the pocketbook. It was marked with the same name, Albert Smith, and contained a roll of notes value six pounds, some of Messrs. Hope Bros. trade cards with 'Mr A. Smith' in small type on the lower left-hand corner, and a few miscellaneous papers, none of which seemed of interest.

The contents of the pockets done with, he turned his attention to the clothes themselves, noting the manufacturers or sellers of the various articles. None of the garments were marked except the coat, which bore a tab inside the breast pocket with the tailor's printed address, and the name 'A. Smith' and a date of some six months earlier, written in ink.

His immediate investigation finished, Sergeant Clarke returned to Dr Bakker in the other room.

'Man's name is Albert Smith, sir,' he said. 'Seems to have worked in Hope Bros. store in Mees Street. Have you nearly done, sir?'

Dr Bakker, who was writing, threw down his pen.

'Just finished, Sergeant.'

He collected some sheets of paper and passed them to the other. 'This will be all you want, I fancy.'

'Thank you, sir. You've lost no time.'

'No, I want to get away as soon as possible.'

'Well, just a moment, please, until I look over this.'

The manuscript was in the official form and read:

'11th November.

'To the Chief Constable of Middeldorp.

'Sir,—I beg to report that this morning at 6.25 a.m. I was called by Sergeant Clarke to examine a body which had just been found on the railway near the north end of the Dartie Avenue Tunnel. I find as follows:

'The body is that of a man of about thirty-five, 6 feet o inches in height, broad and strongly built, and with considerable muscular development. (Here followed some measurements and technical details.) As far as discernable without an autopsy, the man was in perfect health. The cause of death was shock produced by the following injuries: (Here followed a list.) All of these are consistent with the theory that he was struck by the cowcatcher of a railway engine in rapid motion.

'I am of the opinion the man had been dead from eight to ten hours when found.

'I am, etc.,
'Pieter Bakker.'

'Thank you, Doctor, there's not much doubt about that part of it.' Clarke put the sheets carefully away in his pocket. 'But I should like to know what took the man there. It's a rum time for anyone to be walking along the line. Looks a bit like suicide to me. What do you say, sir?'

'Not improbable.' The doctor rose and took his hat. 'But you'll easily find out. You will let me know about the inquest?'

'Of course, sir. As soon as it's arranged.'

The stationmaster had evidently been watching the door, for hardly had Dr Bakker passed out of earshot when he appeared, eager for information.

'Well, Sergeant,' he queried, 'have you been able to identify him yet?'

'I have, Stationmaster,' the officer replied, a trifle pompously.

'His name is Albert Smith, and he was connected with Hope Bros. store in Mees Street.'

The stationmaster whistled.

'Mr Smith of Hope Bros.!' he repeated. 'You don't say! Why, I knew him well. He was often down here about accounts for carriage and claims. A fine upstanding man he was too, and always very civil spoken. This is a terrible business, Sergeant.'

The sergeant nodded, a trifle impatiently. But the station-master was curious, and went on:

'I've been thinking it over, Sergeant, and the thing I should like to know is,' he lowered his voice impressively, 'what was he doing there?'

'Well,' said Clarke, 'what would you say yourself?'

The stationmaster shook his head.

'I don't like it,' he declared. 'I don't like it at all. That there piece of line doesn't lead to anywhere Mr Smith should want to go to—not at that time of night anyhow. It looks bad. It looks to me'—again he sank his voice—'like suicide.'

'Like enough,' Clarke admitted coldly. 'Look here, I want to go right on down to Mees Street. The body can wait here, I take it? One of my men will be in charge.'

'Oh, certainly.' The stationmaster became cool also. 'That room is not wanted at present.'

'What about those engines?' went on Clarke. 'Have you been able to find marks on any of them?'

'I was coming to that.' Importance crept once more into the stationmaster's manner. 'I had a further search made, with satis-factory results. Traces of blood were found on the cowcatcher of No. 1317. She worked in the mail, that's the one that arrived at 11.10 p.m. So it was then it happened.'

This agreed with the medical evidence, Clarke thought, as he drew out his book and made the usual note. Having made a further entry to the effect that the stationmaster estimated the speed of this train at about thirty-five miles an hour when passing through the tunnel, Clarke asked for the use of the telephone, and reported his discoveries to headquarters. Then he left for the Mees Street store, while, started by the station-master, the news of Albert Smith's tragic end spread like wildfire.

Messrs. Hope Bros. establishment was a large building occupying a whole block at an important street crossing. It seemed to exude prosperity, as the aroma of freshly ground coffee exuded from its open doors. Elaborately carved ashlar masonry clothed it without, and within it was a maze of marble, oxidised silver and plate glass. Passing through one of its many pairs of swing doors, Clarke addressed himself to an attendant.

'Is your manager in yet? I should like to see him, please.'

'I think Mr Crawley is in,' the young man returned. 'Anyway, he won't be long. Will you come this way?'

Mr Crawley, it appeared, was not available, but his assistant, Mr Hurst, would see the visitor if he would come to the manager's office. He proved to be a thin-faced, aquiline-featured young man, with an alert, eager manner.

'Good morning, Sergeant,' he said, his keen eyes glancing comprehensively over the other. 'Sit down, won't you. And what can I do for you?'

'I'm afraid, sir,' Clarke answered as he took the chair indicated, 'that I am bringing you bad news. You had a Mr Albert Smith in your service?'

'Yes, what of him?'

'Was he a tall man of about thirty-five, broad and strongly built, and wearing brown tweed clothes?'

'That's the man.'

'He has met with an accident. I'm sorry to tell you he is dead.'

The assistant manager stared.

'Dead!' he repeated blankly, a look of amazement passing over his face. 'Why, I was talking to him only last night! I can hardly believe it. When did it occur, and how?'

'He was run over on the railway in the tunnel under Dartie Avenue about eleven o'clock last night.'

'Good heavens!'

There was no mistaking the concern in the assistant manager's voice, and he listened with deep interest while Clarke told him the details he had learned.

'Poor fellow!' he observed, when the recital was ended. 'That was cruelly hard luck. I am sorry for your news, Sergeant.'

'No doubt, sir.' Clarke paused, then went on, 'I wanted to ask you if you could tell me anything of his family. I gathered he lived in Rotterdam Road? Is he married, do you know?'

'No, he had rooms there. I never heard him mention his family. I'm afraid I can't help you about that, and I don't know anyone else who could.'

'Is that so, sir? He wasn't a native then?'

'No. He came to us'—Mr Hurst took a card from an index in a drawer of the desk—'almost exactly six years ago. He gave his age then as twenty-six, which would make him thirty-two now. He called here looking for clerical work, and as we were short of a clerk at the time, Mr Crawley gave him a start. He did fairly well, and gradually advanced until he was second in his department. He was a very clever chap, ingenious and, indeed, I might say, brilliant. But, unfortunately, he was lazy, or rather he would only work at what interested him for the moment. He did well enough to hold a second's job, but he was too erratic to get charge.'

'What about his habits? Did he drink or gamble?'

Mr Hurst hesitated slightly.

'I have heard rumours that he gambled, but I don't know anything personally. I can't say I ever saw him seriously the worse for drink.'

'I suppose you know nothing about his history before he joined you?'

'Nothing. I formed the opinion that he was English, and had come out with some stain on his reputation, but of that I am not certain. Anyway, we didn't mind if he had had a break in the Old Country, so long as he made good with us.'

'I think, sir, you said you saw Mr Smith last night. At what hour?'

'Just before quitting time. About half past five.'

'And he seemed in his usual health and spirits.'

'Absolutely.'

Sergeant Clarke had begun to ask another question when the telephone on the manager's desk rang sharply. Hurst answered.

'Yes,' he said. 'Yes, the assistant manager speaking. Yes, he's here now. I'll ask him to speak.' He turned to his visitor. 'Police headquarters wants to speak to you.'

Clarke took the receiver.

'That you, Clarke?' came in a voice he recognised as that of his immediate superior, Inspector Vandam. 'What are you doing?'

The sergeant told him.

'Well,' went on the voice, 'you might drop it and return here at once. I want to see you.'

'I'm wanted back at headquarters, sir,' Clarke explained as he replaced the receiver. 'I have to thank you for your information.'

'If you want anything more from me, come back.'

'I will.'

On reaching headquarters, Clarke found Inspector Vandam closeted with the Chief in the latter's room. He was asked for a detailed report of what he had learned, which he gave as briefly as he could.

'It looks suspicious right enough,' said the great man after he had finished. 'I think, Vandam, you had better look into the thing yourself. If you find it's all right you can drop it.' He turned to Clarke with that kindliness which made him the idol of his subordinates. 'We've had some news, Clarke. Mr Segboer, the curator of the Groote Park, has just telephoned to say that one of his men has discovered that a potting shed behind the range of glass-houses and beside the railway has been entered during the night. Judging from his account, some rather curious operations must have been carried on by the intruders, but the point of immediate interest is that he found under a bench a small engagement book with the name Albert Smith on the flyleaf.'

Clarke stared.

'Good gracious, sir,' he ejaculated, 'but that's extraordinary!' Then, after a pause, he went on, 'So that's what he was crossing the railway for.'

'What do you mean?' the Chief asked sharply.

'Why, sir, he was killed at ten minutes past eleven, and it must have been when he was leaving the park. Across the railway would be a natural enough way for him to go, for the gates would be shut. They close at eleven. There are different places where he could get off the railway to go into the town.'

The Chief and Vandam exchanged glances.

'Quite possibly Clarke is right,' the former said slowly. 'All the same, Vandam, I think you should look into it. Let me know the result.'

The Chief turned back to his papers, and Inspector Vandam and Sergeant Clarke left the room. Though none of the three knew it, Vandam had at that moment embarked on the solution of one of the most baffling mysteries that had ever tormented the brains of an unhappy detective, and the issue of the case was profoundly to affect his whole future career, as well as the careers of a number of other persons at that time quite unknown to him.

CHAPTER II

THE POTTING SHED

OF all the attractions of the city of Middeldorp, that of which the inhabitants are most justly proud is the Groote Park. It lies to the west of the town, in the area between city and suburb. Its eastern end penetrates like a wedge almost to the business quarter, from which it is separated by the railway. On its outer or western side is a residential area of tree-lined avenues of detached villas, each standing, exclusive, within its own well-kept grounds. Here dwell the *élite* of the district.

The park itself is roughly pear-shaped in plan, with the stalk towards the centre of the town. In a clearing in the wide end is a bandstand, and there in the evenings and on holidays the citizens hold decorous festival, to the brazen strains of the civic band. Beneath the trees surrounding are hundreds of little marble-topped tables, each with its attendant pair of folding galvanised iron chairs, and behind the tables in the farther depths of the trees are refreshment kiosks, arranged like supplies parked behind a bivouacked army. Electric arc lamps hang among the branches, and the place on balmy summer evenings after dusk has fallen is alive with movement and colour from the crowds seeking relaxation after the heat and stress of the day.

The narrow end nearest the centre of the city is given over to horticulture. It boasts one of the finest ranges of glass-houses in South Africa, a rock garden, a Dutch garden, an English garden, as well as a pond with the rustic bridges, swans and water lilies, without which no ornamental water is complete.

The range of glass-houses runs parallel to the railway and about fifty feet from its boundary wall. Between the two, and screened from observation at the ends by plantations of ever-green shrubs, lies what might be called the working portion of the garden—tool sheds, potting sheds, depots of manure, leaf mould and the like. It was to this area that Inspector Vandam and Sergeant Clarke bent their steps when they left headquarters.

Waiting for them at the end of the glass-houses were two men, one an old gentleman of patriarchal appearance, with a long white beard and semitic features, the other younger and evidently a labourer. As the police officers approached, the old gentleman hailed Vandam.

"Morning, Inspector,' he called in a thin, high-pitched voice. 'You weren't long coming round. I hope we have not brought you on a fool's errand. As I told your people, I would not have troubled you at all only for the name in the book being the same as that of the poor gentleman who was killed. It seemed such a curious coincidence that I thought you ought to know.'

'Quite right, Mr Segboer,' Vandam returned. 'We are much obliged to you, sir.'

The curator turned to his companion.

'This is Hoskins, one of our gardeners,' he explained. 'It was he who found the book. If you are ready, let us go to the shed.'

The four men passed round the end of the glass-houses and followed a path which led behind the belt of evergreen shrubs to the building in question. It was a small place, about eight feet by ten only, built close up to the boundary, in fact, the boundary wall, raised a few feet for the purpose, formed one of its sides. The other three walls were of brick, supporting a lean-to roof of reddish brown tiles. There was no window, light being obtained only from the door. The shed contained a rough bench along one wall, a few tools and flowerpots, and a bag or two of artificial manure. The place was very secluded, being hidden from the gardens by the glass-houses and the evergreen shrubs.

'Now, Hoskins,' Mr Segboer directed, as the little party

stopped on the threshold, 'explain to Inspector Vandam what you found.'

'This morning about seven o'clock I had to come to this here shed for to get a line and trowel for some plants as I was bedding out,' explained the gardener, whose tongue betrayed the fact of his Cockney origin, 'and when I looked in at the door I saw just at once that somebody had been in through the night, or since five o'clock yesterday evening anyhow. The floor seemed someway different, and then, after looking a while, I saw that it had been swept clean, and then mould sprinkled over it again. You can see that for yourselves if you look.'

The floor was of concrete, brought to a smooth surface, though dark coloured from the earth which had evidently lain on it. This earth had certainly been brushed away from the centre, and was heaped up for a width of some eighteen inches round the walls. A space of about seven feet by five had thus been cleared, and the marks of the brush were visible round the edges. But the space had been partly re-covered by what seemed to be handfuls of earth, and here and there round the walls it looked as if the brush had been used for scattering back some of the swept-up material.

Vandam turned to the man.

'You say this was done since five o'clock last night,' he said. 'Were you here at that time?'

'Yes, I left in the line and trowel when I quit work last night.'

'And what was the floor like then?'

'Like it always was before. There was leaf mould and sand and loam on it; just a little, you know, that had fallen from the bench. But it was all over it.'

'You found something else?'

The man pointed to the corner opposite the bench.

'Them there ashes were not there before.'

In the corner was a little heap of burnt paper, and now that the idea was suggested to Vandam, he believed he could detect the smell of fire. Still standing outside the door, he nodded slowly and went on:

'Anything else?'

'Ay, there was the pocketbook. When I was coming out with the line and trowel, I saw something sticking out of a heap of sand just there. I picked it up and found it was a pocketbook, and when I looked in the front of it I saw the name was Albert Smith. I wondered who had been in the shed, for I didn't know anyone of that name, and I slipped the book into my pocket, saying to myself as how I'd give it to the boss here first time I saw him. Well, then, after a while I heard that a man called Albert Smith had been found dead on the railway just back of the wall here, so I thinks to myself there's maybe something more in it than what meets the eye, and I had better give the book to the boss at once, and so I did.'

'And here it is,' Mr Segboer added, taking a small notebook bound in brown leather from his pocket and handing it to Vandam.

There was no question of the identity of the owner, for the same address—that of Messrs. Hope Bros. of Mees Street—followed the name on the flyleaf. The book was printed in diary form, each two pages showing a week. Vandam glanced quickly over it. The notes seemed either engagements, or reminders about provision business. There was nothing in the space for the previous evening.

Vandam questioned the gardener closely on his statement, but without gaining additional details. Mr Segboer could give no helpful information, and Vandam dismissed both after thanking them and, more by force of habit than of deliberate purpose, warning them not to repeat what they had told him.

To Inspector Vandam the circumstances were far from clear. From what he had just learned, it seemed reasonable to conclude that Smith had visited the shed some time between five and eleven on the previous evening, probably near eleven, as the sergeant's suggestion that he had been killed while leaving the

Park after the gates were closed was likely enough. But was there not, at least, a suggestion of something more? Did the visit to the shed not mean an interview with someone, a secret meeting, and, therefore, possibly for some shady purpose. For a secret interview probably no better place could have been found in the whole of Middeldorp. If it were approached and quitted by the railway after dark, as it might have been in this instance, the chances of discovery would be infinitesimal. What could Smith have been doing there?

At first Vandam thought of a mere vulgar intrigue, that he was meeting some girl with whom he did not wish to be seen. But the sweeping of the floor seemed to indicate some more definite purpose. What ever could it have been?

It was fairly clear, Vandam imagined, that the scattering of the earth over the floor was done to remove the traces of its having been swept. If so, it had been badly done and it had failed in its object. Was this, he wondered, due to lack of care, or to haste, or to working in the dark?

He could not answer any of these questions, but the more he thought over them, the more likely he thought it that Smith had been engaged with another or others in some secret and perhaps sinister business.

Inspector Vandam was mildly intrigued by the whole affair, but it did not seem of passing importance. He decided that after taking a general look round, he would return to headquarters and consult his Chief as to whether the matter should be further followed up. He therefore turned from the shed to its immediate surroundings.

At the end of the shed, between the path and the boundary wall, the ground was covered with low heaps of leaf mould. The stuff had evidently lain there for a considerable time, for the surface had grown smooth, almost like soil. Across this smooth surface and close to the end of the shed passed two lines of footsteps, one coming and the other going.

Vandam stood looking at the marks. They were vague and

blurred and quite useless as prints, and yet there was something peculiar about them. At first he had assumed—without reason, as he now realised—that they were Smith's tracks approaching and leaving the shed. But now he saw they had been made by different persons. Those receding were closer together and much deeper than the others, and he began to picture a tall, thin man arriving, and a short, stout one going away.

And there he would probably have left it, had not Sergeant Clarke at that moment walked across the leaf-mould to look over the wall. Almost subconsciously Vandam noticed that his steps made comparatively little impression, about the same, indeed, as those of his hypothetic thin man. But Clarke was not thin. He was a big man, tall, broad and well developed.

'I say, Clarke,' Vandam looked up suddenly, 'what do you weigh?'

'Just turn the scale at sixteen stone,' returned the other stolidly, no trace of surprise at the question showing on his wooden countenance.

'I thought so,' Vandam muttered, turning his eyes again on the footprints. Somewhat puzzled, he walked across the strip himself, and turned to see what marks he had made. Vandam was a small man, thin though wiry, and his weight, he knew, was just under twelve stone. The prints he had left were considerably lighter than Clarke's.

At first he wondered whether atmospheric conditions might not have rendered the leaf-mould softer on the previous night than it was now, but he immediately realised that no such change in the weather had taken place. No, there seemed to be no way of escaping the obvious suggestion. The man who had left the gardens had been carrying a heavy weight.

And this, if true, would account for the outward-bound prints being closer together than the others, so that they might well have been made by the same man. What could Smith have been carrying?

Vandam turned and looked over the wall. Below him was the railway cutting, and his eyes followed the curving line of rails until about fifty yards to the right it disappeared into the black mouth of the Dartie Avenue tunnel. From where he stood, it was just possible to see the place where the body had lain, and Clarke lost no time in pointing it out.

Inspector Vandam nodded absently as he scrutinised the grassy slope below him. Yes, he was not mistaken; a weight had been dragged down the bank. The bent grasses showed a slightly different colour when looked at parallel to the surface. He crossed the wall.

'Stay where you are a minute,' he called to Clarke, as he stooped to examine the ground.

Immediately along the base of the wall, between it and the top edge of the slope, was a flat strip about three feet wide. On it, just opposite the deep footmarks on the park side, the grass was beaten down as if a weight had lain on it, and from this the marks of descent to the rails were unmistakable.

Vandam moved slowly down the slope, noting every indication that he could find. The object appeared to have been something under two feet in width, and at one point it seemed to him that a halt had been made, though of this he was not certain. At the bottom of the bank there were further traces. Vaguely-marked footsteps showed at the edge of the offset, and two faint tracks or scrapes were visible coming on to the offset and turning in the direction of the tunnel. These scrapes were each about an inch wide and ran parallel, a foot apart. They were lost to view almost at once when they passed from the soft ground at the edge of the offset on to the beaten track at its centre.

Calling to Clarke to follow him down and to keep clear of the traces, Vandam scrutinised the ground to the tunnel, but without finding further marks. Then, having reached the scene of the tragedy, he listened to the other's detailed description of what had been found.

'Not much blood about,' he commented, as he stood looking down at the traces which still remained.

'That's so,' Clark admitted. 'I noticed that. It would all be the way he was struck.'

Vandam did not reply. A terrible possibility had suddenly flashed into his mind, and he stood silently considering how far the various points he had learned would fit in with it. At last he turned once more to his companion.

'I take it that body is still at the station?' he asked.

'Yes, sir. I have done nothing yet about getting it shifted.'

'I'd like to have a look at it.'

Twenty minutes later the two men stood gazing down on all that was mortal of the late Albert Smith. But the Inspector did not delay there long.

'Where are the clothes?' he demanded.

Clarke took him to the next room. Instantly the Inspector picked up the shoes, and turning them over, glanced at the backs of the heels. For a moment he stood staring, then laid them down again very deliberately.

'Clarke,' he said slowly, 'it's well that gardener found the notebook. This is neither accident nor suicide. Albert Smith has been murdered by a carefully thought out scheme. How did you come to miss that? You should have spotted it.'

For once the sergeant's face became expressive. Blank amazement amounting almost to awe was stamped on its every feature. He gasped, speechless.

'Let it be a warning to you about taking things for granted,' went on Vandam gravely. 'Here, look at this.'

Once more he picked up the shoes, pointing to the backs of the heels. They were marked with a number of slight scratches, running up at right angles to the tread.

'You see, he's been dragged down the bank with his legs trailing on the ground. The track of the body is quite clear on the slope, and I found where the two heels dropped on the offset and were dragged along towards the tunnel. He was carried over that leaf-mould and dropped on the bank over the wall. And do you know the reason there was so little blood on the railway?'

Clarke recovered himself with an effort.

'He was dead, sir?' he suggested in somewhat shaky tones.

'Of course, because he was dead. You might have thought of that, even if you saw nothing else. And there was another thing that you might have thought of, too, if you hadn't been so darned sleepy; the way the body was torn up. How do you think that happened?'

'I don't quite follow, sir,' the unhappy man stammered.

'No, because you won't use your brains. Think a minute. If the man had been struck when he was standing or walking he would have been thrown clear by the cowcatcher. But if the body was lying on the ground—laid across the rails in all probability—why, it could hardly have escaped the kind of damage it got. See what I mean?'

Clarke murmured incoherently.

'I don't say it would always happen that way,' the Inspector went on after a pause, 'but the thing might have let you smell a rat. Yes, there's no doubt the man was murdered. Murdered, I should think, in that shed, but of that I'm not yet sure.'

'I never thought to doubt—' Clarke was beginning when the other interrupted him.

'Well, you'll know better next time. That'll be all about it, only you've lost your scoop. Now, let us get ahead. We'll go down and examine that ground again while the traces are fresh.'

They retraced their steps down the railway, halting opposite the potting shed.

'Let's see,' Vandam thought aloud. 'We may assume the murderer carried the body down from the shed and left it on the line there, so as to make the thing look like an accident. Then he cleared off. Now, how? Where did he leave the railway?'

He stood for a moment humming a tune, then went on:

'It's unlikely that he would go through the Ballat Road bridge, because the station yard starts at its far end and he would fear being seen by a shunter or signalman. And it's even less likely that he would go in the opposite direction, out of the far end of the tunnel, for about a hundred yards farther on is the Edward Street level crossing, well lighted and with a gatekeeper in charge. Where, then, would he go?'

Sergeant Clarke had recovered from his confusion.

'Over there, sir, I should think. There's a passage for getting to the yards of those houses runs along back of the wall. A man could dodge over there without being seen, and slip out at the end into Craven Street when the coast was clear.'

'Exactly what I think,' Vandam agreed. 'Let us walk along and see if we can't find tracks going up the slope.'

A moment later, Clarke gave a hail.

'Here you are, sir,' he called. 'Plain as you'd wish.'

Stretching up the bank were similar though fainter traces to these leading to the park on the opposite side. Vandam spent several minutes examining them, and at last was satisfied that someone had passed in each direction, up and down.

He worked gradually up the bank and was about to climb the wall to look for traces on the other side when, glancing down, he stopped suddenly. At the foot of the wall, embedded in the grass, lay a few scattered stones. His sharp eye had seen that one of these had been recently moved. Though it was still in its bed, it was not fitting properly, and instead of the grass growing up to it there was a trace of fresh brown earth round its edges. Vandam stooped and with an effort lifted it. As he looked into the hole which it uncovered he whistled.

Beneath the stone lay two objects, either of which would have filled him with interest. One was an ordinary two-pound joiner's hammer, almost new, judging by the varnish on the handle. But it was not on the varnish that Vandam's eyes were fixed. On the head was a dull stain of blood!

The other object looked harmless enough in comparison, and yet to Vandam it seemed even more sinister. It was a tiny roll of stout canvas, not unlike a belt. Vandam picked it up and it resolved itself into a little bag about three inches in diameter and two feet six long. Both ends were sewn up tightly, but near one of them the canvas had been gashed with a knife. Vandam held his hand under the hole and shook the little tube. Some grains of sand fell out.

'Just so,' he thought. 'Sandbagged in that shed. But what in all this earthly world was done with the hammer?' He turned to his subordinate. 'Here, Clarke, bring along that hammer. But don't touch the clean part of the handle; there might be a fingerprint on it somewhere.'

Postponing consideration of his treasure-trove, Vandam continued his search. He climbed the wall and found himself in the lane leading into Craven Street. But its surface was hard, and though he examined it carefully from end to end, he could find no trace of anyone having passed.

Having sent Clarke for an acetylene lamp, Vandam returned to the potting shed and began one of his painstaking examinations. Every inch of the floor and shelf was scrutinised, every grain of the little heaps of soil which lay scattered about was sifted through his fingers. But his discoveries were negligible. One thing only he found, and that a triviality. The ashes in the corner were the remains of newspapers. Beyond that there was nothing.

He stood motionless, pondering over the tragic business.

First of all he wondered at what time the murder had taken place. Before 11.10 on the previous evening obviously, because the body had been struck by a train at that hour. But how much before? The murderer would want some margin of time to get the body into position and to allow for unexpected checks. But he would make this margin as short as possible, to reduce to a minimum the risk of the remains being found before the train passed. It seemed to Vandam that the meeting in the shed must have taken place about half-past ten or a little later. This, of course, was guesswork, but he could hardly picture even so cold-blooded a criminal as this ruffian must be, despatching his victim at an early hour in the evening and then sitting in the shed with the corpse, waiting until it should be time to drag it down to the line.

A further point struck him. It would, of course, be dark at this hour. Would a light not therefore have been necessary in the shed? The burning of the papers, if that had been done at the same time, would certainly have made a light. What chance would there be of that light having been seen.

Quite a good chance, Vandam decided. Though the majority of the evening visitors to the park kept down at the other end near the electric arcs and the bandstand, isolated strollers might penetrate as far as the gardens. And the screen of evergreens, though thick, could not be depended on to prevent a light showing through. Therefore, if the affair was to be kept secret before those papers could have been burned or a light used, the door must have been shut. There was, of course, no window.

Hoskins had opened the door that morning from the outside, but he hadn't touched the inside. The murderer's fingerprints should therefore be intact.

Vandam brought his lamp to the back of the door, and he experienced a shock of real disappointment when he saw that the woodwork was too rough to receive impressions. He would get no help there.

He felt slightly overwhelmed as he thought of the variety of problems which awaited solution. Who was guilty of the murder? What was the motive? Was more than one person involved? How had Smith been lured to the shed? What was the meaning of the sweeping of the floor and the burning of the newspapers? What had been done with the hammer? These were but a few of the salient points, and on not one of them had Vandam the slightest suggestion to offer.

But he realised that this was the position of affairs at the beginning of every inquiry, and he was by no means down-hearted. Rather was he pleased that what would undoubtedly prove one of the most thrilling and important cases of the year had fallen to his lot.

He did not see that he could learn anything more on the ground, and his next business must undoubtedly be to find out as much as possible of Smith's life and personality. No doubt he would thus come across some clue which would lead him to the solution he desired.

Having sent Clarke to get a padlock put on the door of the shed, he returned to headquarters. There he tested the hammer for fingerprints, but unfortunately here again without result. Next he returned to the station, made a further examination of the murdered man's clothes, took prints from the dead fingers, and lastly, having set in order the facts he had learnt, went in and had a long interview with his Chief.

CHAPTER III

GATHERING THE THREADS

INSPECTOR VANDAM, hot on a new case, was a very different person from the same man engaged in routine police work in his office. Not that he was at any time slack or lazy; he was naturally too efficient and hardworking for that. But the interest of a new mystery stimulated him to an enthusiasm which rendered him careless of rest or even food, and drove him on with a tireless energy until he had either found a solution of his problems or satisfied himself that none was obtainable.

In the present case, though it was considerably after his usual lunch hour when he left his Chief's office, he contented himself with a five-minute pause for a sandwich and a cup of coffee in a restaurant before starting the next phase of his investigation. He never drank alcohol, saying that it stupefied him, while hot coffee, he held, stimulated his brain to keener and more incisive thought. Many a criminal was brought to justice, he used to claim, as a result of his coffee habit.

He had decided that his first business must be a call at Messrs. Hope Bros. store in Mees Street. The knowledge gained since Sergeant Clarke had been there earlier in the day necessitated inquiries of a different kind to those already made, and he entered the great building and asked for the manager in the hope and belief that before he came out he would have learned at least the direction in which his subsequent inquiries should tend.

Mr Crawley, it seemed, was again out, and, like the sergeant, he was received by the assistant manager, Mr Hurst.

'I am sorry to trouble you again about this affair,' Vandam began, when he had introduced himself and stated the subject of his visit, 'but our people at headquarters are not quite satisfied that we have really got to the bottom of it. They fear it may not have been the accident it looked like at first sight.'

The assistant manager stared. Vandam, whose golden rule was to give nothing away and distrust everybody, watched him keenly and unobtrusively. But there was neither embarrassment nor undue interest in the man's manner as he exclaimed:

'Now just what do you mean by that, Inspector?'

Vandam leaned forward and spoke confidentially.

'There's a suggestion of suicide.'

Mr Hurst whistled.

'So that's the idea,' he returned. 'What makes you think that?'

'We can't see what else would have taken him to the railway at that time.'

'Not very conclusive, is it? That your only reason?'

'Not exactly,' Vandam answered slowly. 'There are others. But what do you think of the suggestion?'

Mr Hurst moved impatiently.

'I don't think much of it,' he declared. 'Smith wasn't the suicide kind, not by a long way. Too darned fond of himself.'

'A coward, you mean?'

'No, not a coward. I mean he was always out to get the best for himself. Suicide wouldn't be his line except as a last resource, and, so far as I know, he was not in difficulties.'

'You don't seem to have liked him very much.'

'I didn't like him at all,' Hurst returned with some warmth, 'though maybe it's not quite the thing to be saying so with the chap just dead. But his death doesn't alter facts. I didn't like him and I don't know anyone else who did.'

'How do you account for that?'

Mr Hurst shrugged his shoulders.

'Hard to say. Manner perhaps. But he wasn't popular anyhow.'

'It's always an astonishment to me,' Vandam remarked easily, 'what a difference manner makes—a thing, as you might say, that there's really nothing in. However, that's by the way. You tell me this deceased gentleman was not popular. Now, was there anyone he actually had a row with?'

Mr Hurst favoured his visitor with a keen glance.

'Plenty,' he said, dryly. 'I had a row with him myself last week. He has got across most of us at one time or another.'

'I don't mean trifling differences,' Vandam insisted. 'Were there any really serious quarrels?'

'I could hardly tell,' Hurst answered. 'Once, I know, he had a scrap with another man—one of our own staff too. I went into one of the yards and I found him and this chap, a man called Swayne, fighting rings round with half the storemen looking on. Would you call that a serious quarrel?'

'I could hardly tell either,' Vandam smiled. 'Were they in earnest about it?'

'In earnest! They were out for each other's blood. It was the devil's own job to get them separated. They were evenly matched; both big, strongly developed men, and for a time it might have gone either way. Then Smith got Swayne down, and I wouldn't mind betting he'd have throttled him only for the others. They rushed in and dragged him off. Swayne was nearly unconscious. They were both pretty wild at first, and each swore he would do the other in, but next day the thing seemed to have blown over.'

'Which was in the wrong?'

'I don't know. No one ever did know what started it. But Smith was always nagging at Swayne, and I expect he went too far. I don't know how Swayne stood it the way he did.'

'Was that long ago?'

'About a month, I should think.'

'It looks as if Smith had some hold over Swayne.'

'That's what I've thought more than once. Swayne isn't a bad chap and he's certainly no coward, but he always seemed to have the wind up where Smith was concerned.'

'He's on your staff, you say?'

'Yes, he's our sales manager.'

'I'd better see him,' Vandam declared. 'He might know something that would help.'

'Then I'm afraid you'll have some way to look. He's just gone to England on three months' leave to visit his relatives. Lucky chap! I wish I could get a trip like that.'

Inspector Vandam's hopes, which had been steadily rising during the conversation, suffered a sudden drop.

'Oh,' he said helplessly, 'he's gone to England, has he? But you say he's coming back?'

'Yes. We're keeping his job for him. He's a smart fellow, too good to lose.'

'Is it long since he left?'

'Only just gone. He left last night.'

The night before! The night of the murder! Vandam's hopes made a sharp recovery. Certainly he must find out more about this Swayne.

He resumed his interrogation. It seemed that Smith had also been at loggerheads with no less a person than Mr Crawley, the manager. They had had friction over some private business, the details of which Hurst did not know. But Crawley had not allowed the matter to affect their business relations, and Hurst believed it also had blown over.

Vandam asked a number of other questions, but without gaining much more information. In spite of his careful probing, he could hear of no one else whose relations with Smith were really suspicious. Therefore, having obtained the address of Swayne's landlady with the object of prosecuting inquiries there, he thanked Hurst for his trouble, and took his leave.

His next business was at Smith's rooms, and a few minutes' walk brought him to Rotterdam Road. It was a street of comparatively new houses, mostly residential, but with a sprinkling of shops and offices. No. 25 was wedged in between a tobacconist's and an exhibition of gas stoves, and showed in its lower windows cards bearing the legend, 'Apartments.' The Inspector knocked at the door.

It was opened by an elderly woman with hard features and a careworn expression, who explained that she was the landlady. Upon Vandam stating his business, she invited him in, and answered all his questions freely. But here he did not learn a great deal beyond the mere fact that Smith had occupied rooms in the house. Mrs Regan seemed genuinely shocked at the news of her lodger's death, though Vandam suspected this was due more to the loss of a paying client and the unwelcome notoriety which would be brought on her establishment than to personal regard for the deceased.

It seemed that Smith shared a sitting-room with a Mr Holt, a bank official, though the two men occupied separate bedrooms. On the previous evening, the night of the murder, Smith had returned at about six for supper, his usual custom. Holt was later that night and did not turn up until past seven. Mrs Regan in bringing up Smith's tray had 'passed the time of day' with him, as was her habit when either gentleman was alone. Smith seemed restless and excited. She imagined he had something on his mind, and this opinion was confirmed when she found later on that he had eaten hardly any supper. He had gone out shortly after eight; she had not seen him, but he had called through her door that he was going out into the country and might not be back that night. He had never returned, nor had he sent her any message.

Mrs Regan gave her late lodger a good character 'as young men go,' but with a curious reticence in her manner, which Vandam put down to personal dislike. The deceased was rather silent and uncommunicative, but was not too inconsiderate about giving trouble. He did not often drink to excess, nor did he bring undesirables to the house, though he kept pretty late hours. But principally he was a good pay. It seemed that to Mrs Regan prompt payment covered a greater multitude of sins than charity.

The landlady could not give a list of Smith's friends. He had very few visitors, and of those who did come she seldom learned the names. She suggested that Mr Holt would be better able to help, and gave his business address, the Central Branch of the Union Bank.

Neither could she, in answer to Vandam's veiled questionings, suggest anyone who might have had a grudge against the deceased. The Inspector was satisfied from the way she made her statement that she was being as helpful as she could, and thanked her politely.

'I must search his rooms, I'm afraid,' he continued. 'Perhaps you would show me up?'

The rooms, one of which was on the first and the other on the second floor, were typical of the middle-class lodging-house, somewhat drab and dingy as to furniture, but not exactly uncomfortable. Dismissing Mrs Regan, who was becoming a trifle garrulous, Vandam set himself to make a systematic examination of the contents. In the sitting-room he was somewhat handicapped by the fact that he was dealing with two men's belongings, but in any case he found nothing that assisted him. Nor when he went to the bedroom had he at first any better luck. Though he examined everything with the utmost minuteness here also, he came upon nothing of interest until he turned to a small metal despatch case which was on one of the shelves in the wardrobe. It was locked, but locks were but slight obstacles to Inspector Vandam, and with the aid of a skeleton key from a bunch he always carried, it soon stood open. Within were a bundle of miscellaneous papers, some receipts, a few letters, a number of bills and a bank book. The bills caused Vandam to whistle softly. Three were from jewellers; for a pearl pendant, £15 15s., a pair of earrings, £7 10s., a wristwatch, £5 12s. 6d.; several were from fashionable costumiers, among them one for a fur stole at £20, and others for gloves and flowers. Altogether they totalled to over £100.

Vandam metaphorically smacked his lips. When in a puzzling

case he came on what he was pleased to term 'the trail of the woman,' he felt he was moving forward. That Smith was the kind of man these bills revealed him to be did not prove anything, but it was suggestive. A dispute over a woman! What more fruitful source of tragedy could be imagined? An obvious line of inquiry suggested itself. He must learn the identity of the woman or women in question, and find out if other suitors were in the field.

He picked up the bank book. A glance showed that the last balance had been struck a fortnight previously, when some £45 only stood to the deceased's credit.

Smith, then, had been hard up. Not down and out, but still hard up. Though on his £400 a year he could no doubt have paid the £60 odd owing, an examination of the dates of the bills showed that so far from saving, he had been growing rapidly more extravagant during the month or two preceding his death.

'Guess he wasn't murdered for his money anyhow,' Vandam thought with grim humour as he turned to the letters.

With one exception, these were commonplace enough, but as he read this one Vandam smiled with satisfaction. It was a curt note in a lady's rather flamboyant hand, in which 'J. L.' assured 'Dear Albert' that she could not see him that night, but that he might take her out to dinner and a theatre on the following evening if he were good. The letter bore the date of a week previous, but no address. However, taken as an adjunct to the bills, it should lead speedily to the identification of the lady.

He replaced the papers in the box with the intention of taking them to headquarters, then, descending the stairs, he took leave of Mrs Regan and let himself out of the house.

'Now for friend Holt,' he thought, as he bent his steps towards the Central Branch of the Union Bank.

Mr Holt saw him at once. He had heard of the accident and seemed genuinely distressed by the tragic fate which had overtaken the sharer of his room. He scouted the suicide theory which Vandam put forward, saying that Smith was the last man in the world to take his own life. The Inspector's questions he answered with the utmost readiness.

But, like the others interviewed that afternoon, he had but little to tell. He had gone to reside in Rotterdam Road about a year previously, Smith being already there. The two men, while not close friends, got on well enough together. They did not see very much of each other, as Smith was out a good deal, and their associates moved in different circles. Holt was, however, able to give the names of three men with whom Smith had been on fairly intimate terms. Vandam noted their addresses, intending to call on them next day. Generally Holt confirmed what the Inspector had already learned about the deceased's character and habits.

'With regard, then, to last night, Mr Holt,' Vandam went on, 'please tell me what occurred.'

'Last night I was detained up town,' the young fellow answered. 'I did not get to my rooms until about 7.15. Smith had finished supper and was reading the paper when I went in. A word or two passed between us and then I had my supper. When I had about half finished Smith left the room, and I heard him go upstairs to his bedroom.'

'Did you notice anything peculiar about his manner?'

'Nothing, except that he seemed a little excited. He was restless, and kept jerking the paper about.'

'He was quite sober?'

'Absolutely. He seldom drank to excess.'

Vandam nodded.

'And was that the last time you saw him?'

'I saw him once again. When I had finished supper I went up to my room for a book, and as I opened the door he was just passing downstairs. He was carrying a small suitcase. I said, "Hallo, Smith! Going away?" "Only to spend the evening at Pendlebury," he answered, "but if I miss the last train I shall probably stay overnight." I went upstairs and Smith down, and that was the last I saw of him.'

Pendlebury was a residential suburb about four miles south of the city, with which it was connected by electric tram.

'What time was that, Mr Holt?'

'About ten minutes past eight.'

'Smith didn't say to whom he was paying the call?'

'No.'

Inspector Vandam asked a good many more questions, but except that the dead man had seemed a little absent-minded off and on for some weeks past, he learned nothing further of interest.

It was too late on leaving the bank to begin another phase of the inquiry that night. Vandam, therefore, after a call at headquarters, turned homewards, and spent the evening writing up notes of what he had already done and considering his future procedure.

The inquest took place next day. It had been fixed for eleven o'clock, and Vandam spent the whole morning making his preparations and checking over the evidence of his witnesses. After a consultation, it had been decided to keep secret the fact that murder had been committed, in the hope that the assassin might be lulled into a feeling of security which would render him careless and more likely to give himself away.

The tragedy had created immense popular interest, and it was over a crowded court that the coroner was called upon to preside. Punctually to the minute he plunged into business. The jury were sworn, left to view the body, looking self-conscious and important, returned a trifle paler and obviously with less thought of their own dignity, and the taking of evidence began.

Signalman Joseph Ashe first testified as to the discovery of the body and the giving of the alarm, and from the stationmaster and the other railway officials the story of that tragic morning was told up to the arrival of the police. Inspector Vandam then swore that the body so found was that which the jury had just viewed, and Dr Bakker described the injuries.

Evidence of identification having been taken, the court was adjourned, to the surprise of everyone not in the know. The coroner stated that though certain of the details seemed to point to suicide, the police had not as yet succeeded in obtaining sufficient evidence to enable the jury to reach a finding.

The suggestion of suicide sent a thrill through those present, which was quickly succeeded by a feeling of disappointment as they realised that for the time being their curiosity must remain unsatisfied.

The inquest over, Vandam sat down to think out his next move. There were still some obvious inquiries to be made, and he decided he would get through with these at once, before pausing to take stock of his position generally.

First, there was the matter of the hammer. If he could find out where it had been sold and who had bought it, the evidence might lead him straight to his goal. Then there was the sandbag. The purchase of a strip of canvas or a sailmaker's needle would surely be sufficiently uncommon to have attracted attention, and inquiry should bring the transaction to light. A visit to the various shops—jewellers, costumiers, florists—where Smith had made his purchases would probably lead to the identification of J. L., and if so, an entire new line of investigation would be opened up. There was also the matter of the automatic pistol found on Smith's body. If the purchase could be traced it might be valuable. Finally, there were the inquiries into the movements of Swayne upon which the Inspector had already decided.

There was certainly no lack of clues, and Vandam saw a vista of strenuous work opening out in front of him.

He returned to headquarters and instructed Sergeant Clarke to undertake the hammer and sandbag inquiry, put another man on the automatic pistol, and set off down town himself to visit the shops.

His information came more easily than he had anticipated.

Smith apparently had made no secret of his proclivities, and the Inspector soon learned that J. L. was a Miss Jane Louden, the daughter of the owner of a third-rate hotel—or rather public-house—in the poorer quarter of the town. The girl, a dark and haughty beauty, acted as barmaid, and was notoriously given to extracting purple and fine linen from the particular specimen of mankind whom she held in subjection for the time being. She had usually visited the shops with Smith, and had chosen the articles that appealed to her fancy. From the dates of the purchases it appeared that Smith had been a victim for over six months.

Vandam did not obtain all this information at his first call. He spent the afternoon going from shop to shop, and picked it up gradually. But nowhere did he hear of a rival to Smith.

Six o'clock was chiming from the city churches as Vandam left the last shop. His next business would be to go down to East Hawkins Street, where Miss Louden lived, and interview the lady herself. He thought that the evening would be as good a time as any for the purpose, and he went home with the intention of paying the call after he had dined.

But when, some two hours later, he asked for a drink in the bar of Louden's Hotel, he met with a disappointment. The proprietor served him in person, and he soon learned that Miss Louden was unwell. Discreet inquiries produced the information that she was down with an attack of influenza, but was over the worst of it.

There was nothing for it, therefore, but to switch on to one of his other lines of investigation, and next day he determined he would begin the tracing of the movements of Swayne on the night of the murder.

The case against Swayne seemed to him quite strong, and he thought that if he could connect Swayne with Miss Jane Louden, and show that the fight with Smith had been about her, it would be overwhelming. But, even apart from that, it was by no means negligible.

Swayne and Smith had never got on. Smith was continually being offensive to Swayne, and Swayne was apparently swallowing it, until his temper had got the better of him and he had gone for his enemy, fighting seemingly with the object of killing him. That was only a month ago, and the passions then roused would still be strong. The whole thing looked, not only to Vandam, but to Hurst, as if Smith had some hold over the sales manager which made the latter stand treatment he would not otherwise have put up with; just, in fact, the kind of hold which would lead a man to commit murder.

A fact which tended in the same direction was the date of the tragedy. It had occurred on the very night on which Swayne had left Middeldorp for England. If Swayne intended to commit the crime, it was the night he would chose. From the psychological point of view, to complete his revenge would naturally be the thing he would wish to do last before leaving. There might also be another and more practical reason. He might hope that his departure would serve him as an alibi. If the police could be made to believe that the murder had been committed after he had gone, it would meet his case.

All these points were matters for investigation, and Vandam felt he must get at them without delay.

CHAPTER IV

NEXT morning Inspector Vandam began his investigation into the movements of Swayne on the night of the murder, by a visit to his landlady, whose address he had obtained from Mr Hurst on the occasion of his visit to the Mees Street store.

Sydenham Avenue was in a much better district than Rotterdam Road, where Smith had lodged, and No. 18 proved to be a boarding-house of superior type to the average. The landlady, tall and stately as a stage duchess, received him in an office at the back of the lounge, and answered his questions with cold, though polite, efficiency.

Mr Swayne had lived in her establishment, she told him, for three years, during which time she had found him all that a gentleman should be. About a month previously he had informed her that he was going for a holiday to England, explaining that while he was anxious to retain his room, which was particularly comfortable, he did not want to pay for it while away, and asking her if she could let it for the three months. Anxious to oblige him, she had consented to do so if possible, and had succeeded in hearing of an engineer who wished for a few weeks' accommodation while studying conditions in some of the neighbouring mines. This man agreed to take Swayne's room for the three months, provided he could get it by a certain day. As the date was only four days before Swayne's departure, the latter had given it up, and, there being no other vacant room in the boarding-house, he had gone for the period in question to the Bellevue Hotel. About his actual departure from Middeldorp, or his movements on the last day of his stay, the landlady could therefore tell nothing.

Nor did she know anything of Smith nor of the relations between him and Swayne. She had contented herself with her business of running the house, and was not cognisant of the private affairs of her guests.

Before leaving, Vandam asked the landlady if she could show him a photograph of Swayne. It happened that she was able to do so, and while commenting on it, Vandam took a mental note of the photographer's address.

On leaving Sydenham Avenue he went to the studio. There he was able to buy a copy of the portrait, which by another lucky chance was adorning one of the show frames in the window. At the same time he purchased three or four similar sized photographs of men as like Swayne as he could find.

His next business was at the Bellevue Hotel, and returning to the centre of the town, he reached the great building and asked for the manager.

'Mr Royle is in Capetown,' he was told, 'but Mr Buchan, his assistant, is here, if he would do.'

Mr Buchan proved to be an efficient-looking young man with red hair and a Scotch accent. He listened courteously as Vandam explained his business.

'I don't want it to go further, Mr Buchan, but as a matter of fact our Chief has got a bee in his bonnet about Mr Smith's death. He believes it was suicide. Personally I don't, but orders are orders, and I've got to try and settle the point. Now Smith is believed to have seen a Mr Swayne earlier that same day. You knew Mr Swayne? He is in the Hope Bros. firm, and left a few days ago for a holiday in England.'

'I knew him, yes,' Buchan answered. 'He stayed here for two or three days before leaving South Africa, though I had met him before that. We do a good deal of business with Hope Bros., and I've come across most of their staff. Mr Crawley, the manager, I know intimately.'

'Quite. Well, as I say, it is believed that Smith and this Mr Swayne met some time during the day Mr Swayne left. We want to settle this point, because if they did meet Mr Swayne should be able to give us some valuable information as to Mr Smith's state of mind and so on. But we don't want to make a fuss and wireless the boat if there's nothing in it. So I'm to find out first if they did meet. Can you help me in that, do you think.'

Buchan shook his head.

'Why, no, I'm afraid not. I didn't see Swayne that evening at all.'

'Some of your people might know. If you'd be so kind as to put me in touch, say, with your reception clerk, I could make a few inquiries.'

'With pleasure. Will you come this way?'

A young man was working in the reception office. Mr Buchan called him over.

'Ah, Bragg,' he explained. 'This gentleman, Mr Vandam, is making some private inquiries about Mr Swayne, who stayed here recently. You remember him, no doubt?' Mr Buchan turned to Vandam. 'Mr Bragg will do all he can for you, and if you want me I shall be in my office.'

'Mr Swayne left by the south express that same Wednesday night,' the young man said promptly when Vandam had explained his errand. 'It leaves the station here at 3.45 a.m. It's the through train from the north.'

'Did you see him before he left?'

'Not immediately before. I saw him in the afternoon about five. He went out of the hotel about five, and he made some remark to me as he passed the office window. I didn't see him after that, but he must have come in some time later, for he sent a waiter down from his room at about half-past ten for his bill. I sent the bill up and the money came back.'

'Could he have passed in without your seeing him?'

'Oh, yes, he might have done so when I was writing or at the back of the office.'

'You weren't here when he was leaving for the train?'

No, I closed up about eleven and went to bed.'

'When you saw him at five can you tell me how he was dressed?'

'A grey flannel suit and a grey Homburg hat. He always wore grey flannel.'

Vandam produced his sheaf of photographs.

'By the way, is Mr Swayne among these?'

Bragg seemed surprised as he took the cards.

'That's the man,' he said, immediately picking out Swayne's portrait. 'Do you not know him?'

'Never saw him in my life,' Vandam declared. 'I think, Mr Bragg, that's all I want from you. I'm very greatly obliged, I'm sure. Now could I see that waiter who came down with the bill?'

The clerk gave a rapid order on his desk telephone, and presently an elderly, reliable looking man entered. He stated that he recalled the events of the Wednesday night clearly, and answered all Vandam's questions without hesitation.

He had been on late duty, it seemed, that evening, and about half-past ten the bell rang from No. 78, Mr Swayne's room. Jackson, the waiter, had immediately answered the bell, and had found Swayne in his room, packing a suitcase. He had evidently just come in, for he was still wearing his grey Homburg hat.

'Oh,' he said, 'waiter, I wish you'd get me my bill.' Jackson was moving off when Swayne called him back. 'By the way, what time do you make it?' They compared watches and agreed that it was exactly twenty-eight minutes past ten. 'I have to catch the early morning train, and I forgot to check my watch,' Swayne explained, continuing, 'I wish you'd see that the night porter understands about getting me up in the morning, and that a taxi is arranged for. I told him, but I'd like to make sure it's all right.' Jackson then went for the bill. It amounted to four pounds sixteen, and Swayne gave him a five-pound note, telling him to keep the change. Jackson took the money to the office, got the bill receipted, and returned with it to the bedroom. Having assured Swayne that the arrangements for the morning were in order, he left the receipted bill and withdrew, and that was the last he had seen of the visitor.

Vandam slipped a couple of shillings into the man's hand, thanked him, and turned to the clerk.

'Now, if I might see that night porter, Mr Bragg,' he suggested.

'Send Hitchcock here, will you,' Bragg called after the retreating waiter, and presently a second man appeared, this time small, dark and alert looking, not, indeed, unlike Vandam himself.

He had been, he stated, on duty as porter on the previous Wednesday night. He had wakened Mr Swayne and seen him start for the Capetown train.

'Just tell me all you know about his going,' Vandam asked.

'I came on duty at ten, sir,' the man answered, 'and, as usual, I looked at the board to see if there were any early calls. I saw No. 78 was to get knocked at 3.00. "Him for the south train?" I asked my mate, the porter that I was relieving. "Sure," he says. "Is he having a taxi?" I asked, and Morton, that's my mate, said, "Yes," that he had fixed it up. Then at three o'clock I knocked him and brought him up a cup of tea. "Come up for my stuff in twenty minutes," he says. I did so, and carried his baggage down to the taxi. He left the hotel about five-and-twenty minutes past three.'

'Did he speak to you when he was going out?'

'He just said, "Well, goodbye, porter. Thanks for your help," and he gave me a tip.'

'Did you notice anything peculiar about his manner?'

The porter seemed somewhat surprised at the trend of the questions, but he answered unhesitatingly:

'No, sir, I can't say I did.'

'Now, porter,' Vandam went on, 'remember we're talking confidentially and don't jump to conclusions from what I'm asking you. Would it have been possible for Mr Swayne to have left the hotel between 10.30 and 3.25 that night without having been seen?'

Both Bragg and the porter stared, and the latter shook his head.

'It couldn't have been done,' he said decisively. 'Not anyway at all. No one could have got in or out without my knowing.'

'Just explain why, will you?'

'Why, because they couldn't,' retorted the porter, who was getting a trifle nettled by the interrogation. 'The side doors were all locked at dark, and from I came on duty at ten until the front door was locked at 11.30 I was there in the box the whole time, and nobody could have passed in or out without my seeing them. And from 11.30 no one could have got the door open without me. I saw Mr Swayne coming in. He came in about half-past ten, but he didn't go out again, not until he left at 3.25 to catch his train.'

'If you're really keen on that point,' interjected Bragg, who was evidently growing more and more interested, 'it happens you can get some other evidence. Our electrician was working in 70 corridor on that night—that is just outside Mr Swayne's rooms. Some of the bells had gone wrong, and it's not convenient to have the boards up in the daytime. He could tell you if anyone came out of 78 during the night.'

'Thanks, I should like to see him,' Vandam agreed, then turned back to the porter. 'By the way, can you tell me who drove the taxi that night?'

'Jan Voogdt. He drives for Gresham Bros. of 'sGravenhagen Street.'

The porter was dismissed in his turn, and the electrician entered. Him Vandam approached rather differently, asking him to give a list of all the people whom he could remember having passed through the corridor on that Wednesday night. The man would have made an ideal witness, being evidently very observant and having all his facts clear and sharp-edged. He had begun work shortly after eleven, and from that until the night porter arrived at 3.00 no one entered or left No. 78. He described accurately the porter's visit with the tea, his exit in a couple of minutes empty-handed, Swayne's departure some twenty minutes later, and the carrying down of the luggage.

As far as it went, this was conclusive, but it didn't satisfy Vandam. Under Bragg's guidance he interviewed a number of other servants, chambermaids, lift boys, shoeblacks, all of whom confirmed as far as they were able what he had already heard, and all of whom picked out Swayne's photograph from among the others. Then he asked to see No. 78, made certain that no one could have left through the windows—they were thirty feet up and overlooked the main street—went into the question of fire escapes, and at last finally and completely satisfied himself that Swayne had been in the building between half-past ten on the Wednesday night and twenty-five minutes past three on the Thursday morning.

'Now for Gresham Bros., the car owners,' thought Vandam as, after making the polite clerk a friend for life by promising to explain the business later and telling him how much he had helped him, he left the Bellevue and turned eastwards towards 'sGravenhagen Street.

Here, after some trouble, he found Jan Voogdt. The driver remembered the occasion in question. He had driven the fare he had picked up at the Bellevue at 3.25 to the railway station. A porter had there taken charge of the traveller's luggage. He knew the porter and remembered his name. He was a coloured man called Christmas White.

Vandam, methodical and painstaking as ever, went on to the station and looked up White. Like the taxi man, the latter also remembered the midnight passenger. He had arrived in Jan Voogdt's taxi, and he, White, had put his luggage into a sleeping berth on the train. The traveller had had his ticket and the berth was reserved for him.

To make assurance doubly sure, Vandam visited the booking clerk. Here he learned that Swayne, whose appearance the clerk knew, had taken his ticket and engaged his berth on the Monday previous.

Vandam was satisfied. Swayne had certainly left by the train in question. He was doubtless going for the *Warwick Castle,* due out at 7.00 p.m. on the Saturday evening. It would be well, however, to make sure of this, in case his subsequent investigation satisfied him of the man's guilt. He therefore despatched a code wire to the Capetown police, asking them to ascertain the point.

As Vandam walked slowly back to headquarters, he ran over in his mind what he had learned up to the present. Swayne had been staying for some days at the Bellevue Hotel. He had left the building about five o'clock on the fatal Wednesday evening, and had not been seen again until 10.30. Then he had come in, paid his bill, and remained in his room until it was time to leave to catch the south-bound train. He had travelled by that train, and had presumably embarked on the steamer for England.

Smith had left his room about ten minutes past eight that night. The questions, therefore, which still remained to be settled were, first, where was Swayne between 8.10 and 10.30, and second, where was Smith during the same period? In other words, could the murder have taken place between those hours?

Vandam recollected that the medical evidence was not inconsistent with such a supposition. Dr Bakker had examined the body between seven and eight on the Thursday morning, and had given it as his opinion that death had taken place about ten hours previously. The Inspector was aware that such testimony was not conclusive, but so far as it went, it supported the idea.

That evening, when he had finished his day's work and was sitting smoking in his most comfortable armchair, Vandam's thoughts returned to the case. What, he wondered, had taken place in that terrible shed in the Groote Park? What was the sequence of events which had led up to the tragedy? Was

Swayne really the murderer? Had his quarrel with Smith been about the pretty barmaid, Jane Louden? Though at the moment he could not reply to these questions, he swore to himself that it would not be long before he learned their answers.

Presently he began to consider details. How had the victim been lured to his doom? By an anonymous letter? Or by one forged in Miss Louden's handwriting? Vandam's experience suggested something of the kind.

He tried to picture the happening at the shed, Smith's arrival, his feeling his way in through the enshrouding darkness of the night, perhaps his whispered 'Are you there?' the dull thud of the sandbag on the unsuspecting head, the collapse of that powerful frame into a shapeless heap . . .

Vandam, reconstructing the scene, saw suddenly the significance of the sweeping of the floor and of the newspapers. Smith could not be allowed to fall on the earthy floor. Still less could Swayne roll the body over as he searched the pockets for the document which in all probability had been used to lure the victim to his doom. Why not? Simply because the clothes would be stained by earth, stained a different colour from the railway ballast, and would therefore afford a clue to the sharp-eyed detective who would be called in if any suspicion about the 'accident' arose. To lay newspapers on the floor would be an obvious precaution. But newspapers, covering an area on which was spread little heaps of earth and small stones, would tear when pressure came on them. Therefore the heaps of earth and the stones must be removed. The floor must be swept. And when the work of the newspapers was done, when the clothes had been searched and the document removed, and the body dragged down to where the accident was to be staged, these marks left in the shed must be removed. The papers must vanish. And how could this be done more efficiently than by burning? Vandam saw that Swayne would have to burn them. And he would have to throw back the earth over the floor so as to remove the signs of the sweeping.

Smoking feverishly, Vandam believed he could picture the whole scene: Swayne crouching, sandbag in hand and with murder in his heart, behind the door of the shed; Smith, possibly suspecting a trap, but still forced to go on, groping his way cautiously to the place; his sudden instinctive realisation of danger; the dull thud of the sandbag; the limp form falling; the dragging of it in so that the door might be shut and a light used; the search for a possible incriminating document; the extinction of the light, and the terrible, staggering journey with the corpse from that awful shed, across the wall and down on to the railway below. Vandam seemed to see it all; the dragging of the body into the tunnel; the leaving it across the rails; the return to the shed; the burning of the papers and the scattering of the earth; the stealthy crossing of the railway; the hiding of the sandbag cover and the hammer. The hammer! Vandam was brought up sharp in his imaginings. The hammer did not fit in. What had the hammer been used for?

Here was a problem on which at first light seemed unattainable. The Inspector rose to his feet and began silently pacing the room. For twenty minutes he strode up and down, his head bent forward, his lips moving as he put his thoughts into words, and then at last the sought for idea flashed into his mind. Was the hammer not a precautionary measure? Had it not been brought to the site, and used, because there was an element of doubt about the efficacy of the sandbag? A sandbag left no marks. How was Swayne, a layman without medical knowledge, in the imperfect light of the shed and in his hurry and excitement, to be quite sure that the sandbag had done its work? He must run no risk of his victim being merely stunned. He must be certain that there would be no revival in that body before the train came.

The more Vandam thought over it, the better his theory seemed to work in. He now saw why the sandbag had been used in the first instance. There must be no blood in the shed. And blood must not stain the murderer's clothes as he dragged the body to the railway. But the railway once reached, he could complete his ghastly work. Blood on the line did not matter; it would be expected.

As Vandam thought over his theory, he felt distinctly pleased with himself. Starting from nothing, he had evolved a complete conception of what might have occurred, from the original motive almost down to the last detail. Of such an achievement he might be justly proud.

But he was under no illusions on the matter. He fully recognised that his idea was a mere guess, and he quite saw that some new fact might upset the whole of it and leave him as far from a solution as ever. However, his theory was at least something to go on, and he decided that his next step must be to test it. On the following day he would continue the tracing of Swayne's movements on the fatal Wednesday night between the hours of 8.10 and 11.

CHAPTER V

ROBBERY UNDER ARMS

ONE of the things which added piquancy to Inspector Vandam's life was the fact that at no time could he say with any reasonable degree of certainty where he would be or how he would be engaged an hour later. However he might plan, whatever arrangements he might make, he was for ever at the beck and call of the unexpected. His friends knew from experience that it was best to expect him when they saw him, and they were usually more surprised when he kept his appointments than when he broke them.

This attribute of his calling was exemplified when he reached headquarters on the following morning. He had arrived, his mind filled with the importance of finding out where Swayne was between eight and ten on the night of the murder. Fifteen seconds later Swayne was forgotten, and his thoughts were concentrated on a quite different side of his case. The event which produced this sudden change of outlook was nothing more nor less than the fact that he was informed that a Miss Jane Louden was impatiently awaiting the officer who was dealing with the matter of the accident to Albert Smith.

'Show her to my room,' Vandam said, and he looked up with eager interest as a tall, strongly-built girl entered.

She was dark, and her face was of a heavy and immobile type, though it was not without a certain coarse beauty. Her features were set in an expression of arrogance and scorn. After what he had heard of her, Vandam was at first surprised that she was not better looking. But before he was five minutes in her presence he became aware of a certain attraction which to some types of mind, he believed, might easily become irresistible. She was dressed quietly but extremely well in a dark blue coat and skirt, of which even Vandam could not but admire the cut, a small hat, silk stockings and patent shoes. She seemed as eager and excited as Vandam imagined it was her nature to be. He took her measure rapidly and bowed politely.

'Good morning, Miss Louden,' he said. 'Won't you sit down? I am Inspector Vandam, and I have been detailed to make inquiries into the death of the late Mr Albert Smith. I take it from your message you wish to see me?'

'That's so,' the girl answered. She spoke quietly, but there was more than a suggestion of anxiety in her manner. 'I felt I should come to headquarters the moment I heard of his death, but I just couldn't lift my head at the time. I was down with 'flu, and I came just the moment I could stand. I'm not very well yet.'

'I hope you'll soon be all right,' Vandam returned sympathetically. 'In the meantime if there is anything I can do for you, I hope you will just let me know.'

'That's what I came for,' she declared. 'I can tell you in two words. It is not generally known that Mr Smith and I were engaged to be married, but that is the fact.'

Vandam did not see exactly where this was leading, but he made sounds of respectful commiseration and waited for more.

'It was only five days ago, certainly,' the girl went on, 'and it wasn't announced, but it was quite a definite engagement for all that. I wanted it kept quiet for a day or two. A girl does, you know. But I'm sorry I did now, though, of course, I couldn't tell he would be fool enough to get run over. It puts me in an awkward position, right enough.'

Still Vandam did not see what was coming.

'But who would question the fact of your engagement?' he asked.

'Nobody,' she said grimly. 'I'd like to see anyone trying it on. But I thought it would be only right that you people knew.'

'Ah, quite so. Of course. No doubt,' Vandam admitted. 'We'll certainly keep it in mind.'

But this evidently would not meet the case, and she proceeded to explain more definitely.

'I suppose there's no question I'll be all right?' she queried. 'I don't suppose he made a will—it would be just like him not to bother—but there can be no doubt of his intention.'

Illumination came over Vandam. Though a wide experience had made him tolerant of the frailties of human nature, he was unable to keep a slight feeling of disgust out of his mind as he looked at her. She could not show even a decent pretence at regret for the man who had loved her!

'What about his relations?' he asked, to see what she would say.

'He hadn't any.' She spoke with a covetous eagerness. 'I made quite sure of that. There is nobody but me that could have any claim at all. That is, in justice. But I was afraid that perhaps if there wasn't an actual will in writing, that there might be some legal difficulty; that maybe I would only get a part.'

Vandam would have enjoyed telling her that she hadn't the slightest chance of getting a farthing. But that would not be business. He must pump her well first.

'I would hardly like to say off-hand,' he said slowly. 'These lawyers, you know; when once they get started . . .' He shook his head to indicate the futility and meddlesomeness of the profession. 'It would be a matter, I think, of evidence; what evidence there was of the engagement, whether there really were no relatives, and how far the engagement, if admitted, could be held to take the place of a formal will. I don't know that I should like to say how it would go.'

'Do you mean that?' she cried, and there was now no doubt of the genuineness of her emotion. 'But I tell you the stuff is mine! He said so. He said it was for me. Why, it was only on account of it that I promised to marry him. I tell you it was a bargain.'

'Forty-five pounds of assets and a hundred of debts,' thought Vandam. 'What is she getting at?' But aloud he said, 'You speak as if the deceased gentleman had large means. I was not aware that that was so. His salary, I understand, was about £400, and of course that will die with him.'

'Salary!' she repeated scornfully. 'It's not his miserable salary I'm talking about. It's the diamonds I want.'

Vandam automatically controlled a start of surprise, but a moment's thought convinced him that he would gain nothing by pretending a knowledge of her meaning.

'What diamonds are you speaking of?' he therefore asked.

She stared at him.

'Why—' she burst out. Then a look of absolute horror dawning in her eyes, she sprang to her feet and screamed at him. 'You don't mean to say you don't know? You don't mean they weren't on the body? Speak, can't you?'

'Sit down and control yourself,' Vandam said sternly. 'There was nothing of any value found on the body.'

She took no notice of his admonition, but stood glaring at him, crying with a torrent of bitter oaths that her diamonds had been stolen.

Vandam got up, seized her by the arm, and forced her into her chair.

'Sit down there,' he ordered harshly, 'and don't be more of a fool than you can help. If you talk calmly I'll listen to you; otherwise you can get out of here and look for your diamonds yourself.'

The threat had some effect, and the girl stopped shouting.

'Now,' went on Vandam, 'begin at the beginning and explain what you're talking about. And remember you can't do any monkeying with the police force. We've a quick way here of dealing with anyone that gives trouble.'

Somewhat cowed, the girl glanced at him venomously and began to speak.

'It's all very well for you,' she grumbled sullenly. 'You've lost nothing. It's I that have had the loss, and you tell me to keep quiet.'

Vandam, convinced that he was on the eve of some important revelation, was awaiting her statement with keen interest, but all he said was, 'If you don't want our help, you needn't wait.'

'No,' she said hurriedly. 'I'll tell you. Five days ago we were engaged. It's true we didn't—'

'That's no good,' Vandam interrupted roughly. 'You must tell me the whole thing. Begin at the beginning. How did you first get to know Mr Smith?'

'It was about six months ago,' she answered, and as she continued to speak she grew calmer and more coherent. 'He came one night to the hotel—my father keeps a hotel in East Hawkins Street, you know. He was looking for a man who was staying there, a Mr—I forget his name—Jones, I think. Well, anyway, he found him, and they had some drinks in the bar. I served them, and they got talking to me part of the time. After that Albert began to come regularly, but it was a week or more before I knew he was after me. He got more and more friendly, and then one Saturday night he begged me to go for a walk with him next day. I didn't do it then, but after he'd asked me three or four times I went. We went out on Sundays regularly after that, and then he asked me to marry him. I had found out about him by that time, and I knew he had little more than the clothes he stood in, so I told him the truth. I hadn't any use for a poor man. He wouldn't take No for an answer, and implored me not to shut down our acquaintance-ship. I said if he was fool enough to hang round me on those terms I didn't mind. Every now and then he'd ask me to marry him, but I wasn't having any. He might have known I had made up my mind.'

She was talking now in what was presumably her natural manner, with a dull, heavy cynicism that made no attempt to cloak her selfishness and heartlessness. But, repulsive as she seemed to him, Vandam could imagine her possessing enormous influence over any man who might be unlucky enough to fall in love with her.

'Two days before his death,' she went on, 'that was, on last Monday, he came into the bar, and I could see at once that something was up. He was all nervous and upset and was bubbling over with some news. He asked me to go out with him, saying he had something very important to tell me. I confess I was curious, so I agreed and we went to the Groote Park. When we had got away from the crowd, he said that at last he could ask me to marry him with a better heart. He had had a stroke of luck and would now be able to offer me a suitable home and income.

'I asked what had happened, and he drew me over near one of the big lamps in the park and took something from his pocket.

'"Look at that," he said, and he showed me what I thought was a pebble at first, but what I saw then was a diamond. It was a medium-sized stone, not cut. I didn't think much of it.

'"What's the use of that?" I asked him. "That's not worth anything to make a song about."

'"Isn't it though?" he said. "It's worth a tidy £250, and perhaps £300."

'I was annoyed at that, for what was two or three hundred pounds to marry on? I was beginning to tell him what I thought of him when he stopped me.

'"Ah," he said, "but that's not all. That's one stone—it's all I cared to carry on me—but there are more hidden away where that came from. There's a bag in a safe place with forty-seven other stones, and most of them more valuable than this one."

'Well, that pretty well took away my breath. Ten or fifteen thousand pounds! That was talking.

'"If you have that, I'll marry you tomorrow," I told him. He wanted to kiss me, but I wouldn't let him. "No," I said, "time enough for that sort of thing later. Wait 'til we're married. I'll see the money first."

'That sort of made him wild to sell the stones, but after a

time I got him quieted down to tell me some particulars about them, and the more he told me, the more I began to believe in them.'

'Did he tell you how he got them?' Vandam interrupted.

'Yes, that was the first thing I asked him. He said gambling. He said he was in a private room in one of the downtown houses, and there was high play going on and a lot of drinking. There were some men in from the mines, and they were staking stones on the play. Albert joined in. He had a run of luck and began to win their stones. He stood drinks again and again, and they were knocked over soonest, for they were half drunk when he went in, but he was as sober as you are. The stakes got higher and higher and the men drunker and drunker, 'til some of them could go on no longer and dropped out and went to sleep. But there was one big man that wouldn't give way, and he staked and staked and lost to Albert every time. At last when they must all have been pretty mad, the end came. The big man staked all he had, a bag of twenty-one stones against Albert's winnings. Albert by this time had twenty-seven stones in his bag. Albert won this time and collared the lot. Of course, they'd never have let him away alive; the big man pulled a gun on him at once, but Albert had seen the electric switch was just behind him as they sat at the table, and he nipped up and had the light off and was out of the place before they could get him. There was the devil's own row and they fired all round, but he got clear away with the whole forty-eight.'

'Where did this take place?'

'He wouldn't say and I didn't bother to press him; somewhere down east, I gathered. He said it was the greatest piece of luck, for he hadn't gone to the place intending to play. But he was in a rare old stew about it too; said if any of the miners got sight of him they'd have his life for sure. I told him to buy a gun, and he promised he would.'

This, then, was the explanation of the automatic pistol found on Smith's body. Vandam had hoped for great things from the tracing of the weapon, but now it looked as if it would teach him nothing. 'A promising clue gone west,' he thought regretfully as he asked Miss Louden to continue.

'We talked on about the thing, and I told him uncut diamonds were no use to me, and asked him what about getting them turned into cash. He said he'd thought of that, and that he was going to sell them quietly to one of the dealers; Messrs. Goldstein, he mentioned. He said he would go round to old Goldstein the next evening and see if he could fix up a satisfactory price. He didn't want the deal to be known of, for he expected the men that had lost the stones to him would be watching the ordinary buyers, and might find him in that way. He came back on Tuesday night to say he had seen Goldstein, who had seemed willing to treat. Albert was to meet him with the stones the next night, that is, the night he was killed, to fix up the sale. I suppose he was going to the meeting place by the railway so as to avoid meeting people with all that wealth on him, and like the fool he always was he let himself get run over. I would have come and told you all about it this next morning only I had gone down with this darned 'flu, and I didn't know 'til last night what had happened.'

'Where were they to meet?'

'He didn't say.'

For some moments Vandam sat lost in thought. He was not altogether satisfied about what he had heard. That Miss Louden herself implicitly believed her story he had no doubt, but he was not sure that Smith had told her the whole truth. That tale of the gambling for high stakes in the downtown bar seemed to him a little far-fetched, and he wondered whether Smith had not really stolen the stones. The man's choice of an agent was suspicious. Goldstein's reputation was bad. In police circles it was usually assumed that there was no trick too low or shady for him to adopt. He was a clever scoundrel who generally got himself off with his schemes, leaving the penalty to be paid by his dupes. Vandam knew of no one in the city more likely to undertake the sale of stolen diamonds. An obvious line of inquiry would, at all events, be the interrogation of Goldstein.

But with the remainder of Miss Louden's story Vandam was delighted. Here, at last, was an adequate motive for Smith's murder, more satisfying and definite than the possible bad feeling of Swayne! That someone had learnt of the diamonds and murdered Smith for them seemed almost a certainty.

Vandam wondered if he could get any help from Miss Louden by enlisting her self-interest on his behalf. He therefore bent towards her, and sinking his voice confidentially, said:

'This story of yours has made me think, Miss Louden. I'm wondering whether there's not more in the affair than I imagined at first. Seeing there was £10,000 or £15,000 to be gained by Mr Smith's death, well—does that not suggest anything?'

Miss Louden stared at him for a moment, then her dark eyes flashed and she nodded her head emphatically.

'Foul play?' she cried eagerly. 'That's it! I didn't think of it, but that's just what happened. They would think the train hitting him would look like an accident. You'll get them, Inspector! If that's it, you'll get them sure! Get at it quick! Get them before they can unload the stones!'

There was no suggestion of horror at a crime of violence in the girl's manner, no thought of regret for the fate of her former companion and lover. Obviously her sole idea was the diamonds. Even the Inspector was surprised and a trifle shocked at such callousness. But he hid his feelings and continued his confidential mode of address.

'It looks like it, doesn't it? And you're right, too, that if it's murder we'll soon get the guilty party. But I was thinking maybe you could help me a bit there. It seems to me there are two possibilities. Either the murderer knew Smith had the stones on him and murdered him to get them, or he murdered him for some other reason and found the stones on the body by chance. Let us see if we can think of anyone who might fill the bill in both these cases. Suppose, first of all, the thing was done to get the diamonds. Who knew he was carrying them? There was yourself and there was Goldstein. Who else?'

Miss Louden did not seem pleased at the way this was put, and she answered sharply: 'How do I know? Albert was a darned fool. He might have told half the town.'

Vandam shook his head.

'I hardly think so. He's not likely to have mentioned it. But we've to remember the miners, the landlord and waiters in the downtown bar, and other customers that might have been there and seen the gambling. Some of them may have spotted Smith and been following him round.'

'That's so.'

'Now as to murder for some other reason, and the chance finding of the stones. I don't mean to be impertinent, Miss Louden, but a girl as attractive as yourself must have turned a good many more than one man's head. When you took up with Smith, there must have been a good few disappointed. What about them?'

For once the girl did not appear displeased. She laughed as she answered, 'Go on now, Inspector, what next? What do you think you're getting at?'

But Vandam was serious.

'Do you mean to tell me,' he persisted, 'that there was no one who could have been jealous of Smith? This is not a joke. Think carefully.'

But, according to the girl, there was no one. 'Little Johnnie Oswald,' Smith's immediate predecessor, had left the country some months previously; Joe Harrison was married a year ago and she seldom saw him, though he was friendly enough when she did; Willie Deane had gone north; Jack Jenkins had been killed in a mining accident; in fact, the Inspector need not hope to get any help in that line. As soon as he was satisfied he could learn nothing more from her, Vandam dismissed the girl with a warning not to breathe what she had told him to another soul.

He had little doubt that he was now on the high road to a

solution of the mystery. It was true, of course, that since the I.D.B. laws had been more strictly enforced, crime arising from the illicit possession of diamonds had decreased. But it was not by any means unknown. In the Inspector's own experience, murder had been committed on several occasions to obtain stones of less value than were at present in question.

He went over again in his mind the persons who might have been aware of Smith's treasure. There were Smith himself, Miss Louden and Goldstein. If the gambling story were true, there were also the miners, with possibly spectators of the play, the landlord of the bar, the barmaid, the waiters . . . Conceivably several persons might have known or heard of the stones. Smith himself might have bragged.

But the guilt of all these persons was not equally probable. Vandam thought of the details of the murder, ingenious, calculating, subtle. From the mind of which of the above would the scheme have been most likely to spring?

Not from persons like miners, bar loafers or waiters would such a plan materialise. Their methods would be cruder; a knuckleduster, a loaded stick, an automatic pistol. No, some intellectual devil was guilty here.

As Vandam sat pondering, he gradually came to see that of all those of whom he had heard, but one man entirely filled the bill. Goldstein had the necessary knowledge, the required motive, the needful ability. The Inspector began to picture the possibilities.

Goldstein, no doubt, suspected the diamonds were stolen, and he would certainly feel safer if the other party to the illicit purchase was beneath the sod. Further, if he could obtain possession of, say, £10,000 to £20,000 worth of stones, without parting with the £2,000 or £3,000 he would probably have offered for them, he would naturally be so much the better off. In his mind's eye, Vandam saw him preparing the trap. He would tell Smith he could not transact such delicate business at his office or home—the very fact that negotiations were in progress must be kept secret. He would suggest the potting shed as an alternative. Smith would see that no better place could be proposed. He might suspect a trap, but he would go nevertheless. He would feel that he must get through with the business, and that he was armed, and therefore on equal terms with his opponent.

If this theory were true, it supplied an even more cogent reason for the sweeping of the floor and the spreading of the newspapers. The body would have to be searched for the diamonds. They would probably be in a secret pocket, and the remains would have to be rolled over perhaps two or three times before they were found.

Though with his usual caution Vandam recognised that he was entertaining a theory quite unsupported by proof, nevertheless he felt pretty sure that he had stumbled on the truth. At all events, he must apply tests. His obvious duty was to interview Goldstein, ask him where he had been at the time of the murder, and test the truth of his reply.

But he did not abandon his former theories. As this robbery idea seemed the most likely, he would deal with it first, but if it failed he would still have two other strings to his bow, those of Swayne and a possible jealous lover.

He was aware that his immediate quarry did business at 34 York Street, and in less than twenty minutes Vandam was pushing open a door labelled, 'M. Goldstein, Commission Agent.' He sent in his card, and two minutes later was seated in front of the agent in the latter's private room.

Moses Goldstein was dark and oily of countenance, with semitic features and a pair of furtive, shifty eyes. He greeted his visitor obsequiously, as though to propitiate him in advance against the trouble which he appeared instinctively to expect. But Vandam was politeness itself as he began to speak.

'I am sorry, Mr Goldstein, to interrupt you, but I should be greatly obliged if you would give me the benefit of your help in a small matter I have undertaken.'

The commission agent, surprised at this unexpected opening, spread out his hands, and bowing, assured the other of his anxiety to give him any assistance in his power.

'It's just a little confidential information that I want,' Vandam went on, 'to enable me to complete a report for the Chief.'

Again the victim protested his eagerness to assist.

'Thank you, Mr Goldstein, that is very kind of you.' Vandam spoke in his easiest and most confidential tones. 'What I want is merely a complete statement of your recent deal in diamonds with the late Mr Albert Smith.'

If Vandam had leaned forward and politely ignited a squib under his companion's nose, Goldstein could not have started back in greater consternation. It was this effect for which Vandam had been aiming, and he was himself surprised at the completeness of his success. Goldstein's jaw dropped, and he stared at his visitor in something very like panic. Then with an effort he pulled himself together.

'You are mistaken, I assure you,' he murmured in somewhat shaky tones. 'I had no deal with Mr Smith about diamonds or anything else.'

Vandam pretended not to notice anything unusual, and continued speaking as before.

'That may be, Mr Goldstein,' he admitted pleasantly, 'but you cannot deny that you know to what I was referring. Your manner, of course, makes that quite certain. Now, won't you tell me the whole story, seeing that you have admitted there is one?'

Goldstein did not reply at once, and his eyes shone with malice, though his lips remained twisted into the semblance of a smile. Vandam believed he could trace the working of the man's mind. He was anything but a fool, and he would recognise that a mere bald denial would only confirm the suspicion he wished to dissipate. A cleverly constructed story would be the game, one which, while concealing the truth, would cover the facts the Inspector might be presumed to know. Vandam waited with a two-fold interest to see if such would materialise.

Presently the victim came to a decision.

'You are quite correct, Inspector,' he said, with an assumption of candour which instantly increased the other's doubts. 'I know what you are speaking of, or, at least, I think I do. It is true that I discussed a deal with the late Mr Smith, but it never came off. No transaction of any kind took place between us.'

Though the man spoke with an air of assurance, Vandam could see that he was acutely uneasy. His face bore an expression of something not very far removed from terror.

'I think you had better tell me the whole story,' Vandam suggested.

'I will do so. It is but right. On Tuesday night last as I was preparing for bed—I go early as a rule—a ring came to the door. It was Mr Smith, and he said he wished to speak to me in private. I brought him in and he sat in my study. He pledged me to secrecy, and then he drew a small stone from his pocket and asked me what it was worth. It was an uncut diamond of good shape, small, but of an excellent colour. I told him about £100. He said he had a number of others, and he wanted to know if I would buy them. I said I couldn't possibly tell unless I saw them, but that if they were all as good as the one I had seen, and if he could give me proof that they were come by honestly, I probably would deal. He explained that he had forty-eight altogether, but that he hadn't wished to carry so many in his pocket; the others were hidden in a safe place. He said also that he had won them gambling, and that the whole business was honest and above-board. I said that was all very well, but that I would want some proof that the diamonds weren't stolen by the men he had won them from, also that I must see the others before I could decide about them. He admitted that this was reasonable, and it was settled that he would bring them to my house for my inspection at 11.30 on the following night, Wednesday. I was ready for him at the time, but he did not come, though I waited up 'til after one a.m. Next day, of course, I learned the reason.'

'That Wednesday was the night he was killed?'

'Yes. I suppose—eh—you found the diamonds on the body?'

Goldstein had seemed to regain confidence as he was speaking, but he could not quite control his voice when he asked his question. To Vandam his nonchalance seemed over-done, but he answered in the same pleasant conversational way he had previously used.

'Well, no. You could hardly expect a man to take all that trouble to murder Mr Smith, and then to forgo the profits. That would hardly be business.'

Goldstein gave a strangled cry and his face grew ashen.

'Murdered!' he groaned. 'I feared as much. I couldn't believe in the accident. Terrible!'

'Yes,' Vandam went on. 'Now, Mr Goldstein, who besides yourself and himself knew of those stones?'

'Who?' cried the wretched man. 'I don't know. How could I? I don't know who he might have told.'

'Nor I,' said Vandam dryly. 'What were you doing yourself that evening, Mr Goldstein?'

'What I have told you; waiting in my house for Mr Smith's visit.'

'All the evening?'

'No, not all. I was working late part of the time. When closing time came I had not finished, so I decided to dine at Schoof's and go back to the office later. I did so, and worked there from half-past seven 'til nearly ten. Then I came home by street car. I got there a few minutes after ten, had a drink, and sat reading and waiting for Smith 'til about one, when I gave him up and went to bed.'

'Did anyone see you between the time you left the restaurant and the time you went to bed?'

'Yes. My stenographer was in the office all the evening, in fact, I left her behind me there. There were several people in the tram, though I didn't know any of them, but I knew and spoke to the conductor.'

'What tram?'

'One for Coachford, leaving Hovis Street about ten or shortly before.'

'Anyone see you reach home, or after you reached home?'

'No. But I should like to know, Inspector, by what right you are asking me these particularly offensive questions?'

'I don't wish to be offensive, Mr Goldstein. Your own good sense will tell you two things; first, that circumstances have put you into an awkward position, and second, that it is my duty to give you the earliest opportunity to put yourself right. You can easily see that if you refuse to answer me you will arouse unpleasant, though, I am sure, groundless suspicions.'

Vandam had imagined that the man's protest had been enforced by the part he was trying to play, and this opinion was now confirmed by the readiness with which he relinquished it.

'I see that, Inspector,' he admitted. 'As you say, through no fault of my own, I have been placed in very unpleasant and distressing circumstances. Ask what questions you like, and I will answer them without further hesitation.'

He was certainly as good as his word, but the information he had to give was far from reassuring. His wife, it appeared, had been dead for several years, and he lived alone with an elderly housekeeper. As he did not wish anyone to be aware that he and Smith were doing business, he had given this woman leave to spend the night with her daughter, the wife of a foreman in the electric generating station. The child of these people was ill, and the grandmother had asked leave to assist in the nursing, and had already been given it on different occasions. She had not, it was true, asked for a whole night, and Goldstein admitted he had used the child's illness to get her out of the way. No one, therefore, had seen him since he entered his house shortly after ten, nor had he any way of proving that he had been there. Naturally, he had not spoken to anyone about the diamonds.

From the man's manner, no less than from his story, Vandam was inclined to believe in his guilt, but he had to admit to himself that the statement hung together and was by no means impossible. It might, indeed, be true, and Goldstein might be an innocent man, and it therefore behoved him to be very careful in making an accusation or attempting an arrest. After a few moments thought, he decided he would postpone action and pretend that he was satisfied by what he had heard.

He therefore thanked the commission agent for his help, apologised for having troubled him, dropped a hint that his energies would now be turned to an attempt to trace the miners from whom the diamonds had been won, and took his leave. But his first action on reaching the street was to turn into a call-office, ring up headquarters, and arrange for the continuous shadowing of Goldstein.

He next took a tram to the agent's house and saw the house-keeper. Explaining that he was Detective-Inspector Vandam, he told her he had been called in that morning by Mr Goldstein to investigate a robbery of which he had been the victim. By this means he was enabled to make inquiries about the house-hold and about her own and Mr Goldstein's movements on the night of the murder. The replies he received confirmed as far as was possible the statement to which he had already listened.

Puzzled and uncertain as to his next step, he returned to the centre of town and entered his favourite restaurant to partake of a long overdue lunch.

CHAPTER VI

A PROFITABLE EVENING

INSPECTOR VANDAM occupied a solitary table in a secluded alcove of the restaurant, and when he had lunched he sat on for some minutes smoking and sipping his coffee, while he considered what further investigations he could make as to the innocence or guilt of Moses Goldstein.

Three lines of inquiry immediately occurred to him, though from none of them did he hope for much enlightenment. First, there was the conductor of the street car to whom Goldstein alleged he had spoken when returning to his house. Though it would not prove him innocent if the man remembered the incident, it would at least be confirmation of his statement. Next, there was the police patrol on duty in Goldstein's neighbourhood. There was a chance that some of these men might have seen him on his way home at the hour stated. Further, there was also a chance that an officer might have observed him leaving or returning at a later hour—on his way to or from the Groote Park—and, if so, it would be a practical demonstration of his guilt. Lastly, some of the other men on duty between Goldstein's house and the Groote Park might have noticed him passing on his sinister errand.

There were two other points to which Vandam thought attention should be given. He might try to learn if anyone had recently lost uncut diamonds, and he might make inquiries as to whether anyone appeared to have suddenly come in for money.

He returned to headquarters, and began to put his ideas into practice. Summoning three of his men, he put them on the tracing of Goldstein's movements on the night in question. One was to interview the stenographer, another to find the tram conductor and interrogate him, while the third was to make inquiries from the police patrols on duty, or from any other persons who might be in a position to give information.

Vandam then turned to his correspondence. On his desk were two papers bearing on the crime. The first was a memo from the Chief saying he would like to see him at some time during the afternoon, the second a report from the sergeant whom he had detailed to inquire as to the sale of the automatic pistol on Smith's body.

Sergeant Hewitt wrote that he had inquired from several shops, and had at last found that the pistol had been purchased by Mr Albert Smith from Messrs. Frazer & Green, of 127 George Road, on the afternoon of the day before the murder. The assistant who sold it had noted its number and could swear to it positively, moreover, he was personally acquainted with the deceased.

'That's all right as far as it goes,' Vandam muttered as he rose to go to the Chief's room.

'Ah, Vandam,' the latter greeted him as he entered. 'Are you in the middle of anything important?'

'Not for the moment, sir. I am on to a new line,' and he told of Miss Louden's visit and his subsequent activities.

The Chief was a good deal impressed by the story. 'I fancy you're on the right track,' he declared, 'and I agree with you that it's much more likely that Smith stole the stones than that he won them at play. But now you've got your investigation into it underway, you can drop that line for the present and turn your attention to this.' He picked up from behind his desk a small, light coloured suitcase.

Vandam looked his question.

'You reported that Smith had taken a suitcase with him from his rooms on the night he was murdered. What did he do with it? Have you considered that point?'

'Well, no, sir. I haven't had time yet.'

The Chief frowned.

'As far as I understand the situation, we don't know what he did with it? It has absolutely disappeared?'

'That is right, sir.'

'Now, as you see, this suitcase bears the initials A.S. Moreover, it was picked up on the night of the murder. About 11.30 that night a man named Dirk Bechts found it in a narrow passage in Cheyne Street, near the Scala Picture House. He stepped in to light his pipe and fell over it. He gave it to the man on point duty, who brought it here in the usual way, but I didn't hear of it until this morning.'

'Pity we didn't know of it sooner.'

'Our own fault, Vandam. We didn't say we were looking out for a suitcase. You might take it out and see if it is any use to you.'

Vandam took the handbag to his office, and there soon opened it with one of his skeleton keys. It contained a suit of light brown tweed, a light brown felt hat, a brown tie and a soft collar, as well as pyjamas, brushes, shaving tackle, all such as would be required for a night's sojourn from home. The garments were very similar to those Smith was wearing when he was murdered, and Vandam began to believe the case really was that taken out by the deceased on the night of his death.

This, at all events, was a matter which could easily be tested, and not many minutes later Inspector Vandam, suitcase in hand, was standing once more before the door of No. 25 Rotterdam Road. Here his surmise was speedily confirmed. Mrs Regan immediately identified it as Smith's, and said she had missed it when going through his room after the tragedy. Asked if anything else had disappeared, she replied that a suit of clothes had been taken, but that she could not say when. Vandam then opened the case, and she stated unhesitatingly that the contents had belonged to Smith.

'I should like to know also, Mrs Regan,' he went on, 'whether your late lodger took away any more of his things with him. Did you miss anything else?'

'I did not then,' the lady assured him. 'I'm after looking in his room, and all his things are there still, only these.'

'Mr Holt told me about the handbag—he saw Mr Smith going out with it—but of course he did not know what it contained. Are you sure there was nothing else? Come along up to Mr Smith's room if you can spare the time, and just have another look round. I'll help you.'

During the next three hours Vandam more than justified his reputation for thoroughness. With pain-staking persistence he went through each article of clothing in turn, and questioned the landlady 'til her head swam and she wished him in the Groote Park or even farther. But so far as she could discover, nothing else was missing.

Getting rid of Mrs Regan, who was inclined to be garrulous, he turned his attention to a search for the diamonds. With this object, he re-examined each article of clothing, passing them inch by inch between his fingers in the hope of discovering something hard sewn into the lining. Then he started on the rooms, feeling the woodwork, lifting the rugs, and investigating the joints of the floor, examining the furniture minutely. In particular, the suitcase and its contents came in for a thorough scrutiny. But it was all to no purpose. There was nowhere a trace of the missing stones. Disappointed, he took leave of Mrs Regan and left the house.

He was not a little puzzled by this matter of the suitcase. Why had Smith abandoned it in Cheyne Street? This was not on the way to the Groote Park. Unless there was a great deal more in the whole affair than he had yet learnt, Vandam could not see how the thing worked in.

As he walked slowly along in a brown study, a voice said, 'Good evening, Inspector,' and, looking up, he saw Mr Hurst, the assistant manager of the Hope Bros. firm.

'I'm glad I met you,' went on the newcomer. 'I was talking

today to Hindhead, our accountant, about this business of Smith, and he told me he had seen Smith on the evening of his death. He was going into the Scala Cinema. I don't know whether or not you are interested, but I thought as you were making inquiries you might like to know.'

'Thanks, I'm very glad,' Vandam assured him. 'What time was he seen?'

'Between eight and nine, I gathered. But if you are keen about it you should see Hindhead. Besides, he was as good a friend of Smith's as anyone, probably better than most, and you may get other helpful particulars as well.'

'I'll see him at once, and thanks for the tip. Where is he to be found?'

Mr Hurst glanced at his watch.

'I expect he'll have left the office by this time.' he answered, 'but you should get him at his home, I know he doesn't go out much in the evenings. He lives in Ormiston Crescent, off Bulver Avenue.'

'I'll call after dinner.'

A couple of hours later, Vandam left his house, and, walking down to a neighbouring thoroughfare, boarded a west-bound street car to pay his call on Mr Hindhead.

The evening was pleasantly cool after the heat of the day, and the air grew still fresher as the car left the dusty streets, and passed out between the rows of plane trees of the suburban avenues.

Vandam dismounted at the end of a broad boulevard, and turning down a side street, knocked at the door of a tiny semi-detached house surrounded by a scrap of well-kept garden. Mr Hindhead was at home, and soon the Inspector sat opposite to him in a correspondingly diminutive parlour.

The master of the house fitted his surroundings. He was elderly, small and fragile, and his face looked worn as if from chronic ill health. But it lighted up when he smiled, and so kindly was his expression and so sympathetic his eyes that

Vandam felt immediately drawn to him, and his customary distrust was for once conspicuous by its absence.

Introducing himself, he went on, 'I have called, sir, to ask your kind help in investigating an unhappy matter, the death of Mr Albert Smith.'

Mr Hindhead shook his head sadly.

'A very terrible affair,' he commented. 'Poor fellow! The whole thing was just a tragedy.'

'A tragedy indeed, Mr Hindhead, and a sad one. You knew Mr Smith?'

'I knew him well, as well, I imagine, as anyone knew him. I have been closely in touch with him ever since he joined the firm, six years ago. You see, he was in my own department.'

'I understand, sir, that you are yourself connected with Messrs. Hope Bros.?'

'I am their accountant; have been for twenty-five—let's see—twenty-six years. A long time, Mr Inspector.'

'A long time indeed, sir, as you say. And the deceased was your assistant?'

'My second assistant. He was third in the department.'

'A good man?'

Mr Hindhead did not reply. Instead he took a case from his pocket and held it out.

'Won't you keep me company in a cigar?' he invited. 'I usually smoke one at this time.' He settled himself as if for a leisurely chat. 'About poor Smith,' he went on. 'One doesn't like to speak evil of the dead, but I'm afraid I couldn't say that he was altogether satisfactory. He had ability, ability indeed of no mean order, but the poor fellow—' again Mr Hindhead shook his head deprecatingly—'well, he didn't look after himself as he should, and naturally his work suffered.'

'You mean drink?'

'Not so much drink, though there was that too. He got into bad company, I'm afraid, and was always running after people that he would have been better advised to steer clear of; women, you know. But there,' Mr Hindhead shrugged his shoulders, leaving his comment unspoken. 'But, Mr Inspector, I should like to know why you are asking me all these questions. How, exactly, do they arise?'

Inspector Vandam drew slowly at his cigar.

'They arise, Mr Hindhead,' he answered deliberately, 'because we doubt very much whether any accident happened at all.'

Mr Hindhead stared as he ejaculated:

'Good gracious, Inspector, what do you mean?'

'We fear—I mention it in strict confidence only—we fear foul play.'

'Oh, poor fellow!' Mr Hindhead looked deeply shocked. 'You horrify me. How very dreadful!'

'We don't know, sir, for sure, but we think it not unlikely. There is enough suspicion, at all events, to necessitate our making inquiries. Now, sir, you knew the deceased gentleman intimately. Perhaps you would tell me what you can of his circumstances?'

Mr Hindhead answered with the utmost readiness, but he was not able to add much to the Inspector's store of knowledge. It appeared that in addition to the fight with Swayne, there had been trouble of various kinds with others. Smith was of a quarrelsome disposition and made enemies, which did not tend to harmonious working in the business. Once also, Mr Hindhead fancied, an attempt had been made to tamper with the books. He was not sure, and Smith, pleading a genuine mistake, he had let the matter drop. But though no one had a good word for Smith, Mr Hindhead did not believe he had a really serious enemy in the world.

'Mr Hurst told me you had seen Mr Smith that night?'

'I did. I saw him about half-past eight or a little earlier, but he didn't see me. He was standing in front of the Scala Cinema, with a yellow leather suitcase in his hand, as I approached along the footpath. He was looking up and down as if he was waiting for someone. However, just as I got up to him he turned and went into the building.'

'Was he alone?'

'Yes, quite alone.'

'Then he took the suitcase in with him?'

'He did, yes.'

Mrs Regan had stated that Smith had left his rooms about ten minutes past eight. From Rotterdam Road to the Scala was about ten minutes' walk. It looked, therefore, as if the man had walked direct to the picture house. Inquiries at the Scala began to loom big on the Inspector's horizon. For these, some means of identification would be required.

'You don't happen to have a photograph of the late Mr Smith?' he asked.

Mr Hindhead rose and crossed the room.

'Not a professional portrait,' he answered, 'but here is a group of the accountant's staff which contains an excellent likeness of him. Perhaps that would do?'

'Can you lend me this?'

'Certainly. You may keep it if you like; I have another copy.'

Vandam put the card into his pocket, as he considered what other information he wanted from the old gentleman. Then recollecting the other string to his bow, represented by Swayne, he returned to the charge.

'You mentioned someone called Swayne,' he suggested. 'What kind of person is he?'

'A clever man, very ingenious and clever. He made a capital sales manager. Personally, I like him, though I can't say he is a general favourite. Some people think him stand-offish.'

'He went on leave recently?'

'Yes, he's gone to England for three months. The whole story is rather a romance. Swayne told me all about it. One day about two months ago somebody stopped him in the street and asked him wasn't his name John Anthony. "Well," said the man, "there's an advertisement in yesterday's *Cape Times* that you ought to see." Swayne got hold of a paper, and there he found a notice that if John Anthony Swayne would apply to some lawyers in Cape Town he would hear something to his advantage; the usual thing, you know.'

'Good,' said Vandam, as the little man paused to draw at his cigar.

'Swayne wrote to the lawyers, and then it turned out that his grandfather was looking for him. Swayne had always known that his grandfather was an English baronet, but there had been a family feud, and the young fellow knew nothing of him and never expected to hear from him. It seems the old man had a row with his son, that is, our Swayne's father. As usual, it was about a girl. Swayne's father wanted to marry an actress, a girl he met on tour in Newcastle, and the old man was one of your straightlaced, Puritan type, and wouldn't have her at any price. He told Swayne's father that if he didn't drop the girl he would cut him off with the usual shilling. Swayne's father was hot-headed, and instead of trying to humour the old man round, went off then and there and got married. Probably he thought the old man would relent when he found he couldn't stop it. But he didn't. He was that stiff kind. He ordered Swayne's father out of the house, and cut him out of his will.'

'Was she a good girl?'

'Must have been, I fancy. She stuck to her husband anyway. The young couple came out here and made a living, though I don't think much more. They had one child, John Anthony. When he was about fifteen both parents died, and he was left entirely alone. He came to Middeldorp, got a job somewhere, educated himself in the evenings, and at last got a start in our firm. There he began to work himself up, and you have heard how far he succeeded. His grandfather, it seems, is now ailing, and wants to see his grandson. He sent him a cheque for £250 for his expenses, and asked him to go over and pay him a month's visit. Swayne got the necessary leave of absence, and went.'

'It looks as if the old man wanted to see if he was a proper person to whom to leave his money.'

'That occurred to me also,' Hindhead agreed, 'and I mentioned the idea to Swayne. He said that from what his parents had told him of his grandfather, he didn't think it was at all likely. He was inclined to refuse to go at first, but afterwards decided that when a move towards reconciliation had been made, he would not be the one to keep up the ancient enmity.'

'A romance, as you say,' Vandam observed, 'but it'll be a bigger romance if he comes in for the property.'

'Yes, won't it? It's extraordinary the ups and downs you hear of. There's Swayne with a chance of coming into money, and there's our manager, Mr Crawley, a real good fellow, ten times the man Swayne is, getting just as nasty a knock as ever I heard of. It's perhaps not right to talk about it, but everyone knows; it's no secret.'

'What was that?'

'Bergson's. Crawley had all his money in Bergson's, and when they failed he lost every penny. Of course, he has a good position and salary and all that, but it must have been a big blow all the same. And now particularly just as he's going to be married. Fortunately, he has a house and furniture, or I don't know what he'd do.'

'Has the girl money?'

Hindhead smiled.

'She certainly has,' he answered. 'She is Miss Hope, only daughter of Mr John Hope, the owner of our business. But even so, a man doesn't like to lose all his savings and to be even partially dependant on his wife's money. Why, he'll probably have to borrow from his father-in-law for the expenses of the honeymoon. Hard luck, I call it.'

'I've known worse cases,' Vandam declared dryly. 'Smith was harder up than that. By the way, Mr Hindhead, I understand from Mr Hurst that Smith and Mr Crawley had a row at one time. What was that about?'

'Do you mean recently?'

'I'm not sure when it was supposed to take place. Tell me what you know anyway.'

'There isn't much to tell. The incident to which I presume you are referring took place about a week or ten days ago. But I understand it was patched up next day. At all events nothing was said in the office.'

'Tell me anyhow.'

Mr Hindhead paused, and then went on slowly, as if reluctantly.

'It was at our annual dinner. Mr Hope gives a dinner to the office staff every year in the Bellevue Hotel, and after it there is an informal dance. Smith had been unable to resist the champagne and was what you might call "elevated." Miss Hope was there—the girl who I was telling you was to be married to Crawley—and it appears she sent her partner from the conservatory, where they were sitting out, to get her an ice. Smith, who was there, took advantage of her being alone, and tried to kiss her. Crawley came in to see her struggling in his arms.'

'And what happened?'

'Nothing. Crawley took the girl away, and Smith quietly vanished. Crawley apparently recognised he was drunk, and let the affair blow over.'

The conversation rambled on, and Vandam learned a good deal about several of the members of the Hope Bros. staff, though nothing except the one point of Smith's being at the Scala appeared to be of any use to his inquiry. Old Mr Hindhead had seemed glad to talk to him, and the Inspector imagined he was lonely. He had gathered from the conversation that he lived alone, and that his wife had been dead for some years.

But he felt, as he walked slowly home through the brilliantly-lighted streets, that his evening had not been wasted. He had not only gained a jumping-off place for further inquiries as to Smith's movements on the last evening of his life, but he had also tapped a source of information as to the Hope Bros. firm and its staff, which might come in useful should any unexpected development arise.

Next morning, he decided, he would begin work at the Scala Theatre.

CHAPTER VII

THE SCALA CINEMA

On arrival at headquarters next morning, Vandam found an accumulation of routine work which prevented him carrying out his programme of inquiries at the Scala, and it was not until after lunch that he was able to direct his steps to the picture house.

It was a large, flamboyant building in the centre of the town, but newly opened, and palatial in decoration and luxurious in furnishing as befitted a modern city motion picture theatre. Business was in full swing, as was indicated not only by the steady influx of patrons, but also by an electric sign bearing the legend, 'Continuous 2.00 'til 11.00.' In the vestibule, casting a keen eye on those entering, was a huge negro porter, dressed in a uniform of which the chief component seemed to be gold braid. Vandam was not long in taking his measure. He went up to him, determined to try a cast.

'Say, porter,' he began, 'what's your name?'

The negro eyed him doubtfully, but he answered civilly enough, 'Sugah, sah.'

'Well, Sugar,' Vandam went on, 'I'm Detective-Inspector Vandam of the City Police. I want you to answer some questions. If you answer them properly you'll be something in pocket, but if you don't you'll have to come along with me to headquarters and answer them there. See?'

The negro, a monument of offended dignity, saw.

'Now, see here, I'm after a man that's wanted for housebreaking in Capetown. He is believed to have been at the show here on last Wednesday night. Question is, did you see him? There he is.'

Vandam produced the photograph he had obtained from Hindhead. The porter stared at it with a puzzled expression.

'I *have* seen gen'leman like that, sah. Yes, sah,' he said hesitatingly, 'but I'se 'fraid I can't just say where.'

Vandam paused in his turn so as not to hurry the other. Then, the negro shaking his head, he continued:

'Were you on duty here on Wednesday night shortly after eight o'clock?'

'That's right, sah.'

Vandam made his cast.

'I was informed that about half-past eight or shortly before, this man and a friend came into the picture house. Are you sure you didn't see them?'

A flash of intelligence shot across the negro's dull face. He slapped his thigh, then suddenly remembering the dignity of his position, drew himself up stiffly and frowned.

'I 'members him, sah,' he cried in repressed tones. 'I 'members him now. He came in just 'bout the time you say, sah, Wednesday night.'

'Then he had a friend with him?' Vandam queried, trying to conceal his satisfaction.

No, it appeared he was alone, but he was expecting a friend to meet him. The negro had particularly noticed him because he was carrying a suitcase, and as the negro had charge of the cloakroom he had remarked on it. 'Your bag for the cloakroom, sah?' he had asked, and Smith had answered, 'No, I'll keep it. My tobacco's inside.' Smith had stood there in the porch for perhaps ten minutes, and then he had called the negro. 'Look here, porter,' he had said, 'I'm expecting a friend to meet me here, but I've waited for him long enough. If you see a tall man standing about, you might ask him if he's waiting for Mr Smith, and if he says, "Yes," then tell him I've gone inside and to follow me in. He'll know where to find me.'

'And did the friend turn up?'

'No, sah, not that I saw.'

'Mr Smith didn't give his friend's name?'

'No, sah, he say nothing more.'

Had the man really turned up? Vandam began to examine the negro on his duties. He was not, it appeared, continuously in the porch. Besides keeping a general surveillance over those entering, he attended to the cloakroom and was frequently sent messages by the girl in the box office. It would, therefore, have been quite possible for the unknown to have entered without his having seen him.

Vandam thanked the porter for his civility, and with a view to possible future contingencies slipped a few shillings into his hand. Then, crossing to the box office, he bought himself a ticket preparatory to entering the theatre.

It seemed hardly worth while making inquiries of the girl in the box office, as she dealt with such crowds of people, and at best Smith could only have spent a moment at the window. But Vandam was not a man to neglect any chance, however slight, and in a slack interval of business he introduced himself and propounded his question. To his surprise, the girl immediately became interested, saying without hesitation that she had seen Smith on the night in question.

'Then you knew the late Mr Smith?' he asked.

'I knew him well by sight,' she answered. 'Before I came here a year ago I was at the pay-desk in Frederik's Restaurant, and Mr Smith used to lunch there nearly every day. He remembered me when he came here on Wednesday night; knew me at once and smiled and said, "Is this where you are now, Miss Wynandts? Glad to see you again," he said, as pleasant as anything. He wasn't always so pleasant spoken at Frederik's, not by a long chalk.'

'That was about eight o'clock?'

'Later, I think. About half eight, I should say.' She broke off to book some new arrivals. 'I remember, because the house was just about full, and I said I hoped he'd get seats without having to wait.'

'Seats?' queried Vandam, sharply. 'Was he not alone?'

'No, he had a friend with him. At least, he took two tickets—stalls—two and six; best in the house except the gallery.' She waved her hand towards a gilt sign displaying the tariff.

'Then you didn't see the friend?'

'No, I didn't see anyone. But he, or she'—she looked up as if contemplating a giggle, then, as if recalling the gravity of the situation, relinquished the idea—'he or she must have been there, on account of his buying two tickets.'

'Looks like it, certainly,' Vandam agreed. 'By the way,' he went on, taking out his photograph, 'I've never seen Mr Smith. Isn't that the man you're speaking of?' He pointed, not to Smith, but to another member of the group.

'That? That's not him,' exclaimed the girl, regardless of grammar. 'But there he is,' indicating the man mentioned by Hindhead. 'That's him right enough. And a good likeness, too.'

Then the girl really did know Smith. Vandam felt satisfied that her evidence was reliable. He was getting on well. He bowed to her.

'Well, Miss Wynandts, I'm greatly obliged to you, I'm sure. I shall call back if there is anything else I want to ask you.'

Taking off his hat, he turned into the theatre.

'An extraordinary piece of luck, that girl knowing Smith,' he thought as he sat down to wait until his eyes became accustomed to the darkness. 'If I can find out who he met here, it won't be a bad afternoon's work.'

Presently he got up and began to interrogate the attendants, but he was not surprised to find that none of them had seen Smith in the building. Nor had they observed him leaving. It appeared that there were three exits leading directly out, and a fourth through the bar and restaurant. At the first three of these no one was stationed, and, as the attendants pointed out, anyone could leave by these unnoticed.

This was so obviously true that Vandam speedily gave up his inquiries in the theatre and betook himself to the fourth exit, that leading into the restaurant. Here there was a uniformed porter, and Vandam, getting into conversation with him, learned why he was placed there. The restaurant and bar, it seemed, had an entrance from the street and were patronised by many who did not view the pictures. This man's duty was to see that none of these persons entered the theatre from the bar, in other words, without having paid for their admission.

But when the Inspector began his inquiries about Smith he did not meet with so ready a response. The porter could not tell who had left by his door on the evening in question. He had seen that no one had come in; that was his business and he had confined himself to it. Such a man as the Inspector described might have passed out, but among the hundreds he saw daily he could not recall individuals, expecially those whom he did not know.

Vandam saw that he could make nothing of it. The man, though civil enough, was stupid, and his evidence was worthless. The next point of inquiry was the bar, and thither Vandam betook himself.

The bar was a large room with many alcoves and cosy corners, and was furnished and decorated in the same palatial manner as the rest of the building. There were a good number of men and some women sitting or standing about, and it was some time before he could get a word with the barmaid. But at last he saw his chance, and, ordering a cup of black coffee, he engaged the girl in conversation.

She was a pretty creature and, no doubt accustomed to being made much of by more attractive looking men than Vandam, she paid little attention to him until he mentioned his business. Then she seemed interested, and bending forward over the bar, she said in a low tone:

'I can't talk to you now. If you'll sit down there and wait until six o'clock I have an hour off, and you may take me out to supper.'

Vandam, glancing up at the large clock behind the counter

and seeing that he had only twenty minutes to wait, murmured, 'Delighted, I'm sure,' and obediently retired with his coffee to an unoccupied table. There, with a cigar to soothe his nerves and his problem to occupy his mind, time slipped quickly away, and he saw the girl beckoning to him before he realised that the twenty minutes were up.

'Meet me outside,' she directed. 'I won't be long.'

He passed out and almost immediately was joined by the pretty young woman. Meeting the unexpected professional exigency with extraordinary resignation, he asked her where she would like to go, and in five minutes they were seated at a little table in a secluded alcove of a neighbouring restaurant.

'Well, now, what's all this about a man committing suicide?' she demanded, when the waiter had departed with his order, brusquely interrupting Vandam's flow of small talk.

He told her. All he wanted was to know if Mr Albert Smith had visited the bar on that Wednesday night, and, if so, with whom.

Mr Albert Smith? How could she tell whether he had or not? She didn't know the man nor anything about him.

Vandam produced his photograph, and once more, to his delight and amazement, he found he had struck oil.

'Why, yes,' the girl cried the moment she saw it, 'that's the guy with the suitcase. He came in and had a couple of large brandies. I remember him.'

'That so?' said Vandam. 'You might tell me about him. That was Wednesday night, I suppose?'

'Isn't it Wednesday night we're talking about,' she said, with a glance of scorn. 'Yes, it was Wednesday night, if you want to know it again. Just on the stroke of ten I saw him coming up to the counter. He asked for a large brandy, and he put it down nearly neat and asked for another. When he'd had that he began to talk. "Nothing like a little Dutch courage," he said, sort of joking by the way, "I have a nasty job coming on in half an hour," he said, and he looked up at the clock, and then I saw it was just on the stroke of ten. "What's that?" I said, not that I cared any, but just sort of polite. "Oh," said he, "talking of it won't mend it," as much as to say, "Mind your own business and I'll mind mine." So I never looked near him again after that. The impertinence of some people! I can tell you most people are glad enough to have me talk to them.'

'I can believe that,' Vandam assured her. 'I'm like the rest, so please don't stop.'

The girl looked at him distrustfully.

'Oh, you are, are you?' she replied acidly. 'Want to get your little bit of information out of me, don't you? Well, go on. You're paying for my supper.'

'Just a question or two,' Vandam begged. 'Was the man alone?'

'As far as I saw, he spoke to no one and no one spoke to him—bar me. And once was enough for me.'

'You said something about a suitcase?'

The girl nodded and almost laughed.

'Yes, he had a suitcase in his hand, a smallish, light coloured, leather suitcase. I noticed it the way he held on to it; held it there in his hand all the time that he was drinking. I thought to myself, "Why, there's sure something worthwhile in that grip if it wouldn't be safe for five seconds on the floor by itself!" Never let the darned thing out of his hand all the time he was in.'

'And was he in long?'

''Bout ten minutes. I saw him going out about ten minutes past ten.'

Vandam remained silent for a moment, wondering if any further information was obtainable from his fair companion. Then a thought striking him, he leaned forward.

'I have an idea he was meeting someone in the bar,' he declared. 'Did you happen to know any of the people that were present?'

Once again the girl looked scornfully at him.

'I suppose they teach you to be cautious in your trade,' she snapped. 'If you don't believe me, you needn't, and that's all there is to it.'

Vandam, fuming inwardly, with some difficulty pacified her, and at last learned that she had recognised one man, a Mr Lewis Banks, a down-town stockbroker.

As soon as he reasonably could, Vandam got rid of the girl, then returning to headquarters, looked up Mr Banks in the directory. It was seven o'clock and he imagined the man would have gone home. Twenty minutes later he reached the address given. Mr Banks was at dinner.

'I'll wait and see him when he's finished,' he told the boy who opened the door.

When the stockbroker learned Vandam's business he became suddenly interested. Yes, he had known the deceased man, not well, but enough to bid him good day when they met. Yes, he had been in the bar of the Scala on Wednesday evening, and he remembered having seen Smith. In fact, he had spoken to him. Smith had passed out of the auditorium into the bar immediately in front of him, and he had remarked on the play. 'Jolly good show,' he had said to Smith, and Smith had agreed. He had had a drink and had left the bar immediately, and he had not noticed Smith further. That was about ten o'clock. The programme, though continuous, lasted about an hour and a half, so that a visitor entering the theatre about half-past eight would have seen it through by ten.

Mr Bank's testimony seemed to Vandam to be the last link in this particular phase of his inquiry. The whole of Smith's movements on the last day of his life were now established. He had left his office at six, his usual time, having there spent a perfectly normal day, and had reached his rooms in about fifteen minutes, showing that he had walked directly. At eight he had gone to his bedroom, and ten minutes later had left the house with his suitcase. To the Scala was about ten minutes' walk, and about 8.20 he had turned up there in the porch. He had gone into the pictures at 8.30, had seen the programme through, had passed into the bar about 10.00 p.m., and had left to do 'a nasty job' at 10.10. So far as it went, the evidence was complete and conclusive, and there could be no doubt as to its truth.

Vandam went a step further. This information enabled the time of the murder to be closely established. From the Scala Cinema to the potting shed in the Groote Park was from fifteen to twenty minutes walk—even with a taxi to the gates it could not be done in less than ten. Therefore the murder could not by any possibility have taken place before about half-past ten.

The actual performance of the ghastly deed—the sandbagging, the carrying of the body to the tunnel, the burning of the papers, and the hiding of the sandbag and hammer—all these would have taken an appreciable time. Vandam, after making a careful estimate, did not believe it could have been done in less than a quarter of an hour. At the earliest, he felt sure the murderer could not have left the scene of his crime before a quarter to eleven, and in all probability the actual time was a good deal later.

Suddenly the significance of this in connection with Swayne struck Vandam, and he remained motionless, wondering how he had failed to notice it sooner. If the earliest time the murder could have been committed was from 10.30 to 10.45, Swayne could not have been the murderer. Swayne from 10.30 to 10.45 was in his room at the Bellevue Hotel. From the potting shed to the Bellevue was at least fifteen minutes' walk, and had Swayne been guilty he could not possibly have got back before about eleven.

Vandam was cautious about accepting so far-reaching a conclusion without adequate consideration, and he went over again and again each link in the chain of argument. But the more he thought of the matter, the more satisfied he became that there was no flaw. The times were fixed with too complete a certainty. It was absolutely established that the murder had taken place while Swayne was in his bedroom a mile away.

Swayne, therefore, was definitely out of it. Vandam bemoaned the time he had lost on that phase of the investigation, though he recognised that with the knowledge he had possessed at the beginning of the case, he could hardly have acted otherwise than as he had.

Fortunately, he was not at a loose end. There was the matter of the diamonds to fall back on. He decided he must take up that line again and come to a conclusion as to Moses Goldstein.

His thoughts went back to the suitcase. Why had Smith abandoned it? *Had* Smith abandoned it? Ah, that was an idea! What if it was the murderer who had abandoned it? What if Smith had used it as a vehicle in which to transport the stones, and the murderer had discovered the secret? It this were so, it would naturally have been abandoned as soon as its treasure had been abstracted.

Then suddenly Vandam sat back and swore. If the murderer had rifled the suitcase, would he not have left fingerprints thereon? And he, Vandam, one of the best men in the detective service, had never thought of it, and had fumbled all over it himself, no doubt destroying previous marks! He had been obsessed with the idea that Smith alone had used it! Now, perhaps, owing to his own thoughtlessness, a decisive clue had been lost.

Before doing anything else next day, he decided he would critically re-examine the suitcase, and divided between satisfaction at his achievements and annoyance at his oversight, he knocked out the ashes from his pipe and went to bed.

CHAPTER VIII

VANDAM MAKES UP HIS MIND

INSPECTOR VANDAM'S re-examination of the suitcase on the following morning failed to give him the result for which he had hoped. To his unutterable disgust, he found excellent impressions of his own fingers on its surface, but nowhere were those of other persons clear enough to be of use. But there was no good in crying about spilt milk, and he dismissed the matter from his mind, only hoping it would not occur to the Chief to ask awkward questions thereon.

He had intended busying himself on the question of the possible guilt of Moses Goldstein, but as had happened on several occasions before in this case of surprising developments, fresh information unexpectedy came in which turned his attention into a completely new direction. Just as he was going out, a call came through to headquarters from Messrs. Hope Bros. store. It appeared that the newly appointed successor to Smith had discovered a locked drawer in the latter's desk which, on being broken open, was found to contain a number of private papers. As no relatives of the deceased had been discovered, and as the police had the case in hand, it was suggested that if they cared to take over the whole bundle they could do so. Failing this, they would be destroyed.

Vandam, called to the telephone, replied requesting that on no account should anything be destroyed, and saying that he himself would go at once to Mees Street to examine what had been found. He could hardly imagine anything more welcome to an officer engaged in a case such as his, than a gift of the private papers of one of the chief actors in the drama. Private papers were one of the most fruitful sources of clues in existence, and it was with some eagerness that he set out on the short walk to the stores.

The city looked peculiarly attractive in the bright morning sun. There had been a thunderstorm the night before, and now the air was exquisitely fresh and clear. Vandam felt his spirits rise and his step grow more elastic as he walked briskly along the tree-lined pavements.

At Hope Bros. he was introduced to a Mr Lloyd, who had been appointed to Smith's job.

'Here is the drawer,' Lloyd explained, 'and here,' indicating a brown paper parcel, 'are the papers. I did not go through them all. Those that I saw were obviously private—betting records mostly, and I didn't think I was called on to examine them. As you may imagine, I have plenty to do taking over this new job.'

Vandam sympathised with him in his difficulties, complimented him on his wisdom in applying to the police, and took his leave. Then returning to his office, he opened the parcel and set himself to go through its contents.

As Lloyd had said, most of the papers were records of betting transactions, but not all. There were bills, mostly unreceipted, as well as a number of letters. Vandam examined each with care, but it was not until he had gone through nearly the whole pile that he found anything which aroused his interest. But one letter certainly achieved that result, and a look of amazement and mystification showed on his face as he sat reading and re-reading its every word.

It was a note, hidden among the other papers and obviously unnoticed by Lloyd. It was written on an octavo sheet of poor quality paper, headed in memo form with Messrs. Hope Bros. name, and seemed the kind of leaf the firm would use for inter-departmental correspondence. The handwriting was of a bold, masculine character, was done with a broad-nibbed pen and blue-black ink, and was untidy, as if it had been hastily dashed off. It was marked, 'Private and Confidential,' was dated for the day of the murder, and read:

> 'DEAR SMITH,—'I shall be away all day at that railway claim case, so cannot see you at the office.
>
> 'With reference to that which is between us, I have a proposal to make which will either bring the matter to a head or settle it. Will you meet me at 10.30 tonight on the narrow walk which runs behind the south corner of the main glass-house range in the Groote Park. There is a potting shed at the end of it where we can talk undisturbed.
> 'STEWART CRAWLEY.'

Vandam almost gasped. Crawley! Was it possible that Crawley was mixed up in this amazing affair? So far there had not been the slightest breath of suspicion against him, but this note offered up unexpected possibilities. Could it be, Vandam wondered, that up to the present he had been entirely off the track, and that he would have to start at the beginning again and revise his opinions?

He sat quite motionless turning the matter over in his mind, and as he did so little things recurred to his memory which had not struck him as important at the time. Crawley had not been in the office when Sergeant Clarke had gone there to make his preliminary inquiries. Nor had he been there when Vandam himself had called. Was Crawley avoiding the police? It was true that he had been present at the inquest, but by that time he might well have recovered a composure lost on the day after the crime. Then there was that chance remark of Hindhead's, which suddenly became charged with significance. Crawley was hard up—for a man in his position, desperately hard up, if he would have to borrow the price of his honeymoon from his father-in-law. A man might take risks to avoid such a humiliation. But there might be more in it than Hindhead had stated, or even known. Possibly the marriage itself depended on Crawley's obtaining ready money. Once the ceremony was over he would be all right, but it might very well have been that before Mr Hope would give his consent, he would have had to be satisfied as to his future son-in-law's means. With a father-in-law and an employer combined in one and the same person, parental sanction took on a very different complexion than under more ordinary conditions, and Crawley might have had an almost over-whelming need for the money.

But even more significant than any of these was the fact that Crawley and Smith had had a disagreement a few days before the murder. From Hindhead's account, Vandam had not for a moment imagined it could have had any bearing on the tragedy. But now he was not so sure. Considered in conjunction with these other matters, it might indeed have had its effect. Rudeness to the girl to whom a man was engaged would naturally be resented much more than an insult to himself.

At all events it was now as necessary to go into the case against Crawley as it had been to probe that against Swayne, and as it still was to settle that against Goldstein.

The note was a powerful piece of evidence. It definitely incriminated Crawley, so definitely that Vandam did not see how the manager could possibly explain it away. If he were unable satisfactorily to account for his movements at 10.30 on the night in question, his guilt was a practical certainty. With evidence such as this at his disposal, Vandam was assured of a conviction.

At least, so it seemed to him at first sight. But further thought showed that his case was by no means so complete. A good deal more would have to be proved before he could go into court. The genuineness of the note would certainly be ques-tioned by the defence. He would have to be prepared with specimens of Crawley's handwriting, and expert witnesses to prove the note was written by the same hand. These however, should not be hard to obtain. Then he would have to get

Crawley's statement as to where he was at the hour named, test it, and make sure he had no alibi.

He was greatly struck by one point, the amazing carelessness shown by both men. It was the extraordinary characteristic of the average criminal that at some point in even the most carefully planned crime he commits a stupid, unnecessary blunder which gives his whole case away; he gratuitously leaves a trifling clue which leads his pursuers to their goal. Here in the present instance was a man who wished secretly to lure his enemy to a deserted spot where he might the more easily destroy him, and yet he actually puts it on record, in writing, that he is the prime mover in the affair. He sends this record to his victim to leave about for anyone to find, and the victim promptly leaves it about. An astounding oversight, incredible were it not that countless criminals in the past had paralleled it. However Vandam, though he might marvel, had no cause to grumble. From his point of view it was all so much to the good.

He continued turning over the remaining papers, but without finding anything further of interest. Then he pushed them away, lighted a cigar, and began to think out the details of his next step.

For some minutes he smoked lazily, gazing down dreamily into the extremely uninviting courtyard into which his room looked. Then he slowly drew a sheet of official paper towards him and began to write.

'Personal.
'Stewart Crawley, Esq.

'Mr Albert Smith, decd.

'Sir,—'I wish to ask your confidential help on a matter which has just arisen. I would go round to see you on it, but am due at a conference here in a few minutes.

'In the papers handed to me by Mr Lloyd this morning there is constant reference to someone called George Ruff, of Gunter's Kloof. Can you tell me anything about this man, and what dealings Smith had with him?

'An immediate reply would much oblige, as I think of catching the 11.20 train to Gunter's Kloof to see him.

'Yours faithfully,
'JOHANN VANDAM,
'Detective-Inspector.'

He sent his note by a constable, telling him to wait for an answer. In half an hour it was in his hands, and once more he chuckled with satisfaction as he found his little ruse had succeeded.

The note was written on the same memo form sheet as that to Smith, in bold, masculine handwriting, done with a broad-nibbed pen in blue-black ink, and as Vandam eagerly compared the two documents, he saw at a glance that they were from the same hand. Proof of the first portion of his case was thus obtained; that the note making the 10.30 appointment with Smith had really been written by Crawley.

In the second note, Mr Crawley begged to inform Inspector Vandam that he did not know Mr George Ruff, nor could he recollect ever previously having heard the name, which, under the circumstances, was not to be wondered at.

Locking both notes carefully away in his drawer, Vandam turned to the consideration of the next point claiming his attention; how to find out where Crawley had been at 10.30 on the night of the murder.

He spent a considerable time thinking over this problem, then, believing he had hit on a scheme, he began at once to carry it out.

From the directory he found Stewart Crawley's private address—41 Dordrecht Avenue. He knew the street, one of the smaller thoroughfares in the better-class residential area to the north of the Groote Park. To ascertain what the household consisted of would be his first duty.

He left headquarters, and, crossing the end of the park in front of the glass-houses, reached Dordrecht Avenue. Strolling slowly along, he took stock of No. 41, a neat, bijou villa standing in its own tiny but carefully kept lawn, and shut off from the road by a line of evergreen shrubs. His intention was to get into conversation with some of the many chauffeurs employed in the neighbourhood, from whom he could learn of the Crawley menage. But as he sauntered under the leafy plane trees, he noticed on the opposite side a postman on his rounds. 'I'll try him,' he thought, and, crossing over, accosted the man.

'I'm looking for a Mrs Crawley who lives somewhere around,' he announced, drawing his bow at a venture. 'Can you put me on to where she lives?'

The postman pointed to No. 41.

'That's Crawley's,' he responded, 'but you're a month or so previous. If you come back in six weeks you'll maybe see her.'

Vandam smiled.

'I heard some talk of a wedding,' he admitted. 'But it isn't her I want. It's the lady that's on the job now. Who runs the place? Do you know?'

'Sister,' the postman declared. 'Miss Crawley. And I'm thinking there'll be the devil and all to pay when the new one comes in and this one gets the door.'

'Why, what's she like?'

'Terror,' the postman returned laconically. 'You go and you'll see for yourself.'

'I wouldn't miss it after that,' Vandam assured him. 'And are there only the two of them living in that house?'

'Just the two, bar the two girls and the motor man. But I suppose you don't count them?'

Vandam told him that he did not, and after a little good-natured chaff the loquacious postman swung off down the avenue on the continuation of his round.

'That's an unexpected lift,' thought Vandam as he looked at his watch. 'Half-past twelve. Soon time for a bit of lunch.'

He strolled on until he met a policeman walking slowly along his beat.

'Do you do Dordrecht Avenue?' he asked.

The policeman admitted it.

'Do you know Miss Crawley in No. 41?'

He admitted this also.

'Well, see here. I want to know if Miss Crawley goes out. You might hang about the Avenue and keep an eye on the house. I'm going down town for some lunch, but I'll be back and relieve you in about an hour. See?'

The policeman saw, and Vandam left him to his task.

The allotted span had scarcely passed when he was back again. A casual sign between the two men indicated that the lady was still within, and Vandam took over the watch, while the policeman slowly disappeared from view.

Seats were placed at intervals under the trees, and on one of these, some distance from the house, the Inspector took his place. Drawing a newspaper from his pocket, he settled down to enjoy a quiet read and smoke in the pleasant shade. For nearly two hours he remained, then at twenty minutes past three the door of No. 41 opened and a tall lady emerged. He watched her descend the steps and stride masterfully off in the direction of the park.

'Crawley's sister by the cut of her,' Vandam muttered, as he puffed contentedly at his cigar.

He waited for some five or six minutes, and then leisurely approached the house and rang at the door.

It was opened by a rather pretty English servant girl. Vandam dropped his easy manner and became official and businesslike.

'Good afternoon,' he said politely. 'I am Detective-Inspector Vandam of the City Police.' He drew a card from his pocket. 'Would you take in my card, and ask Miss Crawley if she could see me?'

For a moment he held his breath, for he was, of course, by no means sure that the lady he had seen was Miss Crawley. But his fears were immediately dissipated.

'She's just gone out, not five minutes ago,' the girl exclaimed. 'I wonder you didn't meet her.'

'No,' said the Inspector. 'I didn't see her. Do you know when she'll be in?'

The girl thought not until dinner time.

Vandam affected disappointment and hesitation.

'I rather wanted to see her this afternoon,' he said slowly. 'It was a bit important.' He paused, evidently in thought, while the girl, interested, stood holding the door open. A sudden idea seemed to strike him. 'But perhaps,' he went on, 'you could tell me what I want to know, if you would?'

Her curiosity duly responded.

'Come in,' she invited.

She led him to a small room, comfortably furnished as a study.

'This is Mr Crawley's room,' she volunteered. 'We can talk here. If you tell me what you want, I'll help you all I can.'

Vandam thanked her again. He found a little extra politeness a considerable asset in dealing with this class of person. 'It's really a very little thing,' he went on, 'nothing to be making such a fuss about. Two minutes will do all I want.' He drew a notebook from his pocket and pretended to consult it. 'I am trying to get some information for the adjourned inquest on the death of that Mr Smith of Messrs. Hope Bros., who was run over on the railway a few days ago. You remember the case?'

As the girl could hardly fail to have been interested in the affair owing to Smith having been in the same business as her employer, this opening naturally increased her curiosity.

'It is my duty,' went on Vandam, leading gradually on to the bluff he intended to put up, 'to prepare a report saying just how the late Mr Smith passed the early part of the evening on which he was killed. Now I am informed that he called here that night to see Mr Crawley. I have asked Mr Crawley about the matter, and he tells me he did not call while he was in the house. But what has since occurred to me is—and this is where I want your help—that he might have called while Mr Crawley was out. It might very easily happen that whoever opened the door might have forgotten to inform Mr Crawley afterwards.'

The girl shook her head.

'No,' she answered, 'he did not come here. I know because I was in the house the whole of that evening. I remember it well, because of all the talk next day about his being killed.'

She had denied that Smith called, but, as Vandam noted with growing interest, she had not denied that Crawley had been out.

'Don't think me rude,' he went on suavely, 'but the matter is really rather important, and I would like to be absolutely certain no mistake occurred. You didn't open the door to Mr Smith. Very well. Now, is there anyone else who might have opened it unknown to you? Mr Crawley I've already seen, and he didn't. What time did he go out, by the way?'

The girl paused in thought.

'Let's see,' she said. 'He passed through the hall going out just as I was coming from doing some jobs in the bedrooms. That would be shortly after ten, about a quarter past.' She paused, then went on: 'But I can fix it for you if it matters. I was only in the bedrooms four or five minutes, and while I was away our other girl came in. I'll ask her what time it was.'

She left the room, while Vandam sat hugging himself with satisfaction at the information he was receiving.

Presently the pretty servant returned, followed by a companion.

'This is Miss Brown,' she explained, and Vandam rose and bowed.

'Do you remember last Wednesday night?' the first girl continued, 'the night that Mr Smith was killed on the railway. What time did you come in that night?'

'What time?' Miss Brown repeated dully, a slight look of apprehension creeping into her eyes.

This was going too quickly for Vandam. He did not wish the girl to be frightened.

'Let me explain, Miss Brown, what I want to get at,' he interrupted smoothly, and he told her his yarn about Smith's supposed call.

Reassured, Miss Brown became loquacious. She had come in that night at 10.15. She knew because she had left the Empire music-hall at ten, and it was just fifteen minutes' walk.

So far, so good. Crawley had left the house between 10.15 and 10.20. From there to the potting shed would be six or seven minutes' walk. Vandam had difficulty in keeping the satisfaction out of his voice. Things were working in better than he could have hoped.

He wished, if possible, to find out when the manager had returned, and with this view he kept on questioning the girls about the alleged call. He went through the evening carefully until he reached the hour at which they had gone up to bed. Then, as it were incidentally, he asked had Crawley returned by that time. This also worked excellently.

'Yes,' both girls replied, 'because we waited up for him. We did not know if anything else was wanted, for we hadn't heard about the morning. Mr Crawley often goes early to business, and that takes an early call and breakfast.'

'And what time was that?'

'A quarter past eleven,' Miss Brown declared. 'I remember looking at the clock and saying if he wasn't in by half-past I would wait up no longer. He couldn't expect us to stay up the whole night for him.'

'That's so,' Vandam agreed. 'If I may say so, I think you did very well as it was. Then I take it from what you tell me that the late Mr Smith didn't call here that night, and I can only say that I am extremely grateful to you both for your help.'

Vandam had no longer much doubt that Crawley was his man. It was known that he was hard up, that there had been bad blood between him and Smith, and that he had made a

secret appointment with Smith at the place and probable hour
of the crime, at a time when Smith carried a heavy stock of
diamonds. Now it seemed that he had kept this appointment.
All circumstantial evidence, of course, but cumulatively it made
a strong case.

Vandam decided that he must see Crawley before the latter
should be put on his guard by learning of the interrogation of
his servants, and ask him how he spent the fateful hour.

He hailed a taxi and was driven to headquarters. There he
got hold of two plain clothes men, and instructing them to
accompany him, he re-entered his taxi and was driven to Mees
Street. On inquiring for Mr Crawley, the three officers were
conducted to the same richly furnished office in which on his
first call he had been interviewed by Hurst. Vandam entered
alone, leaving the others within call in the passage.

Mr Stewart Crawley was a man of thirty, of more than middle
height, and broad and strongly built. He looked a strong man,
resolute and resourceful, with his dark, curly hair, firm mouth,
and square jaw. Passionate, too, the Inspector thought; the type
that will strike first and consider his justification afterwards.
He rose and bowed slightly to his visitor.

'Good afternoon, Inspector,' he said briskly, his dark eyes
meeting the other's directly. 'Sit down, won't you? What can I
do for you?'

In his intercourse with his fellows, particularly those from
whom he hoped to obtain information, it was Inspector
Vandam's habit to place as much reliance, or more, on what he
called the involuntary answers to his questions, as on the actual
words spoken. A witness's hesitations, starts, changes of colour,
or other expressions of emotion were to him an even more
valuable indication of truth than the statements he received. He
therefore watched Crawley keenly as he began to speak.

'Sorry to trouble you, Mr Crawley. It's about the death of
your clerk, Mr Smith. There are a couple of pieces of information I would be obliged if you could give me.'

'Still working at that, Inspector?' Crawley answered a trifle impatiently. 'It is giving you a lot of trouble, I'm afraid. If there is anything you haven't already asked me, I'll tell it you if I can.'

'We have had some trouble certainly,' Vandam admitted, 'but it has been worth it.' He looked steadily at the other. 'At last we know the truth.'

Mr Crawley did not exhibit any particular emotion, though a certain puzzled interest showed on his face.

'That sounds mysterious,' he declared. 'What have you learned?'

Vandam kept his eyes fixed on the manager's face.

'We have learned, sir,' he said impressively, 'that Albert Smith was murdered in a potting shed in the Groote Park about half-past ten on last Wednesday night.'

There could be no mistaking the genuineness of the emotion which swept over Mr Crawley as he listened to this announce-ment. At first his features seemed to show only incredulous surprise, but speedily this gave place to a look of apprehension. His eyes became anxious and wary as he sat staring at Vandam.

'Good heavens, Inspector!' he cried. 'This is terrible news! Murdered! And in the Groote Park! But what about the train accident?'

'There was no train accident,' Vandam answered grimly. 'That was a plant to cover the thing up. You see, we know all about it, Mr Crawley.'

Crawley had been growing more at his ease, but the last remark of the Inspector's seemed to reawaken his apprehension. He remained silent for a moment, then exclaimed:

'You amaze me, Inspector! I had no suspicion. And have you,' his voice trembled slightly, 'have you any clue? Any idea who did it?'

'We have several clues, sir, but we have not had time yet to follow them up. We are doing so now. It was in connection with that I have just called.'

'Yes, yes, of course. You wanted my help?' Crawley was

evidently striving for composure. 'And what exactly can I do for you?'

'Well, sir,' Vandam went on conversationally, 'for the purposes of my report I should like a statement from you as to how precisely you spent the hour from 10.15 to 11.15 on the night of the murder.'

As the full significance of the Inspector's question dawned on him, Crawley seemed absolutely aghast. His jaw dropped, consternation shone in his eyes, and his face became gradually drained of its colour. For a full ten seconds he sat rigid, gazing at his visitor, then, with an effort, he began to pull himself together.

'Why do you ask me that, Inspector?' he queried in a low voice, as soon as he could trust himself to speak.

'I have to, sir,' Vandam answered. 'I must ask it of everyone whose movements at that time are not accounted for.' He spoke lightly, as if the conversation was trivial and ordinary.

A slight look of relief passed over the other's face. He laughed rather unsteadily.

'You frightened the life out of me, Inspector. I thought at first you suspected me of the crime.'

Vandam became more serious.

'That, Mr Crawley,' he said gravely, 'depends entirely on yourself. If you will answer the question I have asked you, that is an end of the matter. If not, you must see yourself that your refusal will leave you open to suspicion.'

Crawley had by this time recovered himself. He sat thinking for some moments, then said more in his ordinary tone:

'Does that mean that if I don't answer your question you will arrest me?'

'I haven't said anything about arrest,' Vandam replied, 'but all the same I should like an answer. Come now, sir, don't make the mistake of getting on your high horse. It is known that you were on bad terms with the murdered man, and also that you left your house about 10.15 on that night and remained out for an hour. There is strong reason to believe the murder took place about 10.30 or a few minutes later. At that time you must have been somewhere. All I ask is where it was.'

Crawley started when the Inspector mentioned his having left the house. Once more he paused in thought. Then he said quietly:

'I am afraid, Inspector, if your ideas are running in that direction, there is very little use my answering your question; you are not likely to believe what I say, and I am quite unable to prove it. As a matter of fact, on that evening I had been working hard since dinner trying to solve some business problems. By ten o'clock I found I was getting stale and I thought some air would help me. I lit a cigar and went out. For an hour I paced backwards and forwards on the *stoep* in front of my house. At the end of that time I suddenly hit on the solution I wanted, and came in shortly afterwards and went to bed. And that's the whole business.'

Crawley seemed to speak straightforwardly enough, but Vandam's whole instincts cried out that the man was lying. 'He's normally an honest man,' thought the Inspector, 'and therefore he lies badly. He invented that answer on the spur of the moment, and he's as guilty as sin.' But aloud he only said:

'Possibly someone saw you walking there. You say you were smoking a cigar. Someone may have seen the tip glowing in the dark.'

'I hope to heaven somebody did, but I don't know of anyone.'

Inspector Vandam was much dissatisfied. Though he did not believe Crawley's story, there was always the chance that it might be true. There was nothing inherently improbable in it; on the contrary, few things were more calculated to help in the solution of a thorny problem than a quiet stroll with a cigar in the soft darkness of a South African night.

Vandam was puzzled. Should he or should he not arrest Crawley? He did not see his way clearly, but he did see that he might easily make a bad mistake. If he arrested the man and he afterwards turned out to be innocent, it would be a very serious matter for himself. On the other hand, if the man were guilty and he let him slip through his fingers, it would be worse. He had to remember also that he had just given him an effective warning of his danger.

At this stage in his cogitations he was interrupted by Crawley. The man had become more and more fidgety in the silence, and at last had seemed unable to bear it any longer.

'Well,' he said, and his voice had a sharp edge to it, 'are you going to arrest me?'

Vandam reached a decision.

'No, Mr Crawley,' he answered slowly, 'I am not. You have answered my question, and your answer is perfectly reasonable, though, as you admit yourself, you are not able to prove its truth. Confirmation may, however, be forthcoming later.'

Crawley gave a sigh of relief.

'I need not say I sincerely trust so. I may say now that I am absolutely innocent of Smith's death; until you told me I had not had a suspicion that he was murdered. I only hope that you may soon get your hands on the real murderer.'

'We can agree in that, sir,' Vandam smiled, and presently he took his leave.

Calling to his two plain clothes men, he left the building, but as soon as the trio had turned the first corner he stopped.

'I want that man Crawley shadowed,' he explained quickly. 'You two get on the job at once. Arrange your reliefs between yourselves, and if you want further help I'll let you have it. Shadow him day and night, and keep me advised of his movements.'

With a short nod the men melted away, and Vandam looking about until he saw an empty taxi, hailed it and got on board.

'41 Dordrecht Avenue,' he directed, and the vehicle swung off.

He had hurried from Crawley's house to his office so as to interrogate the manager before the latter learned what his servants had disclosed. Now he was reversing the proceeding, hurrying from the office to the house, as he wished to question the servants further before they learned what their master had stated.

The door was opened to him by the same pretty girl, who smiled pleasantly on seeing him. He raised his hat.

'I am sorry,' he apologised, 'to trouble you again so soon, but there is one question I forgot about. Would you mind if I asked it now?'

The girl was interested and had no objection.

'Well, it's this,' he went on, when they had once again reached the diminutive study. 'You told me, I think, that you were upstairs at some time between 10.15 and 11.15 on that Wednesday night, that is, while Mr Crawley was out. Now, were you at the windows of any of the rooms during that time, or did you chance to look out?'

The girl answered without hesitation:

'I was at all the windows in turn. I was pulling down the blinds for the night.'

'Did you see anyone on the lawn?'

'No one,' she answered equally promptly.

'If a man had been there would you have seen him?'

This time she did not answer so quickly.

'I might not,' she said presently, 'unless he happened to be in the light from the window, and even then I might have missed him.'

'It was dark?'

'Yes, it was dark outside. I switched on the light as I went from room to room.'

'Suppose the man had been smoking a cigar?'

'I might have seen the tip if he just happened to draw it as I was there. But I did not.'

'You didn't happen to smell cigar smoke?'

She hadn't, and question her as he would, Vandam could get nothing from her which in any way confirmed Crawley's statement.

Then he tried the cook, Miss Brown. She was more likely to have seen Crawley than her pretty colleague, as she had been out, and in returning had actually crossed the *stoep* from the street to the porch during the time he had stated he was there. But she had not seen anyone.

Vandam decided to wait to interrogate Miss Crawley, who had just returned. From her replies he learned that she knew Crawley had been out, and that she didn't believe anyone had been smoking on the *stoep*, as she would almost certainly have smelt the smoke through the sitting-room windows, which were open.

Not content with this negative evidence, Vandam dressed himself up as an out-of-work mechanic, and striking up an acquaintance with several of the chauffeurs of the district, found three who had passed the house during the period in question. Each of these men stated he had looked carefully in and had seen no one on the *stoep*, and when Vandam not unnaturally inquired the reason of this attention, he learned that the pretty housemaid was the magnet.

Vandam was by this time convinced that Crawley's statement was a fabrication, and that he really was the man for whom he was in search. But negative evidence was unsatisfactory. He had failed to confirm the manager's alibi; could he disprove it.

He spread out a map of the town, and taking the hours at which Crawley had left and returned to his house, and assuming that he had walked to the potting shed and back at a speed of three miles an hour, he noted the exact time at which he would have passed all the salient points *en route*. Then, armed with this timetable, he began to search for people who might have been at some of these points at the given times.

The inquiry was very tedious. He found that a number of the waiters from the refreshment kiosks near the bandstand left off duty shortly after ten. Some of these should have been passing out of the Park at about the hour Crawley would have entered. But though with infinite pains he found half a dozen who had done so, none of them had seen the manager.

He next started on the park officials. Had his inquiry been concerned with any other night than that in question he would have given it up in despair, but the supposed accident fixed it so definitely that he persisted. And at last, after wearisome efforts, his perseverance met with its just reward, though in the end it was rather through a coincidence than as a direct result of his investigations.

It was not until he had almost exhausted the officials that he got his clue. A stoker from the greenhouses, passing homewards out of the park at five-and-twenty minutes past ten, had seen a man such as the Inspector described talking with a friend just inside the Green Gate. But when Vandam showed him Crawley's photograph the stoker said he had made a mistake. The man was like Crawley, but it was not he.

Vandam, disappointed, was unwilling to admit defeat. He questioned the stoker more minutely, learned that he had seen the man on several previous occasions, and at last, with the help of two of the rangers, fixed his identity. He was a certain George Hume, a stockbroker with an office in Mees Street.

Within the hour Vandam had called on him. He could not for some time recollect the occasion in question, but eventually he recalled having met a friend called Lysacht as he was leaving the park. They had stood chatting just inside the gate for some minutes. And then, again after a pause for thought, he thrilled and delighted the Inspector by admitting that while standing there Crawley had passed into the park. Crawley, Hume said, had not seen him, but had hurried past as if late for some appointment.

Vandam was overjoyed. This was the last item he required to make his case complete. Crawley had put forward a false alibi. After that there could be no further question of his guilt.

To make assurance doubly sure, Vandam obtained Lysacht's address from Hume, and he, after some thought, was able to confirm his friend's statement. He also had seen Crawley, and there was no shadow of doubt of the latter's identity.

His case complete, Vandam returned to headquarters to report his conclusions to his Chief. There, waiting for him, he found the men he had put on the Goldstein affair, and their reports indirectly confirmed his belief in Crawley's guilt.

It appeared that Goldstein's story had been fully confirmed, so far as confirmation was possible. The stenographer testified that she had been working late as he had stated, and the tram conductor remembered him travelling by his tram. Further, a police patrolman had happened to be standing opposite his house shortly after ten, and had seen him walk up to the door and let himself in. This man had noticed the electric light being switched on behind windows which were afterwards proved to belong to the commission agent's sitting room. The patrolman was certainly very observant, for it happened that he had passed the house again a few minutes before eleven, and he had then not only remarked that the windows were still illuminated, but had seen a shadow pass across them. If this shadow was Goldstein's, and all Vandam's inquiries tended to prove it could not have belonged to anyone else, the man would not have had time to commit the murder. Vandam felt he might be ruled out of the case. In the light of what he had learned that day, Crawley was guilty, and Crawley alone.

Well satisfied with his results, Vandam sought an interview with his Chief, before whom he laid his discoveries. On hearing the evidence, the latter agreed that the arrest of Crawley was inevitable, though he did not show himself as enthusiastic about Vandam's prowess as the latter could have wished.

'There are a darned lot of points unsettled,' he grumbled. 'Some of these men of yours don't show up very brilliantly, Vandam. You had better get on to them about it. They should have made something of the hammer, for example. They've missed that, and they've missed the sandbag. Then they've made nothing of the diamonds. They've not learnt of any robbery or of anyone showing up unexpectedly wealthy, nor have they found out if old Goldstein got them. I don't blame them for not finding the miners, for I don't believe there ever were any, nor am I blaming you personally. I recognise that you have worked hard and handled the case well, and you're certain of a conviction, but the general standard is too low, and a change must be made.'

Considerably abashed, Vandam made as speedy a retreat as possible. With his two assistants, he once more visited Crawley and formally arrested him, warning him that anything he might say would be used in evidence against him. The manager, after emphatically denying his guilt, took the advice and made no further statement. In half an hour he was lodged at police headquarters.

That afternoon was rich in sensations for the citizens of Middeldorp.

CHAPTER IX

MARION HOPE

INSPECTOR VANDAM'S conclusion as to the identity of the murderer resulted in action which took effect first upon Stewart Crawley, but which did not stop there. It also involved a number of other persons, of whom the existence was in some cases unknown to the Inspector. The first of these was Miss Hope.

Marion Hope was the daughter of John Hope, the junior and only remaining partner of the Hope Bros. firm. Towards the close of the last century, Angus Hope, an enterprising young Scotsman, had ventured forth to try his fortunes in South Africa. Seeing a promising opening in the provision trade, he had sent for his younger brothers, Alexander and John, and the foundations of Hope Bros. had been laid. Under the skilful guidance of the three young men, the firm had prospered until it had become an organisation employing many score of hands and having branches in all the important villages surrounding Middeldorp. Some three years before the present tragic events, Angus, the founder, had died, and then Alexander had taken out his share and gone back to end his days in the old home in Callander, while John remained in South Africa to carry on the business.

John had married a doctor's daughter in Middeldorp, a startlingly beautiful girl, and had gone almost out of his mind from grief when a year later she had died in giving birth to Marion. The child, while she had not inherited her mother's beauty, was still graceful and charming to look upon, and she had, in addition, a sweetness of disposition which made her the absolute idol of her father, and endeared her to those with whom she came in contact. She was, moreover, no fool. Some of the hard-headed, canny business capacity that had built up Hope Bros. had descended to her also, and, though her heart was large, she never allowed it to run away with her head.

When a small child she had formed the habit of frequently visiting her father at his office, and had thus come to be on good terms with the staff at the stores. This intimacy she had refused to give up as she grew older, partly because of her genuine interest in the workers, and partly lest she should be thought superior. Thus it was that she had come to inspire ardent feelings in the breasts of several of the assistants, but it was only in the case of Crawley that these emotions had grown into a deeper passion. He had proposed, and she had accepted him. The engagement was at once announced, and old Mr Hope set the seal of his approval to the project by promising to take Stewart Crawley into partnership on the wedding day. The betrothal had taken place about three months before Smith's murder.

It will be imagined under these circumstances with what incredulous dismay the news of Crawley's arrest reached his prospective father-in-law. That anyone could believe guilty of so atrocious a crime his chief of staff, the man with whom he had been on excellent and intimate terms for so many years, the man he was about to receive into his family! Why, the thing was ridiculous, laughable! Or rather, it would be, were it not so serious. Mr Hope's amazement turned to rage. Who were the dolts, the imbeciles who had done this thing? He knew the head of the City Police. He would ring him up at once. Someone should pay for it, and that immediately.

But the reply from headquarters was anything but reassuring. The Chief Constable deeply regretted the matter, but while he trusted time would prove Mr Crawley's innocence, he was bound to say the case against him was extremely strong. On the evidence in their possession his men had been justified in what they had done.

Mr Hope was dumbfounded, but devastating as the shock was to himself, he saw that it was as nothing compared to that which his daughter would suffer. He left the office and hurried home to break the news to her before she learned it elsewhere.

While his taxi was speeding through the sunlit streets, a further consideration occurred to him. Marion's welfare was paramount; at all costs her name must be protected. Unless this arrest were the most obvious blunder and Crawley was released with appropriate apologies in a day or two, the engagement must be broken off. His daughter could not marry a man who was tried for murder, whose name would be notorious throughout the length and breadth of the land, who would have upon him the blight of prison. Even though he might eventually be acquitted, it would make no matter. The man would be stamped for life, and Marion must have nothing more to do with him. A feeling of thankfulness that the marriage had not already taken place alternated with his resentment. Bad as matters undoubtedly were, they might have been a thousand times worse.

On reaching home he went to his study, and there sent for Marion. Such a summons at such an hour was unprecedented and presaged disaster. That her father was ill seemed to the girl the only possible conclusion.

When she saw his face, her worst fears were confirmed, and she cried out in dismay:

'What on earth is it, Daddy? Are you not well?'

'Well enough, my dear. Shut the door and come here.'

Marion obeyed, the look of anxiety on her face growing.

Mr Hope took both her hands in his own.

'My dear girl,' he said, and she realised that he was deeply moved, 'you have always been my brave daughter, and a call has come on your courage now. It may turn out to be nothing—I haven't any particulars yet—but in any case you must prepare yourself for a shock.'

The girl's face paled.

'Stewart?' she murmured. 'Not Stewart? An accident? Tell me quickly, Daddy.'

'Not an accident, dear girl. Oh, no; in fact, he's perfectly well. But—he has been arrested.'

Marion stepped a pace back and stood staring at her father.

'Arrested?' she repeated dully. 'Whatever for?'

'For the murder of Albert Smith.'

Her face expressed utter incomprehension.

'But Albert Smith wasn't murdered. What *do* you mean, Daddy?'

'I'm afraid, my dear, it is only too true. Poor Smith wasn't run over as we thought. It turns out now that he was murdered.'

She was horror stricken.

'Oh, *poor* Mr Smith! How perfectly awful! But Daddy, they don't—they *can't* suspect that Stewart knows anything of that? You're not saying that they think that?'

Mr Hope shook his head sadly.

'I'm afraid they do, Marion.'

The girl looked at him for a moment and then burst into a peal of hysterical laughter.

'You solemn old dear,' she cried in tremulous tones, throwing her arms round his neck. 'How you frightened me with your silly old nonsense! Why, I never heard anything so utterly absurd. You know Stewart's one of those who literally wouldn't hurt a fly.'

Mr Hope felt both relieved and embarrassed.

'That may be, my dear, and we must hope that all will come right in a few days.'

'A few days?' Marion echoed. 'Why, you don't imagine that they could keep him under arrest for that time? The mistake is sure to be discovered at once. He will certainly be released today.'

Mr Hope took her hands again.

'My dear child,' he said tenderly, 'I'm afraid you don't quite understand. However wrongly, the police really believe there is no mistake. I am afraid he will have to stand his trial.'

Marion stared at him blankly.

'Stewart to be tried for murder,' she groaned at last. 'Oh, Daddy, it's impossible!'

Her voice sank into silence as she stood trying to realise the disaster that had befallen her. But her thoughts did not remain long on herself. If it was bad for her, what would it be for her beloved?

'Daddy, I must see him,' she said presently. 'I must see him at once. He mustn't think that I have delayed. He'll need all the encouragement he can get now.'

This was what Mr Hope had feared. If Marion insisted on going to the prison she would be hopelessly compromised. Her only chance of getting out of the entanglement was an instant and complete repudiation of the engagement.

But he knew his daughter. Though for his self-respect's sake he retained the appearance of authority in his home, he knew that she was in reality the ruling spirit. If she once determined to go—or rather to apply for leave, for he doubted if she would obtain it—he was aware that no protests of his would prevent her. If he were to succeed, therefore, all his diplomacy would be required.

'Well, my dear,' he answered slowly. 'I can understand and appreciate your feelings. But you'll have to wait, whether or no. You see, what happens is this. He will be brought before a special court of magistrates at once, probably tomorrow, and they will decide whether there is sufficient evidence against him to return him for trial. Before the magistrate's court you wouldn't be allowed to see him. After that, if things should go badly, I dare say it might be arranged. But it is too soon to think of that. We must wait and see what happens before the magistrates.'

'Then there is another thing,' Marion went on, as if he hadn't spoken. She was rapidly becoming her cool, practical self again. 'He must have someone to act for him—a lawyer, I mean. Isn't that always necessary? Who's the best man for that kind of thing, Daddy? Mr Griffenhagen, I should think. What do you say?'

Mr Hope had been afraid of this also. He cleared his throat and then said slowly:

'That is a matter for himself, my dear. He must himself obtain advice. A solicitor would only act on receiving his own instructions.'

'But, Daddy,' Marion spoke with more animation, 'that wouldn't do at all. That would look as if we were deserting him in his difficulty; as if we were sitting on the fence to see how things were going to turn out, before we would make a move. I know you never thought of that, but don't you see how it would look? No, if only Stewart can arrange about a lawyer, then I must see Stewart to arrange it with him; or you must. It must be done somehow. Don't you see that it is the only way?'

Mr Hope still counselled patience. 'I tell you things can't be done like that,' he said a trifle testily. 'We must wait and see what happens. There may be no need to do anything. He may be discharged by the magistrates.'

'Yes, but he may not,' the girl insisted. 'You said so yourself. Oh, Daddy,' she threw her arms once more about his neck, 'I can't have him left there without any sign of our sympathy, without even a letter to say we believe in him and are working for him. If I may not see him, you go, Daddy. They would let you, his employer, his future father-in-law.' Mr Hope winced. 'Say you'll go now, right now before you do anything else.'

As Mr Hope still demurred, Marion's expression suddenly changed.

'It's not that you don't want to go,' she cried anxiously. 'Oh, Daddy, say it's not that!' She still clasped his neck.

He tried to soothe her.

'There now, my dear, there now,' he said awkwardly. 'Of course not. But just be content to do as I say. Wait until we know the result of the inquiry tomorrow, and then we can settle what's best to be done.'

Slowly she disengaged her arms and stood looking searchingly at him. He would not meet her eyes, but kept on urging patience. Then reading his mind, she gave a low cry, burst into tears, and, turning quickly, rushed out of the room.

She did not come down to dinner that evening, but next morning she once again opened the attack. She had lain awake all the night thinking. She had looked at the matter from every point of view, even her father's, and she thought she understood his attitude. She saw that consideration for herself had unquestionably been his motive, and she appreciated his devotion and was filled with sorrow that the course she had decided she must take would give him pain. For, during the long hours of sleepless tossing, she had come to a conclusion. Her place, she believed, was by the side of her betrothed, and there she was determined to stand, even though it might mean a breach with her father. Stewart Crawley loved her. She loved him. They had pledged their troth, and though they had not actually pronounced the words 'for better, for worse,' they were as good as spoken. If he had wanted her when all was well, how much more would he want her now when his path was clouded over? At all costs, he would not look to her in vain.

At breakfast they argued it out. Mr Hope again counselled delay, but when he saw she was quite determined, he gave a grudging consent that something should be done. 'When I get to the office,' he said, 'I'll ring up Griffenhagen and see what he says.'

Marion would not admit to herself that she mistrusted her father, but yet she felt this was not enough. She ran round the table and kissed him as she enthusiastically thanked him for giving way to her wishes, but she added, 'And I'll go round and see Mrs Griffenhagen, and get her to speak to him too.' She did not add that it was her real intention to get this lady to accompany her to her husband's office, so that she could herself ensure that the lawyer received the proper instructions.

Mr Hope was displeased, but he knew Marion would have her way, and he contented himself with warning her to do nothing foolish and to take no steps without consulting him. 'What I am really anxious about,' he persisted, 'is that your name should not appear. It is not seemly for a young girl to be mixed up in such sordid matters as police court proceedings. I want you to keep out of it,' and Marion, having won her battle, meekly promised to be a model of circumspection.

But directly her father had left the house, she rang for a taxi and set off to the Griffenhagen's. Though they belonged to an older generation, they were among her best friends in Middeldorp. Mrs Griffenhagen, indeed, sincerely loved the young girl, and had tried as far as she might to take the place of the mother Marion had never known. And Marion, strong as was her affection for the older woman, hardly herself realised what she owed to her goodness and care.

The solicitor had left for his office when she reached the house, but she saw Mrs Griffenhagen, and poured the story of her woes into the good lady's sympathetic ears. But Mrs Griffenhagen knew her neighbours, and her first question was, 'What does you father say?' and until Marion had given her an assurance that Mr Hope approved of the proposal for Crawley's defence, she would not consent to accompany the girl to her husband's office.

'But you know, dear Mrs Griffenhagen,' Marion smiled up at her, 'that if you refused to come with me I should go by myself.'

'I know you would, you naughty, wilful child,' the other returned with an affectionate glance, 'but then I shouldn't be guilty of aiding and abetting you.'

Marion had kept her taxi, and the two women were soon ascending the stairs of Messrs. Griffenhagen and Bondix's office. Two minutes later the door of Mr Griffenhagen's private room closed behind them.

Elias Griffenhagen was a tall, well-built man of about sixty, with a keen, hawk-like face, and eyes which lit up eagerly when he was interested in his subject, as indeed was usually the case. He greeted his prospective client with a quiet kindliness of manner which quickly put her at her ease, and made her feel she had secured a friend at once sympathetic and powerful.

'Oh, my dear Marion,' he said, taking both her hands, 'allow me to say how deeply grieved I am at what has happened. I heard the news last night with absolute incredulity. I don't know what the police have got against Stewart Crawley, but there are two things in his favour at all events, and those are his known character and the fact that he had won the regard of a lady like yourself. I can only say that I hope his ordeal, and yours, may be of very short duration.'

'How kind you are, Mr Griffenhagen,' Marion responded, with a grateful glance. 'I do hope, indeed, that this awful mistake may soon be put right. But now there is not much time, and I want to go on to business at once. You can, of course, guess what it is. Someone must act for Stewart, and I hoped against hope that perhaps you would consent to do it.'

Mr Griffenhagen bowed gravely.

'Anything I can do for you personally will be done as a matter of course,' he returned, 'but to act on behalf of my firm is rather a different matter. In the first place, what does your father say? Have you mentioned it to him?'

'We nearly fought about it.' A fleeting smile passed over Marion's expressive lips. 'But I won. At first he was against our doing anything just for the moment, as he was afraid my name would be mentioned. But at last he saw that it would be impossible for me to stand aside from Stewart at such a juncture, and he gave his consent that you should be asked. Indeed, he said he would phone you when he reached his office.'

'He has not done so.'

'Well, let's ring him up now. May I use your phone?' She crossed to the table and picked up the instrument. 'Hallo! Yes. Seven six, Central.' She turned to the others. 'Dear old Daddy was thinking of me, of course, but what I said to him was, "I am in it anyway, I—" Hallo! That you, Daddy? It's I, Marion, speaking from Mr Griffenhagen's office. I have come round here with Mrs Griffenhagen . . . Yes, he wants to know if you approve of his acting for Stewart. I have told him Yes, but he doesn't seem quite satisfied. I wish you would tell him yourself . . . What? . . . Very well. Here, Mr Griffenhagen, will you take the phone, please?'

'Ah, Griffenhagen, that you?' came Mr Hope's voice in intensely annoyed accents. 'Marion has gone quite mad over this thing. I explained the situation and urged common prudence on her, but nothing in reason will satisfy her. I agreed to consult you on the affair, because if I had not the Lord knows whom she would have gone to. Act for Crawley by all means, if you will, but on my request. And keep her out of it, Griffenhagen; all I ask is that you keep her out of it. Hang it all, she's my only daughter!'

Mr Griffenhagen once more smiled his grave, kindly smile as he assured Mr Hope that he understood the position and would on his request immediately take over the defence of Crawley, provided the latter agreed.

'And now, Marion,' he turned to the eager young woman, 'you must excuse me, for there is a lot to be done and but little time to do it in. First, I must go and see Crawley and find out if he agrees to my acting for him. Then, if that is all right, I must be present in court at the magisterial inquiry. I imagine it will only be formal, but I must be there to make sure. After that, Crawley and I will consult together over his defence.'

'Then you think he will be returned for trial?' she asked, with an appealing look in her eyes.

'Oh, yes; certain to be. The police would not arrest unless

there was evidence enough for that. But you mustn't despair about that. A very large number of innocent men have been tried, acquitted, and gone on afterwards as if nothing had happened. I can't obviously tell you anything more now, but come back to me in—well, say on Saturday next, and I'll let you know how, things are going on.'

'But I shall see you in court today.'

Mr Griffenhagen shook his head.

'Under no circumstances,' he said decidedly. 'You must not come forward in the affair at all. Your every movement and expression would be watched by the other side, and in all probability you would be called as a witness, and you don't know how some start you might make, or some chance word you might innocently drop, would be turned against your fiancé. No, you have asked me to undertake the case and you must trust me to do it in my own way.'

Marion seemed disappointed, but impressed.

'But I may visit him in prison? At least, I may do that?' she begged.

Mr Griffenhagen hesitated.

'That depends,' he answered slowly. 'Certainly not now. But later it might be arranged. I couldn't say definitely at present.'

Marion, despairing, tried again.

'At least I may write to him?'

'If you don't take too long about it,' he smiled. 'Five minutes you may have and no more. There are paper and envelopes.'

Half an hour later Mr Giffenhagen was at police headquarters, putting through the necessary formalities to enable him to have an immediate interview with the prisoner, and presently the door of Crawley's cell swung open to admit his visitor.

'Ah, Mr Crawley, how are you? I am sorry to meet you under these circumstances,' began Griffenhagen as the warder withdrew and the two men were left alone.

They shook hands, and then Griffenhagen explained at whose instance he had come and handed over the note Marion had written. Never had he seen a man change so suddenly from listless, black despair to radiant joy and optimism, as did Crawley when he read that note. He could not contain his emotion, but, leaping to his feet, paced the narrow cell with springy step, while his face shone with a beautiful light.

'I knew she was good,' he cried incoherently, 'but I never dared to expect this. You know what is in this letter, Mr Griffenhagen?'

Mr Griffenhagen did not know, and did not specially want to.

'Why,' Crawley returned, ignoring the other's suggestion, 'she says this affair will make no difference between us, and that I am to feel her and her father's influence and help and confidence are behind me all the time. She says they have asked you to appear for me, and that she will come and see me as soon as it can be arranged! I can tell you, Mr Griffenhagen, it makes me feel small. What have I ever done to deserve such a girl?'

'Not much, I'm sure,' the solicitor agreed, 'but you've got to start now. It's all very well for Miss Hope to write that this will make no difference to your engagement and so on, but you must see it will. Under no circumstances can her name be dragged in. If you're discharged today, why, then, there's not so much harm done, but if you're returned for trial you must release her from the engagement without delay. You see that, don't you, Crawley?'

At Griffenhagen's words the other had ceased to pace the cell and had stood listening with dismay growing on his face. Now he threw himself on his seat once more, and, leaning his elbows on the table, buried his face in his hands. For some minutes he remained thus motionless, then he sat up and faced his visitor with grey and haggard features.

'You are right, Mr Griffenhagen,' he said hoarsely. 'I have realised it all the time. But this note upset me, and for a moment I almost believed it might be as she said. As far as she is concerned, I am dead already. I have thought of nothing else since my arrest, and I see there is no other way. But I must write and tell her so myself.'

Crawley's face had taken on again the expression of black and listless despair which it had worn on the solicitor's entrance. Griffenhagen rose and held out his hand.

'I should like to shake hands with you, Mr Crawley,' he said. 'I don't pretend to realise what this is costing you, but I can imagine something of it. Write what you like to Miss Hope and I will take it back.'

'Thank you,' Crawley answered as he clasped the other's hand. 'I appreciate your kindness.' He paused and then went on despairingly. 'But all we can do won't help matters. Miss Hope's name can't be kept out of it. The police will drag her in in spite of us.'

Griffenhagen looked up quickly.

'What's that you say?' he asked sharply. 'How do you make that out?'

Crawley seemed surprised.

'Well, I take it my row with Smith will be one of their chief points. Don't you think so?'

'I didn't know you had a row with Smith.'

'I had, worse luck! It was on the night of the annual dinner. You know, of course, that Mr Hope treats the staff to dinner once a year?'

Griffenhagen nodded.

'It was at that dinner,' Crawley continued grimly. 'There was a dance after it. I was looking for Miss Hope and I found her in the conservatory with Smith. Smith was drunk, and he had his arm round her and was trying to kiss her. She was struggling and was very much upset. I felt like killing the swine then and there, I admit, but I managed to get Miss Hope quietly away. When she had collected herself and her next partner claimed her, I went to look for Smith, found him in the lavatory, and told him I'd smash his ugly face for him if he wasn't outside the building in two minutes. He must have seen by my manner

I wasn't joking, for he never said a word, just looked black murder at me and slunk out. I don't know whether anyone overheard me, but it got out about his insulting Miss Hope. Everyone knew of it.'

Mr Griffenhagen's expression was grave. If this were true, as of course it was, there was no possible chance of Crawley being set at liberty that day, and very little of keeping Marion Hope out of it either. He thought for a few moments, then spoke again.

'By the way, we have not settled our relation. I take it from what you have told me that you wish me to act for you?'

Crawley laughed mirthlessly.

'I don't think a question of that sort requires any answer,' he declared. 'If you will take on my defence, I needn't pretend to be anything but more grateful than I can say. But I'm afraid,' he wrung his hands with a hopeless gesture, 'you'll find it a tough proposition.'

'Why. What else have they against you?'

'What else? I don't know. One thing they have anyway. Inspector Vandam—it's he that's on the case and he arrested me—he told me that they knew the murder was committed about half-past ten on that night, and he found out from our girls that I was out from 10.15 to 11.15. He asked me where I had been, and I told him walking up and down our *stoep* while I thought out some office difficulties. But he didn't believe me, and I can no more prove it than I can fly.'

Griffenhagen looked very searchingly at his new client, but all he said was:

'Anything else?'

'Nothing, so far as I know. But that's enough, I should think.'

Griffenhagen nodded as he looked at his watch.

'Now,' he said, 'time is getting on. You are to be brought before the magistrates at twelve today. I will be present on your behalf. You can have five minutes now to answer Miss Hope's letter, and then I must be off.'

Ten minutes later Mr Griffenhagen left police headquarters and was driven to his office. Then he sent a clerk to the Hope mansion with Marion's letter, telephoned her a few words of encouragement, and got together some things he would require at the magisterial proceedings. Shortly after he started off for the court.

CHAPTER X

AT twelve o'clock that day the small room in which the magistrates' court was to be held was crowded to suffocation. It was a special court called for the murder case only, but somehow news of it had leaked out, and all who could squeeze their way in had done so.

But those who had hoped for dramatic developments were doomed to disappointment. The proceedings were purely formal and occupied only a few minutes. Inspector Vandam gave evidence of arrest and then asked for a week's remand. This was granted, bail being refused, and the court was over.

Two days' later Griffenhagen received a draft copy of the evidence for the prosecution, in so far as it had up to then been compiled. When he read about the letter from Crawley found in Smith's drawer he was filled with dismay, but when he went on to learn that proof existed that Crawley's statement of his movements between 10.15 and 11.15 on the night of the murder was false, he was utterly aghast.

'A damned blackguard!' he muttered, a hot wave of anger sweeping over him. 'He'll hang, and serve him right!'

For a moment he contemplated writing Crawley a cold note telling him to look for other advice, as he made it a practice only to act for clients who took him into their confidence, but a vision of the eager, appealing face of Marion Hope seemed to float between him and his purpose, and he hesitated. For the man he would not move a finger; a scoundrel who could commit such a murder and then accept the help and sympathy of a girl like Marion deserved any fate that might come on him. But for Marion's sake . . . a girl in a thousand, a girl he had always liked and whom his wife loved almost as a daughter, for her sake . . .

He sat motionless in a deep chair in his private office, drawing at one of his favourite black cheroots as he thought the situation over, and at last he came to a decision. He could not leave Marion in the lurch. He would at all events see Crawley again, put the thing to him squarely, and hear what he had to say. It was well not to be too hasty in such matters. Some explanation of the inexplicable might exist, and, if so, he would give the accused man every chance to make it.

With this object in view, therefore, he set out on the following morning for the State prison, to which Crawley had been removed. The great building was situated on a hill some distance out of the city, and the warm air blew pleasantly on his head as his taxi whirled along the shady, tree-lined road by the river, while the scent of eucalyptus smelt clean and pungent in his nostrils. Occasionally through the foliage he could get glimpses of the grim pile he was approaching, and its presence, with its terrible associations of human sin and misery, seemed to him nothing less than an outrage on the smiling country surrounding it. Well, his efforts had kept many innocent men from the living death of incarceration therein, and he hoped he would live to do the same for many another.

His permit was for admission to Crawley at all reasonable hours, and after but a short delay he found himself once more in the accused's presence. On this occasion he did not spend any time in polite assurances, but directly the door of the cell had closed behind the departing warder, he plunged into the object of his visit.

'I have now received, Mr Crawley,' he began, 'a résumé of the evidence which is likely to be given against you, and I may tell you at once that there are some points in it which will require a pretty complete explanation from you before I can deal with them. I have come out here this morning to learn what you have to say on the matter.'

Crawley, who looked pale and worried, at once sensed the alteration in his visitor's manner, and it was with a look of pained surprise that he protested his anxiety to help in every way possible.

'Very good,' Griffenhagen returned shortly. 'I hope you will. There are three questions that I wish to ask you. I will take them in turn without further preamble, except to explain two things. The first is that I must have truthful answers. No,' he raised his hand as Crawley would have spoken, 'you need not give me assurances. The answers, when I get them, will satisfy me or will not satisfy me, as the case may be. By truthful answers I mean, of course, completely truthful answers. As the legal phrase puts it, you must tell me the truth, the whole truth, and nothing but the truth. If you begin keeping back essential facts, I warn you that I can do nothing for you, and as sure as we are sitting here you will hang.' Again Crawley would have spoken, and again the solicitor raised his hand for silence, continuing: 'The second thing is that whatever you may tell me is safe. Your confidence to me I will treat as sacred as if it were to a priest in the confessional. You need, therefore, have no hesitation in telling me all that is in your mind. Having mentioned those two points, I shall now ask my three questions.'

Mr Griffenhagen paused, but this time Crawley made no reply, but sat gazing mournfully at his visitor.

'The first question is this, Do you care to make a statement as to your guilt or innocence of this crime?'

Stewart Crawley started back as if from a slap in the face. His pale cheeks flushed, and a flash came into his sombre eyes as he answered with some spirit:

'Really, Mr Griffenhagen, I did not expect to get that question from you. You seemed satisfied enough when you saw me last.' He stopped, and the hopeless expression crept back into his eyes. Presently he went on more slowly, 'But there, I needn't be upset. It is what I have to expect. You don't know me and you don't know what happened, and your question is natural. I will answer it.' He stood up and raised his hand. 'I swear by the Almighty above,' he said solemnly, 'that I am completely and entirely innocent of this crime. You can believe me or not as you like, Mr Griffenhagen, but that is the absolute and literal truth.'

Mr Griffenhagen was impressed in spite of himself. He was well versed in the psychology of guilt, and here he saw none of its signs. Unless this man was a much better actor than he had any reason to suppose, he was speaking the truth. At all events, he must suspend judgment until he heard the answers to his remaining questions.

'I'm glad to hear you say so,' he remarked in somewhat more cordial tones. 'I will now proceed to my second question: What was the business about which you and Smith were to consult in the potting shed at half-past ten on the night of the murder?'

Crawley stared blankly at his visitor.

'I don't think I understand,' he said at length, 'or I have heard your question incorrectly. Are you suggesting that Smith and I met that night?'

'I'm asking you a plain question, to which you know the answer perfectly well,' snapped Griffenhagen. 'If you wish me to retain your case, please don't prevaricate any further.'

Crawley's face took on an expression of amazement as he gasped:

'I declare to you, Mr Griffenhagen, on my sacred word of honour, that I have no idea of what you are talking. Smith and I did not arrange to meet, and in point of fact did not meet that night, and there was no business to be discussed between us. I never was at the potting shed in my life. I can't think what you are referring to.'

'Oh, you can't, can't you?' the solicitor returned. 'Then perhaps you will tell me what that is?'

He withdrew an attachment from his pile of papers and smacked it down on the table before his client. It was a photographic copy of the letter found by Vandam among the papers from Smith's drawer.

Crawley's face as he gazed at the print expressed only the most profound mystification. He read the note slowly through, and then raised his horror-stricken eyes to his visitor's.

'What does this mean?' he cried hoarsely. 'It's in my hand-writing certainly, but I never saw it before.'

Remembering his false alibi, Griffenhagen felt a wave of disgust sweep over him.

'Then I should like to know how you account for its being in your handwriting if you never saw it before?' he asked angrily.

'I don't know. I don't know. I never saw it before,' Crawley repeated helplessly.

'But you admit it's in your own handwriting.'

'Yes, but I never wrote it. It's a forgery, Mr Griffenhagen. It's a forgery and a clever one, but who could have written it, and why, I can't imagine.'

Griffenhagen was silent. A possibility had occurred to him, a thing far-fetched and unlikely, but still possible. Could Crawley be the victim of a plot? Could false evidence have been provided by the real murderer to facilitate his own escape at Crawley's expense? It was conceivable. Such things had been done. At all events, before coming to a conclusion, he would sift the suggestion to the bottom.

Then he thought of the alibi. If Crawley had lied to Vandam over the alibi, he was lying now over the letter. The alibi was the crucial point. He would see what he had to say about it first.

'Very well,' he said, 'the letter is a forgery. Let's leave it at that for the present. Now I come to my third question. You said, I think, that from 10.15 to 11.15 on the night of the murder you were smoking on the *stoep* in front of your house?'

'That is so.'

'Now I would ask you if, on second thoughts, you will really stick to that statement, or whether you would not like to modify it in any way?'

Crawley hesitated and seemed momentarily confused, and the solicitor felt his suspicions becoming confirmed. For the first time the young man gave the impression of untruthfulness, and Griffenhagen began definitely to disbelieve him.

'Well?' he queried sharply.

'I do not wish to modify my statement,' Crawley answered, but his voice changed as he said it.

'Then how,' demanded Griffenhagen fiercely, 'do you explain the fact that you were seen during that hour at quite a different place?'

Crawley gave a low cry, and his face paled still further.

'I couldn't have been,' he stammered. 'Where was it—that I was supposed to have been seen?'

Griffenhagen rose to his feet and began to collect his papers.

'Never mind where,' he answered harshly. 'You will learn that in due course. Since you are going to lie to me, I can help you no further. I withdraw from the case, and you can make whatever other arrangements you think best.'

For a moment Griffenhagen meant it, and then once again the eager, beseeching eyes of Marion Hope seemed to float across his vision, and he hesitated.

'Look here, Crawley,' he said more gently, 'I can appreciate your position and your fear of saying anything that might give yourself away. But I assure you that you may trust me. For the sake of Miss Hope I would like to help you. For her sake I beg you to think again and to tell me the truth.'

Crawley groaned, and in his turn springing to his feet, began pacing the cell, his fists clenched and drops of perspiration standing out on his forehead. 'My heavens!' he cried hoarsely. 'What's the good of your saying that? Isn't the whole thing done for her sake?'

'A confession!' Mr Griffenhagen thought in amazement. Then aloud:

'You mean that you killed Smith for her sake?'

Crawley swung round with the light of almost maniacal fury in his eyes.

'Damnation take you!' he roared, 'I mean nothing of the kind. I mean—' he choked, then went on more quietly, 'It doesn't matter what I mean, Mr Griffenhagen. If I am going to receive insults instead of help from you, I think it would be best to bring the interview to an end.'

There was no mistaking the genuineness of the man's emotion, and Griffenhagen once more found himself puzzled. He sat down again and spoke very earnestly.

'Look here, Crawley, I am acting here at Miss Hope's request. For her sake I want to do my best. When you say you have acted for her sake, too, I believe you. For her sake be open with me, and if you have anything to tell me that would throw a light on your statements, for her sake let me know it.'

Crawley had stopped pacing his cell, and now stood as if in doubt. At last he spoke.

'Will you give me your word of honour not to repeat what I tell you without my permission?'

'Yes, I pledge myself.'

'Then I'll tell you.' Crawley sat down and began to speak earnestly. 'There's not much in it, but it was just because it might seem to reflect on her that I hid the thing first from Vandam and then from you. But all the same I'd rather you knew.'

The man's manner had altered, and now Griffenhagen was as certain that he was telling the truth as before he had been that he was lying. He sat eagerly waiting to hear what was coming.

'On that Wednesday of the murder, by the afternoon mail I received a letter at the office marked "Personal and Confidential." It was written in a hand I had never seen before and it was anonymous. It said that solely from the wish to see fair play the writer thought I ought to know of something which would deeply affect my life, and went on to say that'—Crawley hesitated, then seemed to force himself to continue—'well, putting it bluntly, that Miss Hope and Smith were carrying on an intrigue, and were meeting in secret nearly every night. If I wanted to satisfy myself of the truth of this, I was to hide behind the shrubs at the entrance to the rock garden in the Groote Park at 10.30 that night, and I would see them together.'

'And you did?'

Crawley wrung his hands.

'To my everlasting sorrow and shame, I did. But I didn't come to that decision all at once. At first I was furious, and was going to tear the wretched thing up and burn the fragments. Then as I thought and thought, I gradually came to see that I must go. I never believed the lie. Bad and all as I am, I never descended to that. But I felt that unless I had actual proof of its falsehood, the sting would always be there. In after years the doubt might grow. It would be better for both of us that the thing should be actually demonstrated. And so I went. I am being punished now, and I deserve it. I deserve whatever happens to me for allowing even that much doubt of that girl into my heart.'

'And you saw nothing?'

'What in Hades could I see?' Crawley almost shouted, staring angrily at his visitor. 'Of course I saw nothing! How could I, when there was nothing to see?'

'Well, well,' Mr Griffenhagen returned imperturbably, 'I was merely asking the question,' and then he sat for some minutes lost in thought. As far as he could see, the story rang true. He was inclined to build a good deal—though not everything—on the manner in which a statement was made, and it was evident either that Crawley was a superb actor or that he was telling the truth. Further, the story undoubtedly worked in with the hypothesis that Crawley was the victim of a conspiracy—a perfectly reasonable and credible conspiracy of which the object was to make Crawley a scapegoat for the murderer. It was just the kind of tale which would be chosen in such a case and for such a purpose. The writer would not expect his victim to believe it, but he would anticipate arousing sufficient doubt to ensure the test being applied. And this, if Crawley was to be believed, was precisely what had happened. Griffenhagen began to wonder whether the man might not be innocent after all.

'Have you got that note still?' he asked.

'Yes, or at least I think so. After Vandam paid his first visit to me and arrest seemed a possibility, I hid it. I felt I ought to destroy it, but I just hadn't the strength. Even though I didn't mean to use it, I felt as if it would be destroying my last chance of saving my life. I tore one of the maps out of an old guide-book of South Africa, folded the letter, writing inside, to the size of the map, and pasted it in its place. If the police haven't found it, it will be there still—in the top shelf of the bookcase between the windows in my study.'

Griffenhagen was unfavourably impressed by this recital. If the man was sufficiently cunning to devise so subtle a hiding place, would he not be capable of inventing the whole story?

'How did you come to think of such a place as that?' he asked.

'A tale of Edgar Allen Poe's I read when I was a kid suggested it to me. A letter was being searched for by the police, and the owner hid it by turning it inside out, putting seals and writing on the back, and leaving it openly in a rack in his room. It is the same idea.'

Griffenhagen remembered the story, and felt slightly reassured.

'I'll have a look for it,' he said. 'It would be better for me to have it than the police. What about the envelope?'

'The envelope I burned. It didn't seem to be important.'

Griffenhagen nodded and went on:

'In case the letter is gone, I wish you'd write me as exact a copy of it as you can remember. There's paper. Just start in and do it now.'

Crawley obeyed, while the solicitor sat still, thinking over what still remained to be asked. When the letter was finished he resumed his questioning.

'Now tell me about that night. You left your house about 10.15 and went direct to the Groote Park?'

'Yes.'

'By what gate did you enter?'

Crawley looked surprised.

'Why, there was only one gate I could have entered by without taking a long round—the Green Gate.'

'And from your house to the Green Gate would take how long?'

'About five minutes.'

'That works in. I may tell you now that you were seen passing in through the Green Gate at 10.20 that night.'

Crawley groaned.

'Good heavens! No wonder Vandam would not believe me!'

'Nor I either. Now tell me, Mr Crawley, what did you do on entering the park?'

'Just what the note said. I hid behind the bushes at the entrance to the rock garden and watched until after eleven.'

'Did you see anyone during that time, or while you were coming out?'

'No one.'

'Or while you were walking backwards and forwards between your house and the Green Gate?'

'I don't remember meeting anyone.'

'Now, what about your enemies?'

'Enemies? Upon my soul, I don't believe I have any.'

'Rubbish! You needn't tell me a man could get to your age and position without making enemies. Think carefully for this is important.'

'If you mean men I have got across in business at one time or another, there are a good few—men who wanted jobs that I had to turn down, men that I had to sack, others that I refused contracts to, and so on. There was'—and Crawley mentioned the names of some half-dozen whose susceptibilities he had had occasion in one way or another to wound.

Griffenhagen made a note of the names, with the object of following up these men's movements at the time of the murder and of comparing their several handwritings with that of the note Crawley had received. Then gathering together his papers, he took his leave.

He had kept his taxi, and when he reached the city he drove direct to Crawley's house. Miss Crawley was not at home, but his appearance was known to the parlour-maid, and he had no difficulty in gaining access to the study. In ten seconds he had found the South African guide-book, and in five more he saw that the letter was still intact.

Taking the book to his office, he sat down to examine the precious document. It was written on a sheet of poor quality notepaper, with blue-black ink and a wide pen. The handwriting was small and cramped; a man's, he imagined, though he was by no means certain. It had a curious appearance of irregularity, due, he discovered, to the letters not being formed in precisely the same manner each time they occurred. A small r, for example, was written in no less than four different ways, and an e in three. From this it seemed evident that the handwriting was disguised, as would indeed be natural.

He next took up the copy Crawley had written from memory, and placed the two documents side by side. At first sight they looked quite distinct, but as he compared the shapes of individual letters in detail, he saw that several of them were similarly formed. The differences were in slope, curvature, and size, rather than essential shape. Once again doubts of Crawley became uppermost in his mind, as he wondered if the manager had invented his story and himself written the letter to back it up. Finally, he forwarded both documents to a friend of his in Capetown, a handwriting expert of standing, asking him for an opinion on the point.

This matter off his mind, he lay back in his easy chair and lit a cheroot, as he set himself to devise plans for getting hold of specimens of the handwritings of the men whom Crawley had suggested might feel enmity against him. If one of these bore a close resemblance to that of Crawley's letter—well, the affair would be worth looking into.

In due course the week's remand came to an end, and Crawley was once again brought before the magistrates. Vandam did not ask for a further remand, but put in the evidence he had obtained, and when Griffenhagen intimated that the defence would be reserved, only one ending was possible. Crawley was returned for trial at the next assizes, bail being refused.

Then ensued a weary period of waiting, while each side pursued its investigations, prepared its briefs, and retained and instructed its counsel. None of the other points of the investigation had been dropped, Vandam hoping against hope that some fresh discovery might throw new light on the main problem. Thus the search for the purchaser of the hammer and the sandbag had not been abandoned; the look out for a person having lost diamonds or come in for a sudden fortune was kept up; the shadowing of Goldstein was maintained, and inquiries for a possible lover of Miss Jane Louden were still prosecuted. But in spite of all this activity, no fresh facts of importance had come to light, and when the date of the trial drew near neither side was able to produce absolute proof of its case, and neither was confident of victory.

On one occasion only had Inspector Vandam received news which thrilled him with eager anticipation that at last the veil of silence on these matters was about to be lifted, but here again further inquiries resulted in disappointment. About a week before the trial a telephone message was received at headquarters from Mr Hindhead, the Hope Bros. elderly accountant, saying that he had just received some news which might affect the case, and asking to be put in touch with Inspector Vandam.

Vandam immediately called a second time at the old gentleman's house.

'I hope I haven't brought you on a fool's errand,' Mr Hindhead greeted him, 'but now that you are here you must smoke a cigar with me. I have had a letter from John Swayne that I think you should see. He gives some information, but I don't know if it will be of any use to you. It's the middle paragraph I refer to, but you may as well read it all.'

He passed over a couple of sheets of paper and a number of photographs. The letter ran as follows:

'Langholm Hall,
'Norwick,
'Near Newcastle.

'DEAR MR HINDHEAD,—You were always so kind and so much interested in my welfare that I should like to let you know directly that I have decided to stay in England, at least for the present, and am therefore severing my connection with the old firm. I am writing today tendering my resignation to Mr Hope. My grandfather is in poor health, and has asked me to remain with him for a little longer. He has appointed me his secretary, as he is getting too feeble to transact business. I will probably stay with him to the end, which I cannot think is far off.

'I can't say how horrified and distressed I was to read in last week's *Rand News* of the death of Smith and the arrest of Crawley. The latter must be some ghastly mistake, as it is quite impossible to conceive of Crawley's being guilty of such a crime. I had another object in writing you besides telling you of myself, and that is to let you know that I met Smith the night that he was killed. It was the night I left Middeldorp. I was coming down Cheyne Street about a quarter or twenty minutes past ten, when he passed me not far from the Scala Picture

House. I noticed that he was carrying a suitcase. We stopped for a moment and he wished me a good journey. He seemed confused or excited, and was smelling of brandy, and I remember thinking he had had too much. Poor fellow! To think that he was just then going to his death!

'I should be glad if you would tell this to the police, as it might possibly be useful. I am ready to swear an affidavit of the evidence or do anything else they may want.

'Remember me to everyone. I enclose a few photographs of Langholm Hall, also one of myself I have just had taken, to remind you of

'Your sincere friend,
'JOHN A. SWAYNE.'

The photographs showed an extremely ornate old Elizabethan manor house, indeed almost a castle, finely set among great oaks, beeches and elms. That of Swayne was a cabinet portrait marked, 'Wheeler Cox, Newcastle.'

'A splendid old place, and an excellent likeness of its probable future owner,' Mr Hindhead commented as he took them back. 'But is that news about poor Smith of any use to you?'

'As it happens, sir, it isn't much,' Vandam replied. 'It confirms information I had already received, and I'm therefore glad to get it, but as this information was not questioned, confirmation is not essential. But the evidence might have been invaluable, and I am none the less grateful to Mr Swayne and to you, sir, for your trouble, because it doesn't happen to be so.'

Vandam was the more disappointed, because this was the only new evidence he received in the weeks prior to the trial.

During those weeks Marion Hope had haunted Griffenhagen's office, and had followed the preparations for the trial with an almost feverish earnestness, but even she looked forward to the future with a doubt which at times approached actual dismay.

In spite of her eager opportunings, she had been prevented from visiting Crawley in the prison, but she resolutely refused to consider the engagement at an end. Crawley's letter releasing her from it had no effect. She said she appreciated his motives, but that the thing was fixed and would stand.

On one point only had Griffenhagen made headway. After protracted arguments he had prevailed on Crawley to let him tell Marion of the anonymous letter. The girl's relief on hearing of it was so great that it was evident to the solicitor that, in spite of her brave face, a certain doubt of her lover had been gnawing at her heart. She turned on him with glowing face.

'I *knew* there was something like that,' she cried, with a half sob. 'Oh, why, *why* couldn't he have told me before? He might have known me better.'

After this there was no question of keeping the matter secret. It was a point in Crawley's favour, and, as such, Marion decreed it must be used.

The longest periods of suspense come to an end, and, inexorable as fate, the day of the trial at length arrived. Into the already crowded court filed witnesses, jurors, solicitors and counsel, the judge took his place, and finally Crawley appeared between two warders in the dock. The swearing-in of the jurors and other time-honoured formalities were gone through, and the trial began.

Mr Hume Nasmyth, the Public Prosecutor, opened the case. Speaking in a quiet, conversational tone, he assured the jury that on this occasion theirs would be an easy task, that the evidence was clear and complete, and that they would have no difficulty in coming to a just verdict upon it. Then he briefly recounted the discovery of the tragedy, outlined the histories both of Crawley and Smith, told of their association in the provision store, and related the incident of Smith's insult to Marion Hope at the dinner. This incident, said Mr Nasmyth, which would be proved up to the hilt, established the first point in the prosecution's case; that just prior to Smith's death he had given the prisoner mortal cause of offence.

Secondly, a letter from the prisoner to the deceased would be produced, written on the day of the murder, in which the prisoner, referring to 'the matters which were between them,' invited the deceased to meet him in the self-same potting shed in the Groote Park where the murder was afterwards proved to have been committed. When they saw that letter the jury could decide in their own minds whether it was a genuine effort to end the quarrel, or whether a deliberate attempt had been made to lure an unfortunate man to his death. In either case, the result was the same. Smith kept the appointment, and was there murdered in the foulest and most brutal manner possible.

The third of the three main points on which the case for the prosecution hung was that when Crawley was asked to account for his movements during the period in which the murder must have been committed, he put forward an alibi, and that alibi the gentlemen of the jury would please notice, was proved to be a pure fabrication. The prisoner stated that during the fateful hour he was smoking on his *stoep*. But where was he actually? It would be sworn by two witnesses that he, hurriedly and furtively, passed through the Green Gate into the Groote Park at about twenty minutes past ten. That gate, as the gentlemen of the jury were well aware, was in the direct line from his house to the potting shed, and some five minutes' walk from the latter. Whether that entrance, which the prisoner had been so anxious to hide, was to keep his appointment with Smith would be for the jury to decide. Other minor points would come out during the hearing; broadly speaking, that was the case for the prosecution. He would now call his witnesses.

He did so. Signalman Ashe once again testified to the finding of the body, Sergeant Clarke to its position and surroundings, and Dr Bakker to its condition. Then Mr Hope told what he knew of the careers of Crawley and Smith. Other members of the Hope Bros. staff were called to describe the incident at the dance. Lloyd gave evidence as to the finding of the bundle of Smith's private papers in his drawer, and Vandam handed in the letter from Crawley making the appointment, which he had discovered amongst them. Finally, George Hume and Lysacht swore they had seen Crawley entering the park by the Green Gate at about 10.20 on the night of the murder.

When all the evidence had been given, the court adjourned for the night. Hardly one who had been present had a doubt of the prisoner's guilt, and no one thought he had the remotest chance of acquittal. All, therefore, waited with bated breath for Mr Rufus Carrothers, when he rose next morning to make the opening speech for the defence.

Mr Carrothers also began quietly. He admitted at once the completeness of the case for the prosecution and the damaging nature of the evidence which had been given. If that evidence were incapable of another construction than that put upon it by his learned friend, the guilt of the prisoner was demonstrated. But happily for his client, it could equally well bear another and a very different interpretation. He said boldly, and he thought he would be able to prove, that that evidence was not genuine—it was faked. The jury were please not to misunderstand that remark. He made no aspersions on the integrity of the police or of his learned friends opposite. His meaning was quite other. He meant that the prisoner was the victim of a plot; that this evidence was constructed by the murderer to throw the suspicion on an innocent man, and thereby to ensure his own escape. He would deal with the matter in a few words before calling his witnesses.

Reviewing the case as a whole, the first point which would strike any disinterested observer was the complete failure of the prosecution to prove motive. The indication of motive was an absolute essential of criminal proceedings such as they were taking part in, and it was not too much to say that no prisoner could be found guilty of murder unless an adequate motive were suggested. Now, what had the prosecution done? They had proved that on one occasion the deceased and the prisoner had had a tiff—he really could not call it by a stronger name— and he would like to call the attention of the jury to three points about that tiff. In the first place, the insult was offered by a man who had taken more champagne than was good for him. He did not wish in any way to excuse the deceased, but the jury would agree that an objectionable act did not carry the same offence when committed by an intoxicated man as it would were he fully responsible for his actions. That was the first point. The second was that in the tiff the prisoner was the victor and remained master of the situation. He would, therefore, be unlikely to bear resentment. The third point was that on the next day, the day after the tiff, the matter had blown over. He would bring evidence to show that on that next day relations between the prisoner and the deceased were normal. They met in the course of their business and were perfectly polite and friendly.

The prosecution, therefore, Mr Carrothers went on, had failed not only to prove motive, but even to indicate what possible motive there might have been. And why? he asked the jury. The answer was simple; because there was no motive. That alone, Mr Carrothers held, should be enough to acquit the prisoner.

With regard to the second matter referred to by the prosecution, the letter in Crawley's handwriting making the appointment, Mr Carrothers asked the jury if they could seriously bring themselves to believe that anyone intending to decoy a victim to his death would do so by such means; that anyone in his senses would produce a document to prove his own guilt. If Crawley had wished to make such an appointment, there was no need for him to put pen to paper. He was in close touch with Smith—they met many times a day—and there were opportunities for him to have made fifty appointments in complete privacy, and without leaving any record. No, if that letter were the fiendish lure the prosecution stated, Crawley had never written it.

And that was his case: that Crawley had never written it. Why, he would like the jury to ask, had the prosecution not put one of their handwriting experts in the box to prove that the letter was in Crawley's hand? He would tell them. Because no handwriting expert would do so. He would presently call Mr Lewsley, the most reliable expert in South Africa, and he would swear that the letter was a forgery; that Crawley had never written a word of it. So much for the letter.

But there was a third point brought up by the prosecution: Crawley's false alibi. Well, he admitted in the fullest way that the prisoner had made a false statement to the police, and when the jury heard the reason, he, Mr Carrothers, was sure that they would feel nothing but respect and sympathy for his client. On the day of the murder the prisoner had received an anonymous letter saying, not to put too fine a point on it, that his betrothed, Miss Marion Hope, was carrying on an intrigue with the deceased, that that night they were to meet, and that if the prisoner wished to see what was going on for himself he could do so by hiding himself at half-past ten behind the shrubs in the rock garden in the Groote Park. He would presently put the prisoner in the box, and the jury would hear from his own lips how at first he was enraged, how then he gradually came to see that for his own peace of mind in the future he must satisfy himself of the falseness of the suggestion, and how, finally, he did go to the rendezvous at the hour mentioned. Needless to say, he saw nothing. He waited until eleven, then returned home full of shame at having harboured doubt of Miss Hope. Respect for the lady and shame for himself forbade him tell Inspector Vandam of the episode, and he invented a somewhat clumsy lie.

That anonymous letter, Mr Carrothers wished the jury to

appreciate, entirely accounted for the prisoner's actions, both on the night of the murder and afterwards. To satisfy his own mind, he, Mr Carrothers, had submitted it to Mr Lewsley, the handwriting expert, and that gentleman would tell the jury that he was satisfied it was not written by the prisoner. And if it was not written by the prisoner, the gentlemen of the jury would see that the prisoner must have received it as he had said, and that being so, that his whole statement was reasonable and possible.

Mr Carrothers then called his witnesses. First were some other members of the Hope Bros. staff, who testified to certain acts of kindness Crawley had shown Smith in recent times, as well as the friendliness of their intercourse on the day of the murder. Mr Lewsley then gave his evidence about the hand-writings, and, lastly, Crawley went into the box and told his story of the anonymous letter. The two latter witnesses were subjected to a particularly searching cross-examination, but without shaking their statements.

Mr Carrothers then made his final speech for the defence. He briefly summarised the main points of his case, and paid a tribute to the excellent character the prisoner had always borne. He reminded the jury that if an explanation of the facts was tenable which did not involve the prisoner's guilt, they were bound to give the latter the benefit of the doubt, ending up by referring to the extreme responsibility of their office and duty.

The reply for the prosecution was also short. Mr Hume Nasmyth ridiculed the plot theory, saying that common sense would lead the jury to reject it and to return a verdict of guilty.

When the judge had summed up and the jury had retired to consider their verdict it was already past three o'clock. Then ensued a period of waiting, irksome to the mere spectators, but fraught with terrible suspense for the participants in the grim drama. Hour passed after hour, and still the jury remained in consultation. Five o'clock came, then six, then seven, and still they made no sign. At last, at half-past seven, when the strain had become almost intolerable, there was a movement, and the jury, looking careworn and miserable, filed back into court. The judge resumed his place, the prisoner was brought back into the dock, and a rustle of expectancy passed over the building, gradually subsiding into silence. The atmosphere grew tense.

And then came the surprise of the trial. A gasp went up from over the whole court when the foreman of the jury reluctantly announced that they had been unable to agree. The judge, after some further counsel and advice, sent them back to reconsider the case, but in half an hour they returned, saying regretfully that there was no hope of their bringing in a verdict. With something of shortness in his manner, the judge discharged them, the prisoner was put back, and the case was over.

Three months later saw a repetition of the whole weary business. Once again the public flocked to the courthouse, counsel delivered their arguments, witnesses gave their evidence, and the jury retired to consider their verdict. Once again their consultations were protracted. Hour after hour they remained locked up, while the prospect of a second disagreement grew more and more probable to the tired people waiting in the court. And then at last, after deliberations lasting more than five and a half hours, they filed back, to give their auditors an even greater surprise than had their predecessors. Contrary to the expectations of all who had followed the case, they found the prisoner not guilty, and presently, amid an ominous silence, Stewart Crawley was discharged from the dock, legally an innocent man.

But the verdict of the law is not always that of the populace, and the acquitted man soon found that his fellow-townsmen refused to believe in his innocence. His appearance at the court-house door was the signal for an ugly demonstration, and for his own safety the police had to smuggle him out by a back way. Wherever he went, he found more or less active hostility, and his former friends turned in the opposite direction when they saw him approaching.

From Marion Hope there was no sign, and he could not bring himself to thrust himself upon her notice. After two days he was no more seen, and rumour had it that he had left the town.

PART II

SCOTLAND

CHAPTER XI

THOUGH Stewart Crawley did not know it, Marion Hope was very far indeed from being careless of his fate. But her apparent desertion was not her fault. During the concluding day of the second trial, and for nearly a week after it, the young girl was lying in her darkened bedroom, hovering on the borderline of consciousness and hardly able to move. Indeed, those who had witnessed her accident thought it a marvel that she was alive at all. Turning a corner in her little runabout, she had collided with a heavily loaded motor lorry, which was travelling at far too high a speed in the opposite direction and on the wrong side of the road. The big vehicle had crashed through the smaller one, and Marion had been lifted from the wreck bruised from head to foot, with a broken arm and with more than a trace of concussion. At first it had been touch and go with her, but youth and a fine constitution was on her side, and she first rallied, and then slowly began to mend. In a week the doctors were able to report satisfactory progress, and in a second week to pronounce her out of danger.

But by the time she had come out of the condition of semi-coma the trial was over and Stewart Crawley had vanished. In vain she raved and raged, now fiercely rating her father for letting him go, now beseeching him hysterically to find him and bring him back to her. What distressed her most keenly was the fact, reluctantly admitted by Mr Hope as a result of her persistent questioning, that he had not explained to the released man the reason of her absence from court, and that Griffenhagen, thinking Crawley had learnt of the accident from Mr Hope, had not done so either.

'Oh, if I had only been there,' she would moan. 'He will think I deserted him. He will think I didn't care. And you, Daddy, oh, I am ashamed of you. You *did* desert him, just when he wanted help most. Oh, Daddy, how *could* you do it? And now he is gone and I can't make it right with him.' And then she would burst into uncontrollable floods of weeping, long, dry sobs that seemed to tear her very heart, and that irritated her father almost beyond endurance.

To Mr Hope, the whole business, the acquittal, followed by the disappearance of Crawley, had seemed the solution of a vexatious problem, but so violent did Marion's grief become that he was constrained to accede to her wishes and do his best to find the missing man. To his secret relief, his efforts were fruitless. He made inquiries, advertised, even employed a private detective, all to no purpose. Crawley had vanished into thin air.

As Marion's bodily health improved, her self-control returned, and she ceased to give way to the paroxysms of grief which had so distressed her father. But instead, he sensed a permanent change in her feelings towards him which hurt him even more. She was now more polite than formerly, but colder and more self-contained, and the vivacious joy which used to sparkle in her manner was a thing of the past. She became silent, moody, listless. Gradually she ceased to take interest in her former pursuits, and Mr Hope found it increasingly difficult to arouse her attention and to combat the apathy which was creeping over her.

In despair he consulted the doctor who had attended her physical injuries.

'Send her away,' was the verdict of science. 'Send her clean away where she won't be reminded of what has happened. She wants a complete change. Let her travel and see the world.'

But Marion would have none of it. Her place was with her father, and there she would stay. Perhaps, also, there was the lingering hope that news might yet come of her beloved. At all events, she would not go travelling. But all the time she was growing more and more depressed, and though she loathed herself for it, a cold rage against her father, not far removed from hatred, forced its way into her heart.

To do Marion justice, it must be remembered that she had just received a very severe physical shock, which left her badly equipped to withstand the mental one which followed. She fully recognised that her father's action had been prompted by a desire for what he believed was her welfare, and she tried hard not to let him see how deeply she was wounded. But in spite of her efforts, she could not banish from her mind the picture of her lover, publicly declared innocent of the crime with which he had been charged, stepping from the dock after the nightmare months of prison, a free man, with character cleared, stepping forth to meet the congratulations and welcome of his fellow-townsmen, and finding instead that every man's hand was against him, that those whom he had never even known were waiting to injure him, and that her father, *her father*, had taken advantage of her helplessness to abandon him to his fate. Oh! she thought again and again, how could he have done it? Sometimes as she brooded through the long sleepless nights, she felt she could never bear to see her father again; then, shocked at herself, she reminded herself he had meant it for her good.

Mr Hope, who was not without imagination, understood something of what was passing in his daughter's mind, and though he still believed that Marion would live to thank him for his action, he realised the shock that she had received, and saw that if her life and reason were to be safeguarded, something drastic must be done. At a cost of several pounds, he cabled a detailed account of the situation to his brother Alexander, at Callander. It will be remembered that three years earlier Alexander had retired from the business and gone to end his days in the old Scottish homeland. Next day a reply came to Marion containing a cordially worded invitation to pay him a visit. And Marion, with a sudden revulsion of feeling, became aware that it was the thing of all others she wanted—to leave this nightmare town of Middeldorp—to get clear away to some place where she would not at every turn be reminded of her loss. She would gladly have died, or thought she would, but as she had to drag out a miserable existence, she would prefer to do so among strangers.

Her preparations were soon made. A second cable was sent to Alexander, an enthusiastic reply received, and a week later John Hope accompanied his daughter to Capetown and saw her off on the *Dover Castle* for England.

The voyage passed uneventfully, and in due course reached its appointed end. Alexander had come up to town and he met the traveller at Tilbury, spent a fortnight showing her the sights of London, and then took her north to his Perthshire home. There in the pleasant district of Callander she settled down to a quiet and uneventful life which, as month succeeded month, completely restored her physical health, and bade fair in time also to heal the wound her spirit had received.

At times as she thought of her father living alone in far-off Middeldorp, her conscience smote her for remaining so long away from his side. She saw herself selfish, and on different occasions she wrote offering to return. But John Hope, hearing from his brother of the steady improvement in her spirits, was loath to change surroundings which were having so beneficial an effect, and urged her to remain a little longer. This little longer stretched and stretched until considerably more than two years had passed away. Then Marion wrote that no matter what her father might say, she was returning forthwith, and John, secretly overwhelmed with delight, gave an apparently grudging consent.

This was late in September, and the departure was arranged for the middle of the following month, so as to get the voyage over before the winter storms set in, and so that the traveller might follow the summer southwards. And then occurred one of those apparently trifling events which shape the destinies of mortals and give their life histories an entirely unexpected turn.

This was nothing more startling than the fact that Mrs Macpherson, a Callander neighbour, decided to go to Edinburgh for a week's change, and asked Marion to accompany her. Marion consenting, the two women set off on the last day of September, reached the capital and put up at the Waverley Hotel. For three days they did the sights of the charming city, then on the fourth Mrs Macpherson went down to Leith to look up an old servant who had fallen on evil days, and Marion was left alone. During this time Fate intervened.

Marion was strolling slowly along the west end of Princes Street, looking desultorily at the shop windows, when she noticed a figure approaching about whose walk there seemed something familiar. She looked with more attention, then suddenly her heart gave a leap and seemed to stand still. At the same moment the man saw her, stopped, stared with an expression of utter amazement, then stepped forward with a hoarse cry of 'Marion!'

Regardless of the curious glances of the passers-by, who were intrigued by the little drama, she tottered towards him and caught his arm with both her hands, as she murmured, 'Stewart! Oh, Stewart!'

For a moment they stood, too moved to be conscious of their surroundings, then Crawley pulled himself together.

'Get in here,' he said, calling over a taxi which happened to be passing. 'Drive slowly—anywhere—'til I tell you to stop,' he directed, and he handed Marion in.

They moved off, and then the man turned to his companion and gazed at her with hungry yet sorrowful eyes, as his love welled up and made more poignant the bitter sense of loss which had tinged all his thoughts during the past two and a half years. She had aged in the time, he thought. She was thinner, and her face was drawn as if from suffering. She had lost her merry sparkle, but in spite of it she looked ten times, a hundred times more desirable than he had ever before seen her. Heavens, how utterly adorable she was! How beyond belief beautiful! The sight of her and the knowledge that he had lost her was driving him mad. Desperately he strove for composure, but his voice was hoarse with pain as he murmured, 'Marion, you are not sorry to see me?'

'Sorry!' she repeated, the tears swimming in her eyes. 'Oh, Stewart, if you only knew! How I have longed for this! How I searched for you! Oh, Stewart, if you had only come to me that day you were released! What misery it would have saved!'

Crawley looked at her in bewilderment.

'Marion, what are you saying?' he burst out. 'Why did *I* not go? It wasn't my place to go. How could I? You weren't there on that last day of the trial. Your father was, and he avoided me when they let me out. Everyone else did the same. I wasn't wanted by anyone in that accursed town. I wasn't wanted by you. I didn't blame you. You could not have married me. I understood that right enough. For heaven's sake, tell me what you mean?'

She was sobbing, but her eyes were bright.

'My poor Stewart,' she whispered, again putting her hand on his arm. 'Then you didn't know? I feared you mightn't know, and that was the bitterest drop of all. My dear, I was ill then, unconscious. I didn't know anything about the end of the trial for a week afterwards, and then it was too late. You were gone.'

'Ill?' Crawley stared incredulously. 'But you were at the trial on the first day. I don't understand.'

'It was the evening of that day.' She spoke with difficulty between her sobs. 'I took out my little car to go down and see Mr Griffenhagen. I was run into in George Street. My head was struck, and I wasn't properly conscious for over a week.'

Crawley was listening with an excitement so intense as to be almost painful.

'Then you didn't—you didn't *want* to forget me?'

'Forget you!' She laughed happily through her tears. 'My dear! Could I ever forget you?'

He seized her hands in both his own.

'Marion!' he cried hoarsely. 'You don't mean—you can't mean that you love me still?'

She turned and looked straight into his eyes, and in hers he read his answer. In a moment she was in his arms and he was crushing her desperately to his heart.

'My beloved,' he murmured. 'Can you ever forgive me? How I wronged you! Oh, if I had only known! But I never heard. I never suspected.'

Gradually, as the taxi circled slowly along the devious roads round Arthur's Seat, they grew calmer, and told each other more or less connected stories of what had befallen them during the period of their separation. When Crawley had thrilled over the tale of Marion's accident and convalescence, of her father's efforts to find him, of her leaving South Africa, and of the peaceful months she had spent near Callander, he related his own doings. And with the account she was even more thrilled than he had been with hers.

It seemed that before the end of the second day after his release, he had realised that life for him in Middeldorp was no longer possible. His friends would not see him, or turned the other way; his acquaintances cut him dead without any attempt to hide their action; strangers were openly insulting. All agreed in assuming him guilty and in showing their hostility. And Marion, hearing between the sentences, realised that of all these blows the most overwhelming, the most staggering, was her own fancied desertion. What that had cost him, Crawley did not suggest, but his hearer tried to imagine, and clung to him, again sobbing softly.

There being no chance of carrying on in his former job or of obtaining any other work, Crawley decided to leave Middeldorp. He collected what money he could lay his hands on, wrote a note to his sister informing her of his intention, and with a bundle over his shoulder in the traditional manner, left the city that night on foot. For a week he slept by day and tramped by night, until he reached the town of Steinfontein. There, lost in the crowd and passing under the name of James Bright, he took train for the north. After a month's wandering, he joined in the rush to a new goldfield that had just been discovered in Northern Rhodesia, staked off a claim, and for two years put in an existence of heartbreaking, thankless labour. Then suddenly, as if Fate had decided to make it up to him for the blows she had dealt him, he struck gold, and struck it rich. Each day saw his wealth growing, until at last, having accumulated quite a little fortune, he thought he had had enough to keep him for the rest of his days, and left the diggings and came to England to see how he liked the old country. He had bought a car, and, driving leisurely north, had been struck by the appearance of an empty house and place between Newcastle and Berwick. Being in a position to indulge every passing whim, he had called on the agents, and a close inspection of the property proving it increasingly attractive, he had purchased the entire place, lock, stock and barrel. Though the legal formalities were not yet completed, he had moved in, and was now in Edinburgh on the look out for a land steward who could instruct him in the running of the farm.

For an hour more the lovers circled slowly through the suburbs of Edinburgh, talking of themselves and of old times, until Marion turned to a new subject.

'By the way, Stewart,' she said suddenly, 'that place you have bought can't be far away from Mr Swayne's property. Wasn't it somewhere near Newcastle.'

'Right you are, clever little woman,' Crawley smiled. 'I had forgotten all about him when I took the place, but I heard someone speak of Sir Anthony Swayne, and then it occurred to me that it must be our old friend, John A. They tell me the old man died a couple of years ago, and he inherited. I believe he has an absolute mansion there. It's about eight miles from me, eight miles farther inland.'

'You haven't come across Mr Swayne?'

'No.' Crawley hesitated. 'To tell you the truth, I rather funked going to see him. I've got out of the way of looking up old friends. Besides, strictly speaking, it's his business to call on me—the newcomer, you know, and all that.'

'What rubbish,' Marion retorted warmly. 'You know he's not the man to stand on ceremony. I wonder if he knows who his new neighbour is?'

'Shouldn't think so. He's sure to have heard someone called Crawley has taken the Hill Farm, but he'll never connect him with me.'

'I suppose not.' She paused, then added, 'But go and see him, Stewart. I would like you to meet him again. I should like to hear how he greets you.'

Crawley smiled ruefully.

'I dare say. I can see you want me to make you a Roman holiday. I'd rather not, but if you're really dead set on it I'll go and see him when I get back.'

'You're a good boy,' she declared. 'You may kiss me for that.'

When they resumed their conversation it was on another subject—the almost as pressing question of whether or not Marion should carry out her plan of returning to South Africa. For her own sake, she was dead against it—until she could return in triumph as Mrs Stewart Crawley. But she hated to disappoint her father. Though her visit to Scotland had been his suggestion, she knew how he enjoyed her presence and company, and realised something of what his action must have cost him.

In the end, they separated without coming to a decision. Mrs Macpherson was returning to Callander on the following day, and it was agreed that Marion should accompany her as originally intended. After seeing them off, Crawley was to travel down to his new house, the Hill Farm, attend to one or two pressing matters of business, call on Swayne, and then follow the others north. In the meantime, Marion would talk the matter over with her Uncle Alexander, and the three of them would then settle what was to be done.

CHAPTER XII

HAVING seen the two ladies off for Callander by the 10.20 from Princes Street, Stewart Crawley walked down to Waverley and took the 11.10 East Coast express for the south.

To say that he was profoundly moved by his encounter with Marion would be to convey but a slight impression of the state of his feelings. Since that staggering, cataclysmic moment in Princes Street when his eyes first fell on the young girl's face, he had entered into a new existence in a new world. The very physical universe had changed. The sun, pouring down golden glory on the smiling country which hurried past his window, was no longer a brazen orb mocking cruelly at his pain. It was dancing joy incarnate, the overflowing spirit of life and youth. The train no longer clattered dustily and jerkily along, it flew buoyant, as if on the enchanted wings of hope. The terrible months of prison, the horror of the two trials, the stunning loss of the goodwill of his fellow men, the years of hopeless slavery on the goldfields—what were they but an evil dream, a nightmare that had passed into the limbo of things forgotten?

And this in spite of his resolution not to marry Marion while the cloud remained on his life. She knew, she understood, she believed in him; that was what primarily mattered. He had seen her, she loved him, he was to see her again; these were the matters of moment. These were the immediate facts. His renunciation was not yet. Sufficient unto the day!

Had there been other passengers in his compartment, they would surely have been uneasy as to whether this broad-shouldered, powerful man, who jerked himself about so restlessly and smiled so ecstatically at the list of the Company's hotels and refreshment rooms on the opposite wall, was quite a safe fellow-traveller. But Crawley fortunately was alone and needed to pay no heed to the demands of convention.

Presently he turned his thoughts to Marion's suggestion that he should call on Swayne. He found himself looking forward to the interview with strong, but mixed feelings. Though he had never been a close friend of Swayne's, under normal conditions the thought of seeing him again after so long an interval would have brought him real pleasure. But as things were, the paying of the call meant a very real demand on his courage. He marvelled at the intensity with which he hoped for a friendly reception. Its absence would mean more than the actual rebuff. Though not superstitious, he could not help looking on the matter as an omen, as something which would confirm or destroy the hope which had sprung up in his mind that he had entered upon a new and happier stage of his existence. He found himself keenly, feverishly eager to make the test.

His train not stopping at Elswick, the nearest station to his new home, he went through to Newcastle, where he had wired for his car to meet him. During the fifteen-mile run out to the Hill Farm his thoughts continued to dwell on the question of the coming interview, though returning always to what was for him the centre of the universe, Marion.

That evening and the following morning he was occupied with Hill Farm business, but after lunch he set out alone in his small car for Langholm Hall. It was the first time he had passed along that particular road, and as he followed it through the gently undulating country he—with the image of Marion subconsciously before him—thought he had never seen so fair a land.

And in truth it was fair. Though at first a trifle bare, with stunted trees growing thinly in sparse clumps, and a grey atmosphere draining the warmth from the colouring, with every mile that Crawley went inland the country grew more and more attractive, the trees taller and more numerous, the shrubs more luxuriant, and the ground more fertile. Presently he crossed a low range of hills, and in the valley beyond reached the wall bounding Swayne's estate.

A drive of not less than a mile led in a sweeping curve up to the fine old Elizabethan house, which stood peaceful and dignified, looking out over an undulating grassland studded with great trees. The door was opened to Crawley's ring by a grave and dignified butler, who seemed almost part and parcel of the house, so well did he fit his surroundings. He regretted his master had gone out, and was unlikely to return for some hours.

With a feeling of acute disappointment, Crawley wrote on his card, 'In memory of Hope Bros. Sorry not to have seen you,' and took his departure.

But as he drove back to the Hill Farm he began to think that things had happened for the best. It was now up to Swayne to make the next move. If Swayne wished to see him he would call, if he did not desire to be friendly the awkwardness of a meeting would be avoided.

Crawley was not without hope that he might see or hear from his former acquaintance on the next day, but it passed without bringing him news. But just before lunch on the following morning a telegraph boy followed him to the outlying field where he had been discussing improvements with his men, and handed him a message. It had been despatched from the Charing Cross Post Office in London at 10.25 that morning, and read:

'Sorry unexpected summons to London made me over-look your call. Returning Saturday night and hope to call with you Sunday. Looking forward to meeting you again.
'SWAYNE.'

'Good old Swayne!' Crawley muttered delightedly. 'He's a real friend. I believe my luck is going to change!' It was with a feeling of deep contentment that he strolled back to the Hill Farm for lunch.

Some letters which had come by the morning delivery were awaiting him. The first three or four he opened were on trivial subjects, but there was one which immediately attracted his attention. It bore a Glasgow postmark, and though he knew no one in Glasgow, the handwriting was familiar. But he could not place the writer, and it was with a quickening interest that he drew the sheets from the envelope. As his eyes passed along the closely-written lines, an expression of amazement grew on his face, and his lunch remained unnoticed and forgotten. The letter read:

'Kinloch,
'Crianlarich.

'Private.

'Dear Crawley,—I suppose you have not altogether forgotten Sandy Buchan, who used to help run the Bellevue Hotel in Middeldorp? You will be surprised to hear from me now, but as a matter of fact I have been wanting to get in touch with you for a good many months.

'First I must tell you how I come to be here. As you may remember, Janet, my wife, was a Glasgow girl, and she never could stick South Africa. She put up with it for years, but at last got so set on home that I chucked up my job at the Bellevue and came back to the Old Country. At first I had the devil's own luck; couldn't raise a job any place. Things got worse and worse, 'til all my little nest egg was gone and I would have taken any kind of thing that offered. Then this billet turned up and I jumped at it, though it was something of a comedown for the assistant manager of the Bellevue. In brief, Janet and I are housekeeper and man to Colonel Grahame, a widower of over seventy who lives in this shooting lodge and spends his time writing books about ancient Egypt.

'I was in Edinburgh last week and saw someone that I took to be the ghost of Stewart Crawley. Then I thought I was mistaken and I didn't butt in. But when I came back here I learned it was you right enough, for Angus MacTavish, that's one of the foremen on our neighbour's farm, happened to mention he was thinking of applying for the job of land steward to a Mr Stewart Crawley, a gentleman who had just come from South Africa and who had bought the Hill Farm near Newcastle, and who had been in Edinburgh last week interviewing applicants.

'Now you'll be wondering what all this rigmarole is about. Well, I'll tell you. It's about poor Smith. I saw Smith on the night of his death, in fact, I met him by appointment to have a private chat—he told me he was in a difficulty and had asked my help. We met in the Scala Picture House, and during the show there he told me some facts which fairly startled me. He knew then he was in danger, but he had no idea the danger was so close. What he told me has made me suspect what really happened on that night—suspect, you understand, for I have no proof. You will say, why did I not come forward when you were arrested? Well, perhaps I should have. I acted for the best, but I may have been wrong. I held my tongue principally in order to save a lady's good name, but also, I must admit, because if I had spoken I would have been in danger myself. You know the lady, and when you hear the details I believe you will say I was right. But I give you my word of honour had the verdict gone against you I would have told all I knew to Griffenhagen.

'Eighteen months ago the lady died, and since then I have been longing for an opportunity of seeing you to tell you all Smith told me. It may be quite valueless to you, but, on the other hand, it may put you on the right track.

'Now, as you can understand, I don't like to write the yarn, and I can't very well go to see you—I have just been on leave in Edinburgh. Will you therefore call up and see me here? As the story will take some time to tell, and as I want the whole thing kept private, I would rather you would come when Colonel Grahame is out. Friday night next at 9.00 would suit me, if it would suit you. The Colonel is going out to dinner. He'll leave here about 8.00 and not be back 'til 12 or 1.00. I'll have some things to see to after he goes, but we could have an uninterrupted chat from 9.00 to 11.00.

'I would naturally prefer that you would destroy this letter, and say nothing about your visit here—if you come. If you have a car you could drive yourself up from Glasgow in less than two hours. The house is on the road from Ardlui to Crianlarich, on the left-hand side, about a mile on the Crianlarich side of where the road crosses over the railway. The little sketch enclosed will show you the place. Sorry I can't offer you a bed, but you will be back in Glasgow by 1.00 a.m.

'Sorry also for inflicting such an endless screed on you, and looking forward to seeing you.

'Your old friend,
'SANDY BUCHAN.'

When Crawley had finished the letter he at first sat motionless, gazing into vacancy, then as the full significance of what he had read sank into his consciousness he began to tremble with suppressed excitement. He remembered the handwriting now. As Assistant Manager of the Bellevue, Buchan had had large dealings with Hope Bros., and the two men had come into almost daily contact. He had always impressed Crawley as being dependable and straight, and though it seemed cruel that information which might have cleared him had been withheld from the trial, Crawley felt inclined to accept without question

Buchan's statement that his reasons were sufficient. As he wondered what that information was, his pulses quickened, and he sprang from his chair and began to pace the room with short, jerky steps. Could it be that he was really about to learn something which would give him a clue to the truth, which would rehabilitate his character, which would dispel the dark cloud which was brooding over his life? For that would mean— glorious and wonderful thought! that would mean—Marion! He grew more and more excited.

Even at the worst, even if Buchan's story led to nothing, Crawley felt that this was for him a red-letter day. For here, within a few minutes of each other, he had learned that two separate people, old acquaintances, believed in him. Buchan had practically said so in so many words, while Swayne would never have sent so cordial a telegram if he doubted his innocence. It was an omen. Brighter days were coming.

His thoughts turned back to the letter. Buchan, he remembered, had been on intimate terms with Smith. He, Crawley, had heard, partly at the trials and partly through Griffenhagen, of Smith's visit to the Scala on the evening of his death, and the description of the man he had evidently expected to meet there. *Buchan answered that description.* Why, Crawley wondered, had it never occurred to anyone that Buchan might have been the man?

He supposed because Buchan had not come forward. Also it was possible that the question had been asked him by Vandam and that he had lied in answer. If he would hold back his evidence, he would certainly lie. And now it seemed that there was a reason for this.

Well, thought Crawley, he would soon know. He would fall in with Buchan's suggestion and motor out to see him at this place, wherever it was. And possibly—another idea suddenly struck him and he smiled with pleasurable anticipation— possibly Buchan would not lose by his action. It was a big comedown for so important a man on the staff of the Bellevue to become a gentleman's gentleman. Could he not offer Buchan a better job, the business management of the Hill Farm? He could give him one of the larger cottages—quite decent houses they were—pay him a good salary, and have the benefit of his companionship as well as of his professional help. At all events, he would suggest it.

And Marion? Always his thoughts swung back to Marion. Marion must know what was going on. With a sudden impulse he took up Buchan's letter, wrote across the envelope, 'Am going. Destroy when read. Will wire result,' slipped it into another envelope, and dropped it into his letter box. Presently he took down his motoring maps and began to study the country. Ardlui, he saw, was at the extreme north end of Loch Lomond, and Crianlarich some eight miles farther north. The road was marked red, a main, through route, and he could follow it clearly down the western side of the loch, through Alexandria, and along the northern bank of the Clyde into Glasgow.

From the Hill Farm to Glasgow the road was not quite so obvious, but at last he had made out his route, ascertained his distances, and settled the time of his departure.

The meeting was for the following evening, and shortly before eleven next day he set out alone in his two-seater. The day was fine, though there was more than a nip of autumn in the air. He was brimful of anticipation and pleasurable excitement, like a schoolboy starting off home after his first term.

He passed through Jedburgh and Galashiels, stopping at Peebles for lunch at the George. Then on again in sight of the Moorfoots and the Pentlands to Carstairs, Lanark, Hamilton, and so into Glasgow. As he turned into Argyle Street, the clocks were just on the stroke of five.

He had an early dinner at the Central Hotel, and having reserved a room for the night, he started westwards again, and ran out along the Dumbarton Road. Dusk was falling, and before he turned north from the Clyde it was quite dark. The night was fine and starry, and presently there would be a thin crescent moon. It was cold, with a dry, thin air, and more than a touch of frost.

He had not come so quickly as he had hoped, and it was close on eight o'clock before he left Alexandria behind and ran out along the shore of Loch Lomond, with something like thirty miles still in front of him. By the time he reached Luss the moon had risen, and he was able dimly to take stock of his surroundings.

The stretch of road from Luss to Crianlarich is surely the most beautiful in the British Isles. On a clear day it unfolds a gorgeous pageant of mountain and valley, of wood and water, of spray-clad waterfall, of lonely moor. At night the light of even a thin crescent of moon is sufficient to reveal something of its startling grandeur, though Crawley was too much concerned about his coming interview to appreciate it as he otherwise might. But, in spite of his preoccupation, he could not fail to be conscious of the towering heights on his left hand, of the shimmer of reflections on the loch—which here came in to the edge of the road, and of the vast mountain piles across the water. Ben Lomond hung above him as he passed through Inverbeg and Tarbet, he saw the hollow in the skyline where the road from Loch Katrine ran down into Inversnaid, then winding round rocky promontories, he ran past Ardlui at the head of the lake, and began the long climb up the valley towards Crianlarich.

As he zigzagged upwards, he gradually left the densely wooded country of the lower levels and came out on to moorland. He could now get occasional glimpses of the railway on his left hand, and presently he crossed it. Then he stopped the car, and taking the copy he had made of Buchan's sketch map—the original had gone to Marion with the letter—he began to study his position.

The night was intensely still, and a feeling of loneliness swept over him as he sat looking round at the vast space of the valley and the dim outline of the mountains on either hand. Not a light was visible, not a sign of life apparent. A breath of cold wind moaned eerily across the moor, and he shivered with a sudden unreasoning feeling of foreboding. Then, pulling himself together, he moved off again, impatient to see Buchan and hear his news.

Presently he came to the house gate, just where shown on the map, and, pulling the car over to the side of the road, he dismounted and passed up the short drive. The house was in complete darkness, and for a moment he wondered if he had not made a mistake. Then he remembered that the plan showed the porch round at the side. He moved round and saw a beam of light issuing from what seemed to be the glass panel of an inner door. He was stepping up to it past a large shrub which grew beside the path when, with a sickening thud, a crashing blow descended on his head. He gasped, a whirl of stars danced before his eyes, a deep blackness seemed to well up around him, and he fell unconscious to the ground.

CHAPTER XIII

TOUCH AND GO

WE must here go back some thirty hours in our story, and follow the course of the letter signed Sandy Buchan, which Crawley had forwarded to Marion Hope.

It lay until evening in Crawley's letter box, from which it was eventually taken to be posted by one of the Hill Farm labourers. But it happened that this man met a pal outside the Pentland Arms, with the result that when it reached the post office the mail bag for Newcastle was already made up. It therefore remained overnight in the village, journeying up to town by the 7.30 train next morning. From Newcastle it went by an early express to Edinburgh, and thence, after a sojourn of a couple of hours, continued on its way by the afternoon train from Princes Street. Finally the Callander postman pushed it under the door of Mr Alexander Hope's villa at precisely 5.17 that evening.

Two minutes later Marion received it, and she also thrilled with excitement as she began to envisage the possibilities which seemed to be opening up. She recollected Buchan, and was filled with a desire to meet him and to hear from his own lips the story which he had feared to write. Indeed, her cogitations followed very much the same ambit as those of Crawley, some twenty-four hours earlier. In her case, as in his, the need for expression became paramount, and at dinner she could not help broaching the subject to her uncle.

'I should have liked to have seen some more of this country before I went back to South Africa,' she began with feminine directness. 'I haven't been over in the West at all: Oban, Loch Awe, and that district.'

Mr Hope made an inaudible rejoiner.

'Crianlarich, too,' went on Marion. 'Everyone says it's such a lovely place. You know it, don't you, Uncle Alec?'

Uncle Alec knew it.

Marion, pursuing the methods formerly adopted by Red Indians, who, simulating the innocuous sheep, moved in a decreasing spiral round their victim until near enough to leap on him and cleave his skull with a tomahawk, at length reached the radius of Colonel Grahame. She had heard such a name mentioned. Possibly her Uncle Alec had met him?

Uncle Alec had met him, and as the conversation progressed it gradually transpired that he was also aware that the gallant Colonel lived in the villa 'Kinloch,' and that he was elderly, retired, and an undistinguished writer on Egyptian folklore.

Marion suddenly realised that for many years she had unconsciously been interested in Egyptian folklore, and it was in discussing the subject and its aged exponent that she received her first shock.

'Take me to see Colonel Grahame some time, Uncle,' she said, with visions of an unexpected meeting with Sandy Buchan. 'I should like to hear him talk about Egypt.'

Her uncle looked at her.

'I could hardly spare the time to do that,' he said with a chuckle, 'but you might go home overland and interview him on the way.'

'Home overland?' she repeated, raising her pretty eyebrows. 'Home through Crianlarich? I don't understand.'

'If you want to see Colonel Grahame you won't go to Crianlarich. Brindisi, Alexandria and the Cape to Cairo Railway route would be your shortest way.'

'But Colonel Grahame is at Crianlarich.'

'Nothing, as you know, would induce me to contradict a lady, but subject to that reservation I should say that by now he was well on his way to Khartoum.'

'I know just what your politeness is worth,' Marion laughed.

'But this time you are wrong. He is really at Crianlarich, now, at this minute. I know. I heard so today.'

'Will you bet me three kisses to a pair of gloves?'

'Done! I want white suede; long ones, mind.'

'You'll never see them in this world, I'm afraid. Your old friend spends all his winters in Egypt, has done for years. He shuts up his lodge at Crianlarich and lives along the Nile—anywhere between Luxor and Khartoum.'

For the first time a pang of apprehension shot through Marion's mind.

'Oh, Uncle Alec, are you sure?' she said earnestly. 'You *must* be mistaken.'

Mr Hope looked at her curiously as he answered: 'Whatever matter does it make? You surely aren't so badly off for gloves as all that?'

She did not smile at his little joke, but sat gazing at him with a growing expression of anxiety. Seeing her emotion, he went on, 'But I can soon find out. If you really want to know, I'll ring up old Godfrey Sproule after dinner. He's sure to know all about it.'

Marion rose from the table.

'Do it now, Uncle Alec,' she pleaded. 'To please me, do it now. It really is important. I can't explain, but it is.'

Mr Hope demurred, but Marion, as usual, had her way. In five minutes the call was put through. Mr Sproule had just heard from his friend. He had written from Cairo, and was then about to leave for Luxor.

Marion was suddenly panic-stricken. Colonel Grahame's occupancy of the house on the Crianlarich Road was the pivot upon which the whole case for Crawley's visit there turned. If this were a fabrication, what did the letter mean? Why had Buchan written? *Had* Buchan written? . . .

She gave a little cry, and hurrying to her room seized the letter.

'There, Uncle; read that,' she exclaimed as she raced back

to the dining-room. 'Or rather, don't take the time; I'll tell you,' and quickly she gave him an outline of the contents. 'Uncle,' she added, her hands clasped in her excitement, 'there's something wrong! He's in danger! I feel it. Oh, what shall we do?'

Mr Hope was puzzled, but not excited.

'My dear child,' he murmured, 'do calm yourself. There's nothing to be upset about. It's probably a practical joke.'

'No, no, no!' Marion cried. 'He's in danger! I know it! I feel it! We must do something. Look, it's only eight o'clock. We may be in time if we hurry. Quick, Uncle, *do* make a move.'

'But what do you suggest I should do?' Mr Hope, what with the interruption of his meal and this storm in a teacup, was growing irritable.

'Get out the car at once, *at once*,' Marion said imperiously. 'Let us drive to the police station, get a couple of men, and go out to the house. Here, I will ring them up.'

Before her exasperated uncle could interfere she had taken down the receiver and made the call.

'This is Mr Hope's,' he heard her say. 'I am his niece. He has asked me to tell you that he has just got information which leads him to think a serious crime may be in contemplation. If we move at once we may be in time to stop it. Can you have two armed men ready to go with Mr Hope to the place? He will call in his car in five minutes.'

'Really, Marion—' the gentleman in question began, but she was making another call, this time to the chauffeur. 'The large car, immediately, with petrol for fifty miles. *Do* hurry, Duncan. It's a matter of life and death.'

As usual, she had her way, and in less than fifteen minutes they were at the police station, Marion hotly in argument with the sergeant.

'But ye ken, mistress,' the man insisted, 'it's no our district. We canna gae roaming ower a' Scotland. We're bound to keep 'til our ain district.'

Marion retorted hotly, then furiously. But for once she had

met someone who did not fly to do her will. The sergeant rubbed his chin sheepishly and repeated dully that a man was bound to keep 'til his ain district.

The girl knew when she was beaten. She found out from the relieved sergeant that it was to the men of the Tyndrum force that she should have applied, and in ten minutes more had got through to them on the station telephone. But here again she found herself up against officialdom. The officers could not enter a house on such slight evidence unless they had a search warrant. The Tyndrum sergeant doubted indeed whether such could be obtained. He would be glad to help, but . . .

With a superhuman effort Marion controlled her temper, and at last, after spending ten more precious minutes in entreaties, arguments and threats, she prevailed on the Tyndrum officer to agree to two of his men walking into Crianlarich, where the Hopes would pick them up in the car and take them on to Colonel Grahame's house. But the sergeant made it clear that these men could take no action unless they saw for themselves that something was wrong.

'Half-past eight,' Marion moaned in an agony of distress, as they left the police station. 'Thirty miles and half an hour to do it in. Do hurry, Duncan. Take risks and never mind the law.'

Mr Hope, though at first sceptical of danger to Crawley, was by this time as determined as Marion to see the thing through, and it was to his presence and influence that the girl owed such success with the police as she had obtained. He joined in quietly with, 'Ay, give her head, Duncan,' and the big car purred up the hill out of Callander at an ever-increasing speed.

They roared through the Pass of Leny, along the shore of Loch Lubnaig, past Strathyre and Kingshouse, and through a narrow valley with great mountain masses piled up on either hand. The road was good as to surface, but too hilly and too winding for speed, and though Duncan did his utmost, he found it impossible to let the car out. Marion sat tense, with hands clenched and with eyes on the speedometer and the clock, while at intervals she consulted the large-scale touring map, and with Mr Hope's help marked their position.

'Ten miles more,' she muttered as they swung through Ardchyle, 'and we are already ten minutes late. *Do* hurry, Duncan.'

They were now in the wider cross valley, with Crianlarich straight ahead. Here the road was straighter and they made better speed, but in spite of all Duncan's efforts the hands of the clock pointed to half-past nine as they ran past the Caledonian Station at Crianlarich and stopped at the junction of the Ardlui road. The police had not arrived.

'The hotel, Duncan,' Mr Hope suggested. 'Run and telephone to Tyndrum and see if they've started.'

The chauffeur was absent only a few seconds. The sergeant and two men had left Tyndrum on receipt of the news, and were walking to Crianlarich.

'Walking!' Marion groaned with a gesture of despair. Tyndrum, as she had seen from the map, was four and a half miles from Crianlarich. The men had had an hour's start. They could not be far away.

'We'll run out and pick them up,' she said.

It was at this precise moment, had she but known it, that Stewart Crawley, having lost half an hour on his run from Glasgow, walked past the bush in front of Colonel Grahame's house and received the blow on the head which left him stretched senseless on the ground.

She didn't know it, though even if she had she could not have urged haste more insistently. But Fate seemed once more against her. Duncan was familiar with the Tyndrum road, and he shook his head over her suggestion. The road was too narrow to turn the big limousine. If they once started, they would have to run on half-way to Tyndrum before they could get back.

A hasty consultation ensued, and it was decided to turn the vehicle where they were, then push out backwards to meet the police. Duncan objected that he couldn't drive so large a car backwards along such a narrow road in the darkness, but Marion insisted on his trying, and cautiously and sinuously they moved off.

Their slow, halting progress was a nerve-racking ordeal to the girl, who by this time had almost made up her mind that they must arrive too late to save her lover. What the danger that threatened him was she could not imagine, but she no longer doubted that it was real and pressing. Oh, if only the men would come!

Before they had gone half a mile she had an answer to that part, at all events, of her wish. Hurried steps were heard approaching, and a sergeant of police and two constables appeared. In ten seconds they were in the car and the vehicle was moving forward once more.

They ran through Crianlarich with a slight slack for the turn at the hotel, then swung up the hill past the West Highland Station at nearly forty miles an hour. Here they were forcibly reminded that the more haste was often the less speed, for, rounding a curve, Duncan had to jam his brakes on hard to avoid running into a small two-seater with a single occupant, which was coming rapidly to meet them. Both cars swerved and avoided a collision by a matter of inches. But the check was momentary, and in a few seconds they had regained their speed. Marion held her breath. They were getting near their goal.

For a short distance out of Crianlarich the ground rises, then suddenly, on reaching the summit, a far-reaching expanse of country bursts on the view, an expanse of rolling moorland bounded on either side by hills, with, in the distance, the steep cut in the mountains in which Loch Lomond lies hidden. But though, as the car hummed over the crest, the darkness hid this view, it revealed something else, something which thrilled Marion and her uncle with horror, and caused the pulses of even the three policemen to beat more quickly. In the distance, just where Colonel Grahame's lodge ought to lie, there shone a bright, flickering light.

The sergeant swore.

'Yon's the house, right enough!' he cried. 'They have it weel afire!'

On a straighter road their speed still further increased, and within three minutes they pulled up with a jerk at the gate of the drive. Leaping out, they raced for the front door.

The house was long and low, a mere bungalow, with the major diameter at right angles to the road. The fire had evidently started at the back, for there the flames were roaring fiercely, while great tongues came darting out of the windows and lapping round the eaves above. But except for little wisps of smoke which hung round the sashes and roof, the front portion had so far escaped. The scene was already brightly lighted up, and it was evident that the whole house was doomed.

The men threw themselves on the front door, but it was stoutly made and resisted all efforts to break it open. Wasting no further time on it, the sergeant turned to an adjoining window, smashed the glass with his elbow, put his hand in, opened the snib and threw up the sash.

A dense volume of smoke poured out, and the man recoiled. Then seemingly taking a deep breath, he climbed on the sill and vanished through the opening.

For some seconds the others stood motionless in a silence broken only by the hungry crackling of the flames, then one of the constables rushed to the window, shouting, 'He'll be smothered sure.'

'Wait!' Duncan yelled, flourishing a large handkerchief. 'Tie this over your mouth. Wait 'til I wet it at the car.'

He dashed off, and the constable paused irresolute.

'Yes, wait,' called Marion in an agony of suspense.

'Ay, bide 'til Jock's smothered,' cried the constable, and turning again to the window, was half-way through, when a combined shout from the others once more checked him.

The front door was slowly turning on its hinges. A great cloud of smoke poured out, and through it the sergeant reeled forward like a drunken man. Gasping brokenly, he stabbed with his finger in the direction of the hall, as he collapsed in a heap on the grass.

Marion ran to attend to him, and at the same moment the two policemen with Duncan at their heels dashed through the door into the smoke-filled hall.

Some moments of anguish passed, and then they appeared, coughing and gasping, but staggering under a load. In a moment the inanimate form of Stewart Crawley was lying beside that of the sergeant.

His hat was gone, and there was blood on his hair, as if from a scalp wound. He was dead, or at least, so Marion thought, as she tore open his collar and put her hand over his heart. Then hope once more dawned, as a faint fluttering showed that life was still present.

'He's alive!' she cried tremulously. 'Thank God for that anyway!'

The sergeant sat up and began to cough.

'Ay,' he gasped between the paroxysms, 'but it's an ower near shave for a' that. If it hadna been for you, mistress, he'd ha' been a deid man by noo.'

'It's thanks to you, sergeant, and to all of you.' Marion returned with a sob of relief. 'Oh, how can we ever thank you enough?'

'Ay, but you're no out o' the wood yet.' The sergeant was rapidly recovering. 'You'll want to get him to bed and get the doctor. Where'll you take him?'

This turned out to be a question of some difficulty. There was no doctor, it seemed, nearer than Tyndrum, and no hospital nearer than Glasgow. The sergeant advised Glasgow.

'But that's a frightful distance, surely?' Marion queried in dismay. 'How far is it?'

'Twa hours,' the sergeant answered, 'but what better can ye do?'

'Home,' said Marion with decision. 'We'll take him home. We can do it in an hour, and can call for Dr McLeod on the way. What do you say, Uncle?'

Mr Hope concurring, the still form was lifted into the tonneau, and propped up with rugs and cushions to minimise the vibration. Mr Hope turned to the sergeant.

'You'll hear from me again, of course,' he said warmly, 'but meanwhile can we give you a lift back to Crianlarich?'

'Ay, ye can, and thank ye. I'm wishful to phone through to headquarters.' He turned to his men. 'You bide where you are. I'll be back the noo.'

He climbed into the car with the others, and the big vehicle moved off towards Crianlarich. Then he turned to Mr Hope.

'I'll tak' your address,' he said, producing a well-thumbed notebook and a stumpy pencil, 'and the lady's, and that letter she spoke about, if she has it here. And look here, sir, and mistress, and you, driver,' he became impressive, 'dinna any o' you let on about this business—not even to the doctor. Ye can say that ye had an accident, that your car ran into this man, and that you're no wishful to say muckle about it, because it's in the hands o' the police. I'll phone through to the Callander men, and that'll keep you richt. For see,' the sergeant became the embodiment of wisdom and cunning, 'you dinna want them that schemed this thing oot to ken it's no succeeded, else they'd be more watchful to no gie themselves awa'.'

The common sense of this appealed to Mr Hope, and he, Marion and Duncan severally assured the sergeant they would keep the whole thing an absolute secret. At Crianlarich the sergeant got out, and vanished after promising at Marion's request to ring up Mr Hope's and have a bed prepared for the invalid.

Then began the thirty-mile journey to Callander. Terrible as had been the strain to Marion of the outward journey, it was as nothing compared to the return. Then she had been in doubt as to whether or not anything was wrong; now she was in doubt as to whether Crawley would live until they reached home. She was fully aware that the delay in getting him to bed and of providing medical attention might easily turn the balance against him, and she was filled with misgivings that they had done the wrong thing in attempting the journey. Would it not have been better to have taken him to the hotel at Crianlarich, got him to bed there, and sent the car to Tyndrum for the doctor? She did not know, and her lips moved continually in prayer for his safety. It had been decided that a smooth journey was even more vital than a quick one, but in spite of Duncan's most careful driving there were jolts, and every jolt drove the girl's heart into her throat.

Slowly the interminable minutes dragged by, and the never-ending miles dropped one by one behind. Now they had passed Ardchyle and turned south out of the Dochart Valley. A group of lights indicated Lochearnhead, and presently they caught the ghostly reflections from the waters of Loch Lubnaig. At last they were once more clear of the Pass of Leny, and dropping down the long hill into Callander.

Dr McLeod's house was at the entrance to the town, and there they stopped with an urgent request for his immediate help. The doctor fortunately was at home, and in a few seconds he had procured his case of instruments, and joined the others in the car. Ten minutes later, Stewart Crawley lay, white and motionless, on the bed in the pleasant, comfortably furnished room which had been prepared for him.

At first it seemed that only his body lay there, and Dr McLeod shook his head as he looked at the death-like features. But he set to work to do all that medical skill could suggest, assisted by a nurse for whom he had sent the car. Marion and her uncle waited downstairs, the girl's face almost as white and drawn as that of her lover.

At long last the doctor was able to make his report. Crawley had had a serious blow on the head with a blunt weapon of some kind. There was undoubted concussion, but the skull was not actually fractured. The long drive had been unfortunate, but given a strong constitution there did not at present seem to be any reason why the patient should not pull through.

The doctor was politely curious as to how the injury had been caused, but tactfully accepted Mr Hope's statement that an accident had taken place. He was sympathetic towards the old gentleman's position, readily agreeing to report the result of his examination to the police, and to assist all concerned in keeping the matter quiet.

All that night Crawley lay motionless, hovering between life and death.

CHAPTER XIV

INSPECTOR ROSS TAKES CHARGE

WHEN Sergeant Blair stepped out of the Hopes' car at Crianlarich he was still feeling a good deal shaken from his adventure in the burning house, but he realised that his big chance had come, and that if he were to profit by it he must not give way to physical weakness. He therefore hurried to the hotel and drank a single whisky to steady his nerves, before calling up the Chief Constable of his county.

After a short consultation that official decided that expert assistance must be obtained from the detective headquarters in Edinburgh, and half an hour later he rang up the sergeant to say that he had arranged that Detective Inspector Ross would be sent to take over the case. By a stroke of good fortune, it happened that a train conveying through sleeping cars from King's Cross to Fort William ran on Saturday mornings, and Ross would take advantage of this train, leaving Edinburgh at 4.45 a.m., and reaching Crianlarich at 7.48.

While waiting for a reply from the Chief Constable, Blair had carefully read the letter from Sandy Buchan to Crawley. That it was a forgery seemed obvious to him, for he knew that Colonel Grahame had left the country, and he did not believe that any caretaker had been left in charge of the house. The fire being the one and only topic of conversation, he had an obvious opening for discreet inquiries, and he speedily satisfied himself that not only had the bungalow been empty for the past fortnight, but that there had never been anyone in it with a name remotely resembling Buchan.

He went back to the house on receiving the Chief Constable's message. In the amazing way in which crowds materialise from nowhere, there was now a mob of black figures moving round the burning building. Since he had left the fire had made rapid headway. The whole house was now a glowing mass, and as he came up the last portion of the roof collapsed into the inferno below with a vast outburst of flame and sparks. Towards the rear, where the conflagration at first was fiercest, it was now dying down, the walls with their empty windows standing black and gaunt against the smouldering debris within.

There was nothing to be done, and Blair stood discussing the affair with those whom the spectacle had attracted to the spot. He explained casually that he and his men had happened to be in the locality and had seen the glare. Hurrying up, they had found that the flames had taken too great a hold to save the house, and they had broken in with the object of trying to get out some of the furniture. The smoke, however, had been too dense to allow of this. He agreed warmly with the sentiment expressed by all, that it was fortunate that no one had been in the building, and was as mystified as the rest as to how, under the circumstance, the fire could have originated. Sergeant Blair, in fact, was something of an artist, and none of those with whom he spoke that night had the slightest suspicion that the man's brain was seething with the consciousness of the tragedy which had been enacted in their midst.

Slowly the night dragged on. By two o'clock the flames had died down and the spectators had disappeared. Blair had borrowed a bicycle, and believing that his presence was no longer required on the scene, he left his two men to keep watch 'til morning, and rode back to Tyndrum. He wanted to be at his best to meet Inspector Ross, and he felt that a few hours sleep would be his most effective preparation.

At 7.48 a.m. he was back in Crianlarich at the West Highland Station. Inspector Ross proved to be a tall, stoutly built man, blue-eyed, fair haired, and of the traditionally Norse type. Blair had never met him before, but he knew his reputation as one of the most trusted officers of the Scottish service, and he hugged himself on his luck in thus coming into personal touch with so influential a member of his profession.

'I don't want to be seen talking to you, Sergeant,' was the detective's somewhat uncompromising greeting. 'I don't want anyone to suspect my business. I'll go to the hotel for breakfast, and give out that I'm from the Insurance Company. We'll meet at the place in an hour.'

Blair, grasping the situation, made no reply, but continued walking down the train looking into the carriage windows as if expecting a traveller. Then, apparently satisfied his friend had not arrived, he slowly left the station and returned to the house. An hour later he was joined by Ross.

'Now give me an idea of this business.'

Sergeant Blair had foreseen the demand, and he had spent some time in rehearsing to story. He was therefore able to put the facts succinctly before the other. Ross nodded approvingly, glanced rapidly over the decoy letter, put it away in his pocket-book, and went on:

'The first thing is a search round the house. I suppose you have made one already?'

'Ay, sir, but I didna find anything.'

'We'll look again.'

But the new inspection, meticulously thorough though it was, revealed nothing helpful, and Blair, who had been on tenterhooks during the process, breathed freely again.

'Seems to have been a pretty near thing for this Crawley?' Ross muttered.

'If it hadna been for the lassie, sir, he would be a corp noo. Anither five minutes an' we couldna ha' got him oot.'

'It was a clever scoundrel that fixed the thing up. You were right, Sergeant, to keep the thing quiet and to warn the Hopes to do the same. I'll remember it in your favour. Are those men of yours reliable?'

The sergeant glowed with delight as he murmured his thanks and expressed his confidence in the constables' discretion.

'Very well. Come down now to the road and we'll have a look for traces of Crawley's car.'

'Ay, there's wheel marks down by the gate.'

A few yards on the Crianlarich side of the entrance to the drive impressions in the soft ground at the side of the road showed that a small car had been driven in near the fence from a southerly direction and out again in a northerly. There was not much to learn from the traces, but such as there was Ross noted. The gauge of the wheels, the length of the wheelbase, and the width and make of the tyres were all discernable at the point where the vehicle had stood, and all pointed to a small car of the runabout or two-seater type. The non-skid ribbing on the tyres was also clearly marked, and Ross discovered signs of wear on some of the ribs which, he hoped, would enable him to identify the machine should he be lucky enough to find it. Having made dimensional sketches of the defective ribs, he turned to Blair.

'Who can have taken the thing?' he muttered. 'Did Crawley bring a driver with him, and if so, where has he gone?'

He paused in thought. Then quickly the solution occurred to him, and he burst out:

'But of course it would be taken! That would be part of the scheme. The man or men we want went off in that car. We can see that they had to. They daren't leave it here. No one was supposed to know that Crawley had come, and it would give the show away at once. Incidentally it gave a fine means of escape.'

Inspector Ross stood whistling a little tune as he considered how he should carry on the inquiry. The main facts of the attempted murder seemed clear enough. Someone, desiring Crawley's death, had forged a letter luring him under cover of darkness to this lonely house where he could be done away with by an unexpected blow. This person—or persons—had then set fire to the house, unquestionably with the object of getting rid of the body and destroying all incriminating evidence.

It had been part of the plan to make Crawley come by himself in his car, and this, Ross could see, had obvious advantages. For one thing, it enabled Crawley to start off without letting his destination be known. Again, his actual journey would be more secret and, in the event of suspicion being aroused, much harder to trace. There was also the point he had already thought of, the excellent way of escape the car offered to the murderer.

Ross went a step further. Supposing he were right so far and that the assassin had indeed taken the car, what would he do with it? Though he could use it during the night, he could hardly risk being seen in it. As soon as Crawley's disappearance became known, a description of the vehicle he had left in would be circulated, and all the police in the country would be on the look out for it. No, Ross thought, the car would have to be got rid of before daylight, and if so, there lay his first clue.

Lighting his pipe, he puffed slowly as he followed out his argument. There was still more in this matter of the car. Would its desertion at some carefully selected spot not also be part of the scheme? Would the finding of the vehicle at some point far removed from Crianlarich not indicate to the unsuspecting that Crawley had himself gone there? It would certainly tend to draw attention away from Crianlarich, and to prevent a connection being suspected between Crawley's disappearance and the fire.

Inspector Ross felt that these ideas worked into a connected scheme sufficiently well to justify him in following them up. He turned to his companion.

'Look here, Sergeant,' he said, 'I want you to make discreet inquiries about the neighbourhood. Find out if a small car was seen last night, and, if so, where it was going. Make inquiries about strangers, or any other inquiries you think might help. But all quietly, you understand. Don't give away what you're after.'

The sergeant, delighted at the chance of showing his metal, hurried off towards Crianlarich, Ross following more slowly.

From the hotel he telephoned to Edinburgh, asking that the police be advised to look out for a car of the kind in question, particularly if such had been deserted during the night. Then, finding he had just time to catch a train for Callander, he went to the station and got on board.

He lunched on arrival, then calling at the police station, learned that Dr McLeod had been called in by the Hopes. An hour later he was seated in the doctor's consulting room, explaining his business to that somewhat dour though efficient-looking practitioner.

'The man is still alive,' he was told, 'at least, he was an hour ago when I saw him. He has had a bad blow on the back of the head. The skull is not fractured, but there is undoubtedly concussion—serious, I'm afraid. But there is certainly hope.'

'He is unconscious?'

'Oh, yes.'

'I suppose, Doctor, such injuries could not be self-inflicted?'

'Quite impossible.' Dr McLeod shook his head decidedly.

'Nor could they result from an accident? I mean, could Crawley have broken into the house, set fire to it accidentally, and in his excitement have tripped over something and struck his head as he fell?'

'Out of the question, I should say. The injury is to the top of the head. The skin is but slightly broken, though the blow was undoubtedly severe. The man has been struck, if you ask my opinion, by someone behind him, with a blunt weapon— possibly a sandbag.'

'I may take it then it is attempted murder?'

'In my opinion, there is not the slightest doubt of it.'

Inspector Ross rose.

'Thank you, Doctor. You won't mind my impressing on you the need for secrecy? We want the murderer to think his scheme has succeeded. The injured man must absolutely disappear. You follow me?'

'Quite,' the doctor answered as they shook hands.

'Now for that girl that carried out the rescue,' thought Ross as he walked in the direction of Mr Hope's villa. Marion was lying down, but she got up eagerly when she heard who had called. She was pale, and dark rings below her eyes indicated a night of stress.

'I trust you have good news about your patient, Miss Hope?' Ross began when he had introduced himself. 'I have just seen Dr McLeod and he was encouraging.'

A rush of tears came to the girl's eyes, but she smiled wanly.

'Oh, *was* he?' she cried. 'I couldn't get him to express an opinion. He tells me the skull is not fractured but he fears concussion.'

'But concussion is not necessarily fatal,' Ross went on reassuringly. 'As Mr Crawley has lived so long, I should say he's pretty certain to pull through. Cases of this kind are very much a matter of nursing, and he's all right in that respect. And now, Miss Hope, I want your help. As you must know, a deliberate attempt has been made to murder Mr Crawley. I have been instructed to find the criminals. As a beginning, I want to know all that you can tell me about Mr Crawley. Please take your time and let me have everything in detail.'

'I will do my best, Mr Inspector. As you may imagine, I am as anxious as you that such fiends should be brought to justice. I suppose you know,' a faint colour mounted her pale cheeks, 'that Mr Crawley and I are engaged to be married?'

'I didn't know,' Ross returned. 'In fact, I know nothing about the affair at all. So please begin at the beginning.'

She did her best, and by dint of discreet questionings he gradually learned the whole story. Then, with further polite references to Crawley, he rose to take his leave.

As he strolled about, waiting for his return train to Crianlarich, Ross pondered over the history he had listened to, and tried to get its salient features clear in his mind. On the face of things, it seemed not unlikely that these two tragedies were connected, that this attempt on Crawley's life had its roots in that murder of Smith in far off Middeldorp. He thought it would be worth while obtaining from the South African police fuller details of that first crime than Miss Hope had been able to give him. He would have to cable them in any case to learn if Buchan had left the country, and he might ask for a copy of the evidence to be sent.

But whether or not the tragedies were actually connected, it was at least certain that the writer of the decoy letter was fully aware of what had taken place in South Africa. The amount of knowledge that this person possessed impressed Ross. He took a fresh page of his notebook and jotted down the points as they occurred to him.

In the first place, it was clear that the writer knew Buchan intimately, and possessed specimens of his handwriting. Equally intimately he knew Crawley, the details of his life in Middeldorp, and the whole story of the Smith murder. He was aware also of Crawley's history since he had returned to England, that he had taken the Hill Farm, that he had a small car, and even that he drove it himself. Finally, he knew of Colonel Grahame and of the house on the Crianlarich Road.

Surely, thought Ross, there couldn't be many persons possessed of all this knowledge, and, if so, it materially narrowed the field of his inquiry. All the same there was no one in Miss Hope's story who completely filled the bill. Buchan might, and if Buchan had left South Africa it would undoubtedly be necessary to find him and trace his movements on the night of the murder. His very next business must be to cable to the South African police to settle this point.

He took the decoy letter from his pocket and examined it thoughtfully. The postmark showed that it had been posted in Glasgow on the previous Wednesday morning, but though he re-read it with care, he could not find any further clue.

If for the moment he assumed Buchan innocent, was there anyone else upon whom suspicion might reasonably fall?

His thoughts at once turned to Swayne. Swayne knew

Crawley intimately, as also Middeldorp and the life that had gone on there. He had known Smith, and must be familiar with the details of the murder trial. Even if he had left South Africa when the latter took place, it was inconceivable that, being so closely connected with the actors in the sordid drama, he would not at least have had local papers sent him. He had also known Buchan; these men had all seemed to be in pretty much the same set.

The farm Crawley had taken lay near Swayne's domain, and it was therefore not unlikely that the latter had learned the identity of his new neighbour, as well as the facts that he had a car and could drive it himself. There was, of course, no proof of this, but a few inquiries would settle the matter. Still less was there reason to believe that Swayne had known Colonel Grahame and his lonely bungalow, but here again discreet questions would produce the information. Swayne, Ross felt, was undoubtedly a person to be kept in view.

If Buchan and Swayne were both innocent, Ross felt that so far he was up against it. There was no one else whom he had reason to suspect.

Still pondering over the problem, he took the train to Crianlarich and returned to the hotel, intending to call up headquarters and get his cable about Buchan and the Crawley case despatched. There a note was handed to him, which proved to be from Sergeant Blair. It read:

'SIR,—In accordance with your instructions, I made inquiries in the neighbourhood. I am informed that a stranger left the Edinburgh train which reached Crianlarich at 7.58 last night. His description is tall, stout, with round cheeks, a dark moustache, and glasses, and dressed in a khaki waterproof and soft hat. He left the station immediately, and I have not yet been able to trace him farther.

'I should have told you that last night as we were going out to the house in Mr Hope's car, just beyond the West

Highland Station we were nearly run into by a small two-seater coming down the hill. There was only the driver in it, and I was thinking that maybe it was the car you wanted. I made inquiries at Tyndrum, and a car of same description was seen at about 10.00 p.m. heading towards Bridge of Orchy. It was specially noticed because that is a deserted road at night at this time of year.

'Yours obediently,
'JOHN BLAIR.'

'Bully for you, Sergeant,' Ross muttered as he went to the telephone and put through his call. Headquarters, it appeared, were also anxious to speak to him, and he listened with growing satisfaction as he heard the subject.

'We think we've found your car,' the distant voice explained. 'Last night about midnight a car was heard approaching the hotel at South Ballachulish, then a cry and a splash. Search was made, and it was found that a small two-seater had run off the ferry wharf into the sea. The driver appears to have been drowned. You had better go and find out if it's the one you're looking for.'

Inspector Ross swore a fierce oath. If headquarters were correct and the would-be murderer of Stewart Crawley were dead, his case had collapsed; a case, as he had fully realised, that had bade fair to be a *cause célèbre*, perhaps the most famous that had taken place for many a long year. He felt himself badly used, cheated of his just due, duped.

Had the message not stated that the driver had been drowned, he would have felt no doubt that the lost car was that in which he was interested. Tyndrum and Bridge of Orchy were on the direct road from Crianlarich to Ballachulish. The time of the accident also worked in. The run should have taken a couple of hours, and apparently just this time had elapsed between the criminal's departure from the burning house and the disaster at the ferry.

But the death of the driver was not in the picture, as Ross saw it. If this had actually taken place, there was here a very remarkable coincidence, a dramatic stroke of poetic justice such as seldom obtained in real life. Of course it was by no means impossible. A man who had been through the experiences which that traveller had undergone, might be excused if he made an error of judgment in his driving.

But there was no doubt as to Ross's own procedure. He must go at once to Ballachulish, make sure if the wrecked car was that which had stood outside Colonel Grahame's shooting-lodge, and try to find the body of its occupant.

He looked at his watch. It was just half-past eight, too late to do anything that night. He therefore ordered a car for the next morning, and, turning in early, did his best to make up for his loss of sleep on the previous night.

CHAPTER XV

THE BALLACHULISH FERRY

INSPECTOR Ross was a Sabbatarian to the extent of never doing any work on Sunday which he could possibly postpone to later in the week, but when he looked out next morning across the Crianlarich valley at the range of sunlit mountains showing up clear-cut as a cameo against a sky of lightest blue, for once he did not regret the chance which had decreed for him a motor journey through such a country on the day of rest.

He had once before visited Ballachulish, and had been greatly struck by the beauty of its surroundings. That had been by steamer from Fort William. Now, apart from the interest of his quest, he looked forward to seeing it again, and especially to approaching it through the historic Pass of Glencoe, of which he had often read, but which he had never had the opportunity to visit.

The car was waiting for him when he had finished breakfast, and soon he was being whirled westward through the broad valley in which Crianlarich is situated. At Tyndrum the road turned north, leading up speedily to the bare moorland. Ross took out the large-scale touring map he invariably carried, and followed the route as they ran through Bridge of Orchy, and began the long, slow climb up the sides of the Black Mount. Reaching the summit, he gazed with interest out over the vast panorama of Rannoch Moor, wild, melancholy, forbidding; the bare undulations broken by lochs which, even on that sunny morning, were dull with the dead colour of lead. At the Kingshouse Hotel the road turned west, until, crossing the last divide, they began zigzagging down into the dark and gloomy Pass of Glencoe. As they dropped deeper into the narrow defile, the stony wastes gave place to grass, trees appeared, and soon they passed the Obelisk, memorial of the massacre, and got their first glimpse of Loch Leven. Five minutes later they reached the shore of the estuary, and pulled up at the Ballachulish Hotel.

Ross remembered the place. Loch Leven, a long, narrow estuary, bit deeply into the country in an easterly direction. Near the mouth was Ballachulish, and there the shores drew together, forming a strait no wider than moderately-sized river. Along the southern edge was the road by which they had come, leading eastwards back to Glencoe, Kingshouse and Tyndrum, and westwards along the shore of Loch Linnhe to Oban. On the northern shore immediately opposite was North Ballachulish, and there a road started which led northwards to Fort William. There was no bridge at the place, and these roads were connected solely by a ferry, a motor pontoon which could carry a large-sized automobile. For embarkation purposes, there were two wharves down to which connecting roads led from the main roads on the north and south shores respectively. It was evidently from the southern wharf, that beside which the Inspector was standing, that the car had fallen.

The hotel was only a few yards from the wharf. Ross went in and leisurely ordered lunch and a room for the night. A passing reference to the accident produced the information that the car had been dragged ashore and was then in the hotel yard. With a natural curiosity, Ross went round to have a look at it.

It was a small two-seater of a popular though expensive make, and as Ross glanced at the tyres he was able to identify certain irregularities in the treads. There was no doubt it was the car of which he was in search.

The yard happening to be deserted, he took the opportunity to give the vehicle a rapid examination. But beyond the fact that it seemed none the worse for its adventures, he could learn nothing of interest.

He re-entered the hotel, lunched, and after smoking a pipe in the lounge, sauntered out 'to take a turn before tea.' But his aimless strolling brought him in due course to the local police station, and after a rapid glance round, he disappeared within. There he saw the sergeant in charge, introduced himself, and asked for details of the accident.

The sergeant stated he had been on the scene within half an hour of its occurrence, a boy from the hotel having ridden down to bring the news. It appeared that a valuable cow belonging to the hotel was sick, and the herd, this boy's father, had gone late to the hotel out-buildings to see it. He was delayed longer than he had expected, and it was midnight before he was free. He had just stepped out of the cowshed into the hotel yard when he heard the sound of an approaching car. He had paid no special attention to it, but the thought had crossed his mind that if the traveller were coming to the hotel he would have some trouble in waking up the staff. The car had suddenly seemed to slow down as if for a corner, and then had got up speed again. Almost immediately after there had come a terrible cry, followed by a splash, and then silence. The herd had rushed down with his lantern to the shore, and there he had seen the windscreen of a motor-car sticking up above the surface, some twelve feet away from the ferry wharf. No one was in sight, and though he had shouted, there had been no response. His cottage was close by, and he had roused his son and sent him for the police. The tide, though nearly at low water, was still running strongly out to sea through the narrow channel.

The sergeant, on realising what had taken place, had taken a boat and rowed down in the direction of the current, though owing to its speed he had not thought there was much hope of finding anything. He had cruised about for a couple of hours, and at last had come on a hat. It had been sold by a well-known Edinburgh firm, and bore the initials in gold letters, S. C.

Returning on the flood tide to the wharf, the sergeant had had a rope put round the rear axle of the car, and with the help of a number of sightseers whom the news of the accident had attracted to the spot, had pulled the vehicle past the wharf and ashore up the shelving beach. The licence showed that it belonged to a Mr Stewart Crawley, of Hill Farm, Elswick, near Newcastle. The clutch was found to be in, and the controls set for what on the level should be a reasonably rapid speed, say, twenty miles an hour. Nothing had been found to throw light on the disaster, the steering-gear being in perfect order, but in the pocket was a largescale motoring map of the district, with the name, Stewart Crawley, written in ink on the flyleaf.

'An' that map, sir, is what in my humble opeenion caused the accident,' the sergeant concluded, as he took from a cupboard a water-stained and still damp road book. 'See here.'

He turned over the sodden pages, until the district of Ballachulish was revealed. 'See,' he repeated, 'see the way that ferry's shown.'

The map was published by a celebrated firm of motor accessory suppliers, and showed good roads on through routes coloured red. At Ballachulish this red line was drawn without a break. The suggestion was certainly that of a bridge, and there was no correcting indication of a ferry.

'See that, sir,' the sergeant continued. 'That map would ha' misled anyone. It shows a bridge as clear as anything, and I'm thinking the driver took the road doon to the ferry wharf for the end o' a bridge, and when he saw his mistake he couldna stop.'

Inspector Ross agreed outwardly with all that the sergeant had said, but he was in a thoughtful frame of mind as he walked back to the hotel and sat smoking in the lounge. Had it not been for the special information which he possessed, he would unhesitatingly have agreed that an unfortunate accident had taken place, possibly due to the driver's having depended too much on the small details of his map. But knowing what he knew, could he accept that theory? The car he had *expected* to find deserted. It was true he had not expected to find a suggestion of the driver's death. But was not that merely because the mysterious actor in the drama had devised an even better scheme than he, Ross, had thought of? To have arranged matters so that it would seem that Crawley had been killed accidentally was surely not far short of a stroke of genius.

The more Ross thought over the whole affair, the more probable it seemed that this was indeed the explanation. The episode of the hat confirmed it. It was too much to assume that S. C. should also be the initials of the murderer, and this granted, it followed that Crawley's hat had been brought from the burning house with the express purpose of aiding the deception. The ownership of the hat could easily be settled. Crawley's servants should be able to identify it were it their master's, and Ross decided the application of this test must be an early part of his investigation.

But the point that rather bothered him was how the actual accident could have been arranged. Had the driver gone into the sea with the car? If so, had he escaped, or was his body now floating out in the waters of Loch Linnhe? Or had he been able to jump out before the car went in?

Inspector Ross pulled hard at his pipe as he turned over the details in his mind. He remembered that the herd had stated the car slackened speed, then increased it just before the splash. Had the driver leaped out during that slack?

Gradually a possible solution seemed to shape itself in his imagination. Suppose when approaching the place the driver had slackened speed, climbed out on the footboard, set the car straight for the wharf, put on full power, and jumped off. The car, even without a steadying hand on the wheel, would run straight enough in the short distance to drop off the wharf at the place intended. As it went over the man would have uttered his cry and then fled before anyone could arrive. Yes, it seemed possible. It was at least likely enough to form a provisional starting-point for investigation.

But suppose he had thus escaped. In what direction would he have headed?

Ross again took out his large-scale map and considered the

possibilities. Escape could be made from Ballachulish in five ways: by road, railway, steamboat, row-boat, or across country.

It did not take Ross long to eliminate two of these methods. The quarry must have recognised the possibilities of suspicion being aroused, and he would never risk an open departure by rail or steamer. In the tourist season it would be a different matter, but now when strangers were few and far between, to attempt it would be courting disaster. Such was Ross's opinion, at the same time he took a mental note to have the matter inquired into.

An escape by row-boat seemed almost equally unlikely. The boat could not be returned, and its removal would rouse the very suspicion it was desired to avoid. But here again a few inquiries by the sergeant would set the point at rest.

A recourse to the open country was no more promising. Ballachulish lay in the centre of a wild, mountainous district, trackless to all but natives. Immediately behind the hotel was a range of more than 3000 feet in height, which rose precipitously from the shores both of Loch Leven and Loch Linnhe. In the dark of a winter's night the place would be impossible.

At first sight an escape by road had seemed the obvious thing, and now Ross felt more than ever certain that this method had been adopted. Besides being the safest plan, it was the only one which could have been entered upon immediately on getting rid of the car and before an alarm could be raised. Assuming, therefore, that he was right so far, the next question became: by which road had the fugitive gone?

There were three: that by which Ross himself had come, leading to Kingshouse and Tyndrum; its continuation in the opposite direction to Oban; and that from the other side of the loch to Fort William.

The advantage of taking the train from a town was obvious, and at Fort William a stranger might pass through the station without attracting attention, but the difficulty was the ferry. There was no way in which the quarry could have crossed without taking a boat, and without being observed by those whom the supposed accident had aroused. He would therefore have had to walk up to the head of the loch and cross the Levin at Kinlochmore. This would have meant seven miles along a rough footpath to Kinlochmore, where the road was not yet made, and twenty-one more miles of road to Fort William; total, thirty miles.

Inspector Ross said, 'H'm,' dubiously, and turned his attention to the Kingshouse direction. This, he soon saw, was, if anything, even less likely. Here there was a good road all the way, but the objective was bad. The first collection of more than half a dozen houses was Tyndrum, and Tyndrum and Crianlarich were too near the scene of operations to be exactly healthy. Besides, from Ballachulish to Tyndrum was thirty-one and a half miles. Ross said, 'H'm' again, and looked at the Oban road.

This, he saw at once, was more promising. Oban was the largest town in the district, and a stranger would be much less likely to be noticed there than even at Fort William. The fugitive would try, he felt sure, to head to Oban.

And there was nothing to prevent him that Ross could see. There was a good road all the way, running through sparsely populated country; indeed, but for Connel Ferry, there was no village of any size all the way. The distance was considerable, of course, about thirty miles, like the other two routes, but thirty miles was well within the power of a resolute man spurred on by the fear of the scaffold, supplied, doubtless, with a flask and sandwiches, and walking in the sharp, invigorating air of a frosty night.

The more he thought over the matter, the more Inspector Ross felt assured that the fugitive had walked to Oban. He therefore decided that in the morning he would himself follow in that direction. At the same time he would telephone the police on the other two roads to make inquiries, and arrange for the Ballachulish men to investigate the possibilities of the local stations and piers, as well as the disappearance of a rowing boat.

Accordingly, after dinner, he slipped out and went down once more to the police station. There, after warning the sergeant of the extreme secrecy of his business, he took him into his confidence and gave him his instructions.

'But remember, Sergeant,' he concluded, 'it is absolutely necessary that the public think an accident has happened. You will report so to headquarters (I will keep you clear afterwards), and without advertising it, let it be known locally that that is your opinion. Indeed I think you had better get some drags and drag the loch about the wharf for the body. As a matter of fact, you may find it. All that I have told you is only guesswork on my part.' He paused, then went on, 'There is another thing. Who does the local news for the papers?' The sergeant told him. 'Then see him, and make sure a proper report of the affair is sent in. Let him understand that you are satisfied it was an accident, and explain that business of the map and that you are dragging for the body. See? Got the idea?'

He returned to the hotel, and ringing up the police first at Fort William and then at Tyndrum, gave them their instructions. Then engaging a car for the next morning, he turned in.

He was early astir on the following day, and by eight o'clock was out on the Oban road. The sun, hidden by the mountain behind the hotel, was lighting up with a thin, yellow radiance the northern and western shores of the lochs. It was a fine autumn day, but the air was sharp and biting, and Ross felt his moustache grow stiffer as the vapour from his breath froze upon it. But the motion was exhilarating and the scenery charming. Had the Inspector not had the weight of his investigation on his mind, he would have looked upon the trip as a delightful holiday.

At Kentallon, the first station on the single line of railway which ran parallel to the road, he explained to the stationmaster that he was Inspector Ross of the Detective Service, and that he was after an absconding bank manager who had been traced to Fort William and there lost sight of. A row-boat, it seemed, had disappeared from the town two nights previously, and it was thought that the fugitive might have landed near Kentallon and taken the train to Oban. Could the stationmaster tell him if a stranger had left by the early train on the previous Saturday morning, or indeed by any train on that day? There were, of course, no trains on Sunday?

The stationmaster, visibly thrilled, was all eagerness to help, and his reply was given with an assurance which left no doubt of its truth in the Inspector's mind. There were no trains on Sunday, moreover he was positive that no one had boarded any of those on Saturday who was not personally known to himself. To make the matter even more certain, he looked up the total number of tickets which had been sold on the previous day— they numbered seven—and after a little thought he was able to recall the seven persons who had used them.

Ross parted from him with polite thanks, and at each of the other little stations he came to told the same story and asked the same questions. So he worked on through Duror and Appin and round Loch Creran, until he crossed the toll-bridge over the entrance to Loch Etive and stopped at Connel Ferry.

Inquiries from the toll-keeper produced no result, but Ross was not disappointed, as he felt sure that, had the unknown crossed, he would have somehow managed it without being seen. He therefore pushed on to the station.

Here the Ballachulish line branches off from the Oban-Crianlarich-Edinburgh line, and Ross realised that his quarry might have taken a train from this station instead of walking the extra six miles to Oban. It was, of course, a smaller place, and therefore more dangerous, but, on the other hand, a man who had walked twenty-four miles might be disposed to take some extra risk to avoid another six.

Here also Ross saw the stationmaster and told his story, but this time without getting a satisfactory reply. The official had seen no tired-looking man board the 8.40 a.m. from Oban, nor any such descend from the Ballachulish connection. But there was an earlier up-train than that with which the first from Ballachulish connected. The 5.30 a.m. from Oban passed his station at 5.46, though the stationmaster had not been on duty at that hour. If the Inspector wished to inquire about that train he must take the head porter into his confidence, as he had then been in charge.

The head porter heard Ross's story with an unmoved expression, and replied stolidly that he hadn't taken notice of anyone of the kind. To the further inquiry as to whether any other of the men were about who might have seen a stranger, the man shook his head gloomily, but as Ross was turning away he called him back.

'Bide a wee,' he invited. 'This man, he would be comin' frae the Ballachulish Road?'

The Inspector agreed.

'An' gangin', maybe, 'til Oban?'

'Quite likely.'

For a moment there seemed almost the suspicion of a wink in the head porter's wooden countenance, then he turned slowly and hailed a man in blue dungarees, who leisurely detached himself from a group of loungers and came forward.

'Here, Sandy,' the head porter adjured him, 'the boss here,' with a sidelong nod of the head towards Ross, 'will let you see the colour o' his siller for that tale o' yours aboot the man you lifted Saturday morn.'

Ross was alive to the hint. He took half a crown from his pocket.

'That's right,' he agreed. 'I'm connected with the police, but I'm willing to pay well enough for information for all that. That's yours for the yarn, and if it's any good to me there'll be that amount more to follow.'

Thus encouraged, the man in dungarees, prompted at intervals by the railwayman, told his story.

It appeared that shortly before seven on the morning in question, the man, who was a van driver employed in the principal shop in the little town, was loading up the Ford lorry of the establishment with some goods which he was about to take into Oban. The vehicle was standing in front of the shop, which was situated on the road which led to the toll-bridge on the way to North Connel and Ballachulish. Just as he was about to start his engine, he noticed a man approaching from the direction of the bridge. His face was white and drawn and he was limping painfully. He beckoned to the porter, and the latter waited 'til he came up. 'Are you going into Oban?' the stranger asked, and when the other admitted it, he offered him five shillings for a lift. He explained that he was on a walking tour and had just started from Ledaig, where he had slept the night with a friend, but that he had slipped on a piece of ice and fallen, hurting his foot. He climbed on the Ford and they ran into Oban. He asked to be put down at the intersection of George and Stafford Streets, opposite the North Pier. He paid the five shillings, thanked the driver for the lift, and limped off in the direction of the pier, and that was all the driver knew.

'What was the man like?' Ross asked.

'Gey an' big. Tall an' strongly built, wi' fat cheeks an' a moustache.'

'What colour?' Ross demanded eagerly.

'Dark.'

'And his dress?'

'A licht broon waterproof coat an' a grey felt hat an' broon shoes.'

Ross was extraordinarily pleased. There was no mistaking that description. The man who had driven to Oban in the early hours of Saturday was the man who had alighted at Crianlarich from the Edinburgh train on the previous evening. And there could be no doubt as to his movements in the interval. He had gone out to Colonel Grahame's house, sandbagged Crawley, dragged him within and set fire to the building, then taken his car and staged the accident at Ballachulish.

'He's made an oversight,' the Inspector thought delightedly; 'forgotten to soap his socks, and his twenty-four mile walk has started a blister. All the easier for me.'

He rejoiced the hearts of the two men with five shillings apiece, then re-entering his car, drove on towards Oban. What, he wondered, would his quarry have done on reaching the town? He would get there about 7.20 a.m. and his train—if he went by train—would not leave until 8.40. How would he spend that hour and twenty minutes?

It seemed to him that the circumstances indicated a hotel for a wash and breakfast, and a chemist's for a box of ointment.

He dismounted at the corner of George and Stafford Streets, and paid off his car. Then looking idly about, he took stock of his surroundings. The hotel, he thought, would probably be the first call, as at 7.20 hotels would be open, but not chemists. The man had walked towards the pier, but this, Ross imagined, might only have been a blind, and he prospected equally carefully in the other direction.

Down all the four streets he could see hotels, but as no one of them seemed to be more promising than its neighbours, he began systematically to work through them. He drew blank at the first six, but at the seventh he had a stroke of luck. A lame man had come in about 7.20 on the Saturday morning, apologising for calling so early, and saying he wanted some breakfast before catching the 8.40. He looked pale and tired, and it was evident his foot was giving him a good deal of pain. He had had a wash and breakfast, and had left about 8.00 a.m., saying he had to make another call before reaching the station.

A waiter and a maidservant had each seen the man at close quarters, and described him in terms similar to those of the Crianlarich sergeant and the Connel Ferry lorry driver, both saying they would recognise him if they met him again.

As Ross came out he noticed a chemist's at the opposite side of the street. Here the recital of his story brought an instant response. The man had called and had his foot bathed and bound up. There was a painful blister on the heel, caused, in the chemist's opinion, by taking too long a tramp when out of condition.

As Ross walked to the station he was well pleased with his progress. His case, he believed, could not be far from completion, for it was incredible that a man whose description he now had so completely, particularly who was lame, and who had little more than forty-eight hours' start, could long remain undiscovered.

At the station he made systematic inquiries, with equally satisfactory results. The quarry had been seen entering one of the Edinburgh through carriages on the 8.40 a.m. train. Ross immediately rang up headquarters, described his man, and asked for the Edinburgh force to be put on the job.

As he went back into the town for some lunch he bought a *Scotsman*. His Ballachulish friends had done their business well. There was a paragraph headed, 'Tragic Affair at Ballachulish,' which read:

'An unusual accident occurred at Ballachulish about midnight on Friday, whereby Mr Stewart Crawley, of Hill Farm, Elswick, near Newcastle, lost his life. It appears the deceased gentleman was motoring alone in his two-seater from Glasgow to Fort William by the Crianlarich-Glencoe route. At Ballachulish the road is intersected by the narrow opening into Loch Leven, the crossing being effected by a motor ferry. It is presumed that the unfortunate gentleman imagined there was a bridge, for he drove his car down the road to the ferry wharf, off which, before he could retrieve his mistake, it plunged into the estuary. A herd who was engaged in the hotel yard adjoining heard the car pass at a fair speed, then a cry, followed immediately by a splash. No trace of the body has been found, though Mr Crawley's hat was picked up nearly a mile out to sea, where it had been carried by the strong tide. The police are dragging the loch in the vicinity of the wharf.'

'Nothing could be better,' Ross muttered. 'That Sergeant has done well.'

He left Oban by the next train, and on reaching Edinburgh went straight to headquarters. There he found that a number of men had been put on the case, and intimation of the fugitive's arrest was momentarily expected. But so far nothing had been heard of him, and Ross went home feeling sure that before morning the man would be in his hands.

CHAPTER XVI

INTRODUCING SIR ANTHONY SWAYNE

WHEN Inspector Ross came on duty next morning he was surprised and disappointed to learn that no news of the tall, stout man with the black moustache had yet come in. It seemed impossible that anyone of such distinctive appearance should so long elude pursuit, and Ross began to suspect that the methods of his subordinates must leave something to be desired. He therefore took charge himself, and spent a busy two days organising the search. But his efforts were crowned with no greater success than those of his predecessors. No trace of the stranger was forthcoming.

On the morning of the third day he reached headquarters to find a message waiting for him from Callander. Stewart Crawley had been less seriously injured than had at first been supposed, and he was now sufficiently recovered to see the Inspector, should the latter desire to question him. Ross had been anxious all along to learn his story, and he lost no time in travelling down to Callander and presenting himself at Mr Hope's villa.

Marion saw him first, and inquired eagerly as to the result of his investigations. Ross was cheery and confident, but vague as to actual achievements. He would, however, be sure to let her know of any discovery at the earliest possible moment.

With repeated warnings not to tire the invalid, she took him upstairs. Crawley was in bed, his head swathed in bandages, and his face pale and wan, as if from a long illness. Marion introduced the visitor, then left them together.

'Now, Mr Crawley,' Ross began, 'you've had a nasty experience and I don't want to trouble you more than I can help, but just tell me what you can about this business. There's no hurry, so take your own time and don't tire yourself.'

Thus adjured, Crawley entered upon the story of his adventures, speaking in a weak voice and pausing frequently for breath. Touching briefly on his life in South Africa and his settling down in England, he told of the receipt of the decoy letter, his journey to the lonely house, and his alarming experience there. Ross, leaning back luxuriously in an easy chair, listened quietly, occasionally asking a question or taking a note, while his disappointment grew keen at the paucity of the news. When Crawley had finished, he directed the conversation to the murder of Smith in the Groote Park, pressing the sick man for all the details he could recall.

'Seems a bit of a coincidence that, what you tell me,' he remarked, when at last there seemed to be no more to be learned. 'If I understand you right, first this Swayne and then yourself were suspected, and both, one after the other, were proved innocent. And now here's an attempt on your life, and one of the two men *I've* suspected is this same Swayne. I can't very well suspect you, or no doubt I should.'

'Swayne?' Crawley remonstrated feebly. 'But that's impossible. Swayne was in London at the time,' and he went on to tell of his call at Langholm Hall and of the telegram he had received from the Charing Cross Post Office.

'You haven't got the telegram, I suppose?'

'Look in my coat pocket there.' Crawley pointed a trembling finger.

A search revealed the message, and Ross, after reading it carefully, put it away in his pocket-book.

'Who's the other you suspect?' Crawley asked faintly. Ross saw that he was tired, but he could not resist trying for further information.

'Buchan, of course,' he answered. 'If Buchan wrote you that letter, he's certainly guilty. Question is, did he?'

'Well,' Crawley declared, 'it's not my business in a way, but

I reckon if you're after Swayne and Buchan, you're as far off as Vandam. It's no good, Inspector. I know these two fellows, and they're just about as likely to be guilty as you are. They're both white men all through. If you don't want to waste your time you may give it up and start again.'

'Probably you're right, Mr Crawley. You know them and I don't. If so, it leaves me—I don't mind confessing it in strict confidence—it leaves me just a little uncertain about my next move. Now tell me, Mr Crawley, is there no one you suspect yourself.'

The sick man moved feebly.

'Not a soul, Inspector; not a single soul. I'm fairly mazed about the whole thing; can't make anything out of it.'

It was fortunate for Ross that he had learned all he could from his visit, for at this juncture it was brought to an abrupt end. Marion suddenly appeared, looked at Crawley, declared that he was exhausted, rated the Inspector for letting him talk too much, and insisted on the latter taking an immediate leave. To make sure he obeyed her she saw him to the door, and Ross, after a word of congratulation on her patient's recovery and a reminder of the urgent need of still keeping his existence a secret, made a virtue of necessity and departed.

He was surprised and disappointed on arriving back at headquarters to learn that no news of the tall, stout man with the black moustache had yet come in, and he began to fear that his series of lucky discoveries in Oban was going to bring him no nearer his objective. But there was nothing more he could do to expedite matters. Now that the search was in full swing on the lines he had laid down, his own efforts would not appreciably supplement those of the men engaged in it. He therefore turned back to the considerations which had previously occupied his mind. Should his next step not be to find out where Buchan and Swayne had been on the previous Thursday night?

The matter of Buchan was already in hand, and until he received a reply from the South African police it would not be wise to spend more time on him. Some inquiries into the recent movements of Swayne seemed therefore his immediate business. Since Crawley had told him of the telegram from London he was much less hopeful of Swayne being his man, but he recognised that the telegram was not an alibi, and that something more definite would be needed to prove him innocent. Indeed, if he were guilty, the sending of such a telegram would be a likely enough ruse to divert suspicion.

Next morning, therefore, arrayed in a black suit and a bowler hat, and carrying a small black handbag, he left Waverley at an early hour, and shortly after midday he was motoring out through the grey-coloured country north of Newcastle. In due course he drew up at the door of Langholm Hall. It was opened by the same gravely dignified butler who had answered Crawley's knock. He bowed with an old-fashioned politeness to Ross as he informed him that Sir Anthony had gone down to the farm.

'If he won't be too long, I should like to wait,' Ross answered. 'I am a solicitor, Mr Cairns of Messrs. Cairns & McFarlane, of Edinburgh.'

'If you will come in, I'll send a message to Sir Anthony.'

Ross was shown into a comfortably furnished waiting-room, and there he skilfully detained the old man in conversation. He was acting for that unfortunate gentleman who had just lost his life, Mr Crawley, of the Hill Farm. Mr Crawley had had some business with Sir Anthony which he, Cairns, wished to discuss. Could the butler tell him had Mr Crawley seen Sir Anthony lately?

Not to the butler's knowledge. Mr Crawley had called on the previous Tuesday afternoon, but Sir Anthony had just gone out; in fact, he was just leaving the house when the ring came. He had evidently heard the ring, for he had called to the butler: 'If that's anyone to see me, you may say I'm out. I have an appointment at four and I'm late as it is.' Mr Crawley had pencilled a few words on his card, and when Sir Anthony came in he had seemed very sorry to have missed his visitor. Sir Anthony had not, however, given the matter as much thought as he otherwise might, for his letters were waiting for him, and after reading one of them he had said that he found he had business in London next day, and must go up by the night train. Locke, the chauffeur, had therefore been sent for, and had driven his master into Newcastle to catch the 10.35 p.m. sleeping-car train to King's Cross. On Friday the butler had received a letter from Sir Anthony, written from the Hotel Splendide, in which he said he was returning by the 1.40 p.m. from King's Cross on the Saturday, and for Locke to meet him at the Central in Newcastle on the arrival of that train at 8.31. Locke had done so, and they had arrived at Langholm Hall shortly after nine. On the following day, Sunday, Sir Anthony had motored out to see Crawley, and had been greatly shocked by the news of his death.

The butler had not volunteered all this information, but Ross, by adroit questioning, had gradually extracted it. Indeed, so long had he kept him talking that he had left the room but a few moments before the door opened and the master of the house entered.

Inspector Ross's first feeling was one of profound disappointment. Sir Anthony Swayne was a tall man, but there his likeness to the walker of Connel Ferry and Oban ceased. All the witnesses Ross had questioned had agreed as to the stoutness of that other, the roundness of his cheeks and the breadth of his chest. But this man was not stout, nor were his cheeks round. Though powerfully built, he was not corpulent. That other had worn a dark moustache cut rather long; this one also wore a moustache, but it was fair and of the type known as a toothbrush. Ross felt he was hopelessly off the trail.

But second thoughts made him less certain. The feature that a man couldn't alter—his height—was the same in both cases. The others—the round cheeks, the corpulence, the dark moustache—were all attainable by disguise; moreover, they constituted the kind of disguise an amateur would attempt. The disguise of the professional had to do more with things such as the subtle shaving of the eyebrows or the substitution of a differently shaped set of teeth. But rubber fillers for the cheeks, padded clothes, and false moustaches were dear to the heart of the novice. Though perhaps it was unlikely, it was still conceivable that Swayne was his man.

'Good morning. You wished to see me?' Sir Anthony spoke courteously, with the manner and accent of his class.

Ross rose. 'I'm sorry to trouble you, Sir Anthony,' he answered, 'but I am in search of some information, and you are, I think, the only person who can give it to me.'

Sir Anthony looked his question.

'It is in connection with the death of Mr Stewart Crawley, of the Hill Farm.'

While Ross was speaking he glanced unostentatiously at his host. Was it fancy that Sir Anthony started slightly, and that a look of alarm shot into his eyes? He recovered himself so quickly that Ross for a moment questioned that he had seen it, but on second thoughts he felt sure he had not been mistaken. There remained at all events a careful, wary expression on the man's face, such as it might have worn had he steeled himself to meet a serious crisis. Nevertheless he answered calmly:

'Yes, I knew poor Crawley. A terrible business.'

Sir Anthony had certainly not given himself away in his reply, and Ross realised that his bluff had failed. It was now necessary for him to remove any suspicion that he might have raised.

'I should have explained, sir,' he went on, 'that my firm has acted for Mr Crawley since he came to England. But we are now at a loss; we don't know if he has any relatives living to whom we should apply, and to whom his property should go. When looking through his papers, I found a telegram from you in reference to a call he had paid here and one you intended to pay at the Hill Farm. It seemed, therefore, that you might be on terms of some intimacy with him, and might be able to give me the information.'

Sir Anthony took a cigar case from his pocket.

'Won't you smoke?' he invited, and when both men had lit up he went on: 'Before my grandfather died and I came in for this property, Crawley and I were employed in a large provision business in Middeldorp in South Africa. As a matter of fact, he was my boss; he was manager, while I was head of the sales department. I didn't know him very well except in connection with the business, but I believe there was a sister, a Miss Crawley, who kept house for him. I don't know if she has left Middeldorp, but you could find out through the provision store people, Messrs. Hope Bros., of Mees Street. Poor Crawley had trouble there, you know?'

'No,' said Ross, 'I know nothing.'

'There was a murder there. A man called Smith, an assistant in the Accountant's department of the same business, was murdered, and Crawley was suspected. It was just after I had left, and I only know the details that I saw in the papers. Crawley was arrested and brought to trial. The jury disagreed and he was tried again, when he was acquitted. Personally, I never for a moment believed him guilty and I wrote congratulating him. But there was no answer, and I learned from a correspondent that he had left Middeldorp. Then I heard that someone called Crawley had taken the Hill Farm, but I never imagined it was my old acquaintance until last Tuesday he called here. I was unfortunately out. That evening I had unexpectedly to go to London on business, and in the hurry of the journey I forgot his visit. I remembered it in London, and I wired him I would call on my return. That, I presume, was the message you found?'

Ross agreed. He asked a number of other questions, all of which Swayne answered readily and without in any way incriminating himself. Ross had a growing feeling that he was speaking to an innocent man, but he was loath to give up one of the only two strings he had to his bow, and he hesitated to come to a conclusion until he had actual proof.

Though at first disappointed with the result of his interview, as he thought over the situation during his drive back to

Newcastle he became less dissatisfied. He had, after all, gained some vital information, information which ought to establish the guilt or innocence of Swayne. The butler's letter surely gave him the lead he required.

On the Friday, the day of the tragedy, the butler had received a letter from Swayne, written from the Hotel Splendide in London. Inquiries at the Splendide should establish Swayne's movements. If he was in London on the Friday, he was certainly not at Crianlarich.

Ross pictured himself arriving at the hotel and asking his questions. He would require two things, a photograph of Swayne and a sample of his handwriting. He spent the remainder of the drive working out schemes for obtaining these.

On reaching Newcastle, he drove to the Metropole, and going to the writing room, drew a sheet of the hotel paper towards him and wrote as follows:

'DEAR SIR,

'*Stewart Crawley, deceased.*

'With reference to my call today re above, I quite forgot to ask you if you knew from what country or place the deceased gentleman came originally. Such information, if obtainable, would materially assist my search.

'Apologising for troubling you, and hoping to receive as early a reply as your convenience will allow.

'I am, Sir,
'Yours faithfully,
'WILSON CAIRNS
'(CAIRNS & MCFARLANE).'

Ross then turned his attention to a second note. Opening his despatch case, he searched through a number of sheets of paper which, on expeditions of the kind, he always carried, and which bore the bill heads of firms of many kinds, both real and imaginary.

Selecting one, he went to the office and there succeeded in borrowing a typewriter. Slowly and painfully he typed his letter, signed it 'Kenneth Munro,' placed it in an envelope bearing the typewritten address, 'Sir Anthony Swayne, Bart., Langholm Hall.' Then slipping the note into his pocket, he called for a directory of Newcastle and made a note of a few of the principal photographic studios. With this he sallied forth, and in a few minutes was interviewing the manager of the first on the list.

'My name is Munro,' he told him, 'and I represent *British Homes*. We have an article set up on Langholm Hall. The thing was written up and the views taken before this present Sir Anthony succeeded, but owing to our "Swiss Chateaux" series, we haven't had space for it until now. We want a portrait of Sir Anthony to complete it. Can you get it for us?'

'Certainly,' the manager answered. 'I suppose Sir Anthony is expecting me?'

'No, but I've a note here from the firm to him, which will introduce you and explain matters.'

He took from his pocket the letter he had typed with such pains, and handed it to the other.

'Right,' the manager said. 'I'll send out first thing tomorrow.'

'You might let me have the portrait at the Metropole as soon as you can,' Ross directed as he took his leave.

Next day he took a half holiday. The morning he spent writing up his notes of the case, then, having notice that a play which he had long wished to see was billed for the afternoon, he went to the matinee. When he returned to his hotel, two letters were waiting for him.

The first was written on grey cream laid paper in a strong masculine hand, and read:

'Langholm Hall.

'DEAR SIR,—In reply to your letter of yesterday, I regret I am unable to inform you from what country or place the late Mr Crawley came originally. I cannot recall his ever having spoken in my hearing of his early history.

'Yours faithfully,
'JOHN A. SWAYNE.'

'That's a bit of luck,' Ross muttered. 'He might have dictated it to a secretary. Well, that's his handwriting at all events. Now for the photograph.'

The second letter was as follows:

'The Clayton Studio,
'Newcastle.

'DEAR SIR,—With reference to your call and commission to us to do a cabinet portrait of Sir J. A. Swayne, we beg to inform you that our representative duly called on Sir Anthony next morning and presented your note. In reply, Sir Anthony stated that he fully appreciated your kind thought, but that as he did not take a prominent part in the social life of the county, he would prefer not to figure in the article.

'We presume after this you will not care to pursue the matter, but should you do so we might point out that a small-size photograph of Sir Anthony is already in our possession. By chance he happens to figure in a view taken of Mr Lloyd George's arrival at Central Station when he was Prime Minister. I enclose a copy for your inspection.

'Trusting to be favoured with your commands.

'We are, dear Sir,
'THE CLAYTON STUDIO, LTD.'

'Good old Clayton Studio!' Ross mentally ejaculated. 'This is better and better. Here I have a quite good photograph of my man, and he doesn't even know one has been taken.'

He was now armed for the next stage of his investigation, and he determined to proceed with it without delay. He telephoned to the station for a sleeping berth, and at 10.30 p.m. left the Central Station for London.

He had bought himself a Bradshaw, and before turning in he set himself to look up the trains between London and Crianlarich. The tall, stout man for whom he was searching had arrived at Crianlarich at 7.58 on the Friday night. His immediate problem was therefore, what was the latest time at which a traveller would have to leave London, in order to reach Crianlarich at 7.58.

He was characteristically thorough and painstaking, looking up all the possible routes and checking his results again and again. At the end of an hour he had established the fact that the hypothetical traveller must have left London by one of the evening trains on the Thursday, the previous night. Leaving by the earliest trains on Friday morning would not have got him to Edinburgh or Stirling in time to catch the connection to Crianlarich. If, therefore, Swayne was in London on either Thursday or Friday night, it would be conclusive proof of his innocence. To ascertain this would, he felt sure, be a simple matter.

On reaching King's Cross he drove to the Splendide, and when he had breakfasted he asked to see the manager, to whom he explained his business.

'I should think we can help you, yes,' that suave official replied. 'We'll have a look at the visitors' book to begin with. Do you mind coming through to the office?'

The haughty goddess in charge, adddressed as Miss Bushe, hastened to produce the book, and the manager ran his eye down the list of names.

'That looks like it,' he said presently, pointing to the words, 'Sir Anthony Swayne, Newcastle.'

Ross laid the letter he had received from the baronet beside the entry, and studied the two signatures, first with the naked eye, and then with a lens.

'It's the same signature,' he said, after a prolonged scrutiny.

'I'll swear both those names were written by the same man. What do you say, sir?'

'I certainly agree with you, but then I am not an expert like the gentlemen of your profession.'

'But this is not the date I want,' Ross went on. 'This was written on Wednesday, the 9th, but the nights I am anxious about are Thursday and Friday, the 10th and 11th. How can I find out if he remained over?'

'We'll ask the clerk.' The manager turned to the young lady, pointing to the item. 'Miss Bushe, do you happen to remember this gentleman, Sir Anthony Swayne?'

The girl glanced at the signature, then answered readily, 'Oh, yes, quite well; a tall gentleman with a short, fair moustache.'

'Is that he?' Ross asked, producing his photograph.

'Yes, that is he. I should know him anywhere.'

'How do you come to recall him so distinctly?' the manager asked.

'He spoke to me two or three times. When he came in on'— she looked down at the date in the register—'on the 9th, that was Wednesday, he stopped here and talked for a minute or two. "I shall want to stay for three nights," he said. "I haven't any luggage, it went astray on the way up"—he had only a small attache case in his hand—"so I'll make a deposit of five pounds." "Thank you," I said, "I'll give you a receipt, but it's perfectly all right in any case." He chatted on while I was filling out the receipt, then I put him down for Room 130 and rang for the porter to show him up.'

Inspector Ross's heart was slowly sinking. This was not at all what he had hoped to hear.

'And did he stay for the three nights?' he asked anxiously.

'No, for two nights only. He left on the Friday morning.'

Friday morning! Then he could not have been at Crianlarich on Friday night! Ross was suddenly conscious of a feeling of the bitterest disappointment. He had been counting much more than he had realised on Swayne being his man. And now the brilliantly successful termination to the case to which he had looked forward was jeopardised, if not lost altogether. His time for the last three or four days, his trouble at Newcastle, and his visit to London were lost at all events. One of the two strings he had had to his bow was gone, and if the other, represented by Sandy Buchan, failed to materialise, he would be utterly at a loss; he would be back at the beginning of the case without having made any progress whatever.

But his thorough-going nature asserted itself, and he went on trying to obtain all the information available. He turned back to the girl.

'I think you said Sir Anthony spoke to you more than once. Perhaps you would please tell me of the other occasion?'

'I didn't see him again on the night that he arrived,' Miss Bushe went on, 'but next morning he came to ask for letters and stayed chatting for a minute or two. Then he came up again that evening—that was Thursday—and he complained that he had a nasty chill and had had some whisky, and was going to bed to try to sleep it off. He asked me to give orders that he was not to be called on the following morning, as he would not get up until he felt inclined. He also said that a friend had asked him home for the Friday night, so that he would be leaving on the following morning.'

'And he did so?'

'Yes.'

'You saw him that morning?'

For the first time the girl hesitated.

'I don't remember that,' she said at last. 'I may have, but I rather imagine a waiter got his bill.' She brightened up. 'Yes, though, I do remember after all. Giuseppe, that's one of the waiters, came for the bill; there was a balance due Sir Anthony, and I handed Giuseppe the money and the receipted bill. You can see a copy of the bill if you like.'

Ross saw it, and not only the bill, but the carbon of the receipt which had been pasted on it.

It seemed useless to inquire further, but Ross went on in his methodical way. He would like to see the waiter.

Giuseppe proved to be an elderly Italian with an intelligent expression and a polite manner. He gave his evidence clearly, and replied to Ross's questions without hesitation. He remembered the original of the photograph; he had waited on him for two mornings. He recalled being sent to the office for the bill after breakfast on the second morning. He recalled is specially because he was given no money to pay it, but told instead to bring money back from the office. He brought back the money and handed it with the bill to the gentleman. The latter tipped him and left, and that was all he knew of the matter.

Though convinced by this time of Swayne's innocence, Ross still persevered. While he was at it he might as well see the chambermaid.

The girl in charge of Room No. 130 also remembered Swayne. He had slept two nights, though she could not say for certain what two nights they were. Her attention had been specially called to him because, early on the second night, he had rung for her, explained that he had a chill, and said he did not wish to be called on the following morning. That was about 9.30 or perhaps 10.00. She had heard him bolt the door of his room after she left. Next morning she had gently tried the door about ten o'clock, but it was still locked. Swayne must have left shortly after, because when she tried it again about a quarter before eleven it was open and the room empty. The bed had been slept in and the washhand basin used.

It was enough! There could no longer be any doubt of Swayne's innocence. He had been at the Splendide on the Thursday night, and Ross had already found that by no possible means could a man who had been in London on Thursday night be at Crianlarich at 7.58 on the Friday night following. No, he was up against it. He might go back to Scotland and begin again. His present line was a washout.

However, with a kind of lingering hope in his mind, he

occupied part of the time until his return train in visiting the Charing Cross post office and looking at the original of the Crawley telegram. But an inspection of the form only confirmed what he had already learned. The handwriting was undoubtedly Swayne's.

In a deeply despondent frame of mind he joined the 8.15 p.m. sleeping-car express from King's Cross to Edinburgh.

CHAPTER XVII

MR SANDY BUCHAN

WHEN Inspector Ross reached headquarters next morning he found he was being anxiously sought for. To his relief, the story of his failure in London was not demanded.

'That Swayne business a dead end?' his chief merely remarked. 'I thought it might. Well, this looks better.'

It appeared that news had come in, important news from no less than two sources. The first was South Africa. The Chief of the Middeldorp police cabled: 'Alexander Buchan left here ten months ago to take up job in Glasgow. Sending Crawley papers next boat.'

'Yes, sir, that should be a help,' Ross admitted.

'Ay, but wait 'til you see this.' The Chief picked up a type-written slip. 'This is a phone message from Murdoch, who's been after that man you traced to Oban.'

Ross eagerly took the slip. It was dated for the previous evening and read:

'4.48 p.m. D.-Sergeant Murdoch phones from Buchanan Street Station Public Call Office: "I came on a trace of the wanted man at Stirling. A commercial I met in the refreshment room had seen him get off the 8.40 a.m. ex Oban on the Saturday. As Stirling is the junction for Glasgow, I came on here, and after trying for half a day, got news of him. A porter, Andrew Burns, had seen him leave the 1.15 p.m., the connection of the 8.40 a.m. ex Oban, at Buchanan Street Station, and go towards the exit. I am sure from the porter's description it is the man we want. I am trying to follow him up."'

*

Inspector Ross was greatly cheered by the news.

'Looks like it, sir, right enough,' he exclaimed. 'It's all tending the same way. Here's this man Buchan, apparently, at all events, writing the decoy letter to Crawley. That letter was posted in Glasgow. Buchan went to Glasgow ten months ago. The man who attempted the murder went to Glasgow. It seems to me that when we get hold of Alexander Buchan of Glasgow our job'll be done.'

'Well, get ahead with it,' the Chief advised, as he turned to other business.

Having wired to Murdoch, Inspector Ross took the next train to Glasgow, and by eleven o'clock was discussing matters with Sergeant Murdoch on the circulating area of the Central Station.

'You've heard the news from South Africa, of course?' he asked, when the other had reported his proceedings to date. 'We've got to find this Buchan if he is in the city.'

'I have two men on it, sir,' Murdoch answered. 'Headquarters phoned me late last night, and first thing this morning I started Steele and McDuff round the hotels to make inquiries. It seemed to me that if this chap was in a hotel in South Africa and left there to take over a job here, it would likely be in the same line. At any rate, I didn't see any better way of getting at it.'

'I think you're probably right, Sergeant. We'll work that line first anyway, and if we get nothing, we can try something else. Where are your men now?'

The sergeant pulled a notebook from his pocket, and turned the somewhat dog's-eared leaves with a thick and moistened thumb.

'Here's a list I made out,' he explained. 'Steele is working this lot here, and McDuff this other lot. I was just going to start the Central, St Enoch's, and round this neighbourhood when I got your wire to meet you.'

Ross grunted.

'Do them quicker by telephone,' he suggested. 'There's no

need for a personal call. Let those men carry on as they are, but you and I'll work the phone. Get hold of a directory and we'll take the hotels in order, so we'll not leave any out.'

Having obtained street and telephone directories and ten shillings' worth of coppers, the two men squeezed with some difficulty into a public telephone booth and the work began. Murdoch looked up the hotels and found their numbers, while Ross rang up each in turn and asked if their Mr Buchan was engaged. When they replied there was no one of that name on their staff, Ross apologised, said he might have mistaken the name, but he wanted the gentleman who had come to them ten months ago from South Africa. When they still assured him no such person existed he apologised again, explained that the error was evidently in the address, and asked if they knew of anyone of the name in another hotel.

The work was tedious, though much quicker than driving round from building to building. But though they were very conscientious and omitted none of the names on the list, their luck was out. Nowhere in the Glasgow hotel business could they hear of an Alexander Buchan.

Over a belated lunch Ross was pessimistic. 'If the darned chap came to the town at all, there's fifty odd jobs he might have started in on. If we don't get him by tomorrow night we shall have to advertise.'

'Would that not give us away?'

'Not if we did it right. "If Alexander Buchan, late of South Africa, would apply to Messrs A. and B., he would hear something to his advantage." That's the idea. Pass me that directory.'

He slowly turned the pages.

'See here,' he said presently. 'We'll have a try at some of these institutions before we give over. An assistant in a hotel would likely take on managing one of these places if he could get it. There's a Blind Asylum and a Cripples' Home and a Sailors' Home and the Lord knows what all. Take a note of them, Murdoch, and we'll ring them up on spec.'

They returned to their booth and resumed their monotonous work. They rang up Inebriate Homes and Private Asylums and Welfare Canteens, but it was not until they were nearly at the end of their list that they had a stroke of luck. When Ross asked the office of a high-class boarding school for boys whether their Mr Buchan was engaged, he was electrified to receive the reply, 'Mr Buchan speaking. Who are you, please?' Indeed, so taken aback was he at this unexpected answer that he hesitated perceptibly before continuing: 'Mr Alexander Buchan, late of South Africa?'

When the answer came, 'That's right. Who is speaking, please?' a wave of exultation swept over him. But he controlled himself and spoke in a quiet, business-like tone.

'This is Frazer & Muirhead's office; Messrs. Frazer & Muirhead, solicitors, Sauchiehall Street. I'm one of the clerks. I am instructed by Mr Frazer to ask you if you could find it convenient to call and see him here as soon as possible. He wishes to see you on some business that has just arisen in connection with the school. He thinks that a short, personal interview at this stage might save a mass of correspondence and perhaps litigation. Could you manage this?'

'Why, yes,' came Buchan's voice. 'Would tomorrow at 3.00 do?'

'Certainly,' Ross replied, 'if you couldn't come this afternoon. I suppose it would be impossible for you to come down now?'

'I couldn't come now, but if it's very urgent I could come in an hour's time. How would that do?'

'Excellently, sir. Mr Frazer will be very grateful to you for meeting his wishes so promptly. You know the office? Sauchiehall Street, just at the corner of Leven Lane, upstairs.'

'We've got him, Murdoch, we've got him now,' Ross cried in high delight when he had hung up the receiver. 'Come along out to this place, wherever it is.'

The school was situated not far from Kirkintilloch, and thither the two men betook themselves. It proved to be a large, red brick building set back a quarter of a mile from the road, and standing in well-kept and well-wooded grounds.

'He'll not be out for another half hour,' Ross remarked. 'Come round and see if there's a back entrance he might use.'

They satisfied themselves that anyone going in the direction of Glasgow would pass through the large, beaten iron gates they had first seen, then Ross gave his instructions.

'Now, Murdoch, you've got to shadow this man without letting him see you. You remember Miss Hope's description of him: middling tall, sallow, clean-shaven, with dark eyes and thin features? He'll probably come straight back here when he finds he's been hoaxed. I'll be waiting for him.'

They took up a position behind some trees, from where they could see the road without being themselves exposed to view. Presently they noticed a man leave the building, walk rapidly down the drive, and turn off in the direction of Glasgow. Murdoch slipped quietly after him, and when Ross reconnoitred again a few moments later both figures had disappeared.

Ross was not in any hurry to come out himself. Nearly half an hour had elapsed before he moved from behind the trees, and walking up the school drive, knocked at the door. It was opened by a porter in uniform.

'Good evening,' said Ross. 'Is Mr Buchan in?'

'No, sir,' the man answered. 'He went out about half an hour ago.'

'Will he be in soon?'

'He said about six, sir.'

Ross looked at his watch and hesitated.

'Not for an hour,' he said, as if to himself. He paused in apparent thought, then turned again to the man.

'You could help me, if you would, and I should be very much obliged. Mr Buchan thought of spending last Friday night week in Edinburgh, in connection with some business in which we are both interested. I wanted to see him to know if he went and, if so, how he got on. Perhaps you could tell me if he was away that night, because, if he was, I'll wait to see him, and if he wasn't I'll not.'

The porter, possibly scenting backsheesh, was communicative.

'He was away on Friday night week, sir,' he answered. 'He left about three o'clock on Friday afternoon, and came back about the same time or a little earlier on Saturday. Of course, I don't know if it was Edinburgh he went to, but he was away right enough.'

'Thank you, then I think I'll stay and see him. I'm an old friend. I'll go to his room, if you'll show it to me.'

The porter hesitated, but Ross at that moment slipped half a crown into his hand, and it had the necessary effect.

'I shouldn't perhaps take you to his room,' the man said doubtfully, but leading the way. 'But if you are an old friend, I suppose it's all right.'

'Of course it's all right,' Ross declared cheerfully. 'It's what Mr Buchan would wish.'

Left to himself, Inspector Ross acted warily. Mindful of the questioning look in the man's eye, he lit a cigarette, took up a book which was lying on the table, and threw himself into an armchair. Not many minutes had passed when his perspicacity was rewarded. With just the semblance of a knock, the door suddenly opened and the porter appeared carrying a newspaper. Ross was amused as well as pleased to see the suspicion on his face change first to relief and then to confidence.

'I thought you might like to see the paper, sir,' he said civilly.

Ross thanked him, and was interested to notice that though he had not heard anyone approaching, the man's steps as he walked away were clearly audible. He smiled, and getting up noiselessly, began to make a silent, though thorough, search of the room.

He busied himself more particularly with his unconscious host's papers. The desk was unlocked, and he lost no time in running through the numerous drawers. But neither in them nor on the various tables the room contained could he find anything suspicious or in any way bearing on the tragedy.

Presently, hearing footsteps in the distance, he sank back into the chair and picked up the paper. It was characteristic of him that not only did he look consciously to see that it was right side up, but he also made sure it was opened at a page containing news paragraphs and not merely advertisements.

The door swung back and Buchan stood framed in the opening. He seemed annoyed, and for some seconds remained motionless, staring at his visitor. Then he stepped forward and spoke sharply.

'Good evening, sir. The porter tells me you stated you were an old friend of mine. I do not remember ever having seen you before. You have, I am sure, some explanation of this somewhat mysterious circumstance.'

Ross got up.

'I have, sir,' he answered, 'a very complete one, and if you will come in and shut the door behind you I shall be glad to give it to you.'

Mr Buchan shrugged his shoulders, closed the door, and sat down at his desk.

'Now, sir,' he invited.

Inspector Ross was experiencing once more the feeling of disappointment to which he had been a prey when first his gaze had fallen on Sir Anthony Swayne. This Buchan could by no means be described as stout, fat-cheeked, and with a dark moustache. Though fairly tall, he was in fact slight, thin-faced and clean-shaven. But here again Ross recognised the possibilities of disguise. In the dull and uncertain light of early morning, and dealing with the uncritical observers of Connel Ferry and Oban, Ross believed that this man could have made himself up to such an extent as to merit the description given. As in the case of Swayne, Ross had to admit to himself that this man's appearance decided nothing. As far as that went, he might or might not have been the murderer.

'Before I offer my explanation and state my business,' Ross
went on, 'I must ask you to excuse me if I make sure you are
really the gentleman I want to see. May I ask where in South
Africa you were before coming here?'

Mr Buchan answered readily enough though shortly.

'Middeldorp. I was assistant manager of the Bellevue Hotel
for seven years.'

'Thank you, that's what I want. My name,' the Inspector
squared his shoulders and gazed sternly at the other, 'is Ross,
Detective Inspector Ross of the Scottish Service.'

Mr Buchan looked neither impressed nor embarrassed.

'That so?' he said coolly. 'Well, Mr Detective Inspector Ross
of the Scottish Service, I'm pleased to meet you, but that does
not explain why you forced your way into my private room on
false pretences, when a waiting-room is provided for visitors.'

'I didn't wish it to be known I was here,' Ross explained,
'and instead of questioning my action, I think you should be
grateful for it. However, that's by the way; let me come to my
real business. Did you ever hear of a man called Stewart
Crawley?'

The Inspector, watching the other keenly, saw him start, but
he answered without hesitation.

'I knew a Stewart Crawley in Middeldorp, if that is the man
you mean. He was manager of a big provision store.'

'Hope Bros. of Mees Street,' Ross returned. 'Yes, that is the
man I mean. But it is not of South Africa that I want to hear.
You knew, of course, that this Crawley had returned to England?'

Buchan seemed to the Inspector to be about to fall into the
little trap, then suddenly checked himself.

'I saw that a man called Stewart Crawley had been accidentally drowned at Ballachulish some days ago,' he said in a
changed voice, 'but I had no reason to connect the two.'

Ross was not favourably impressed with the man's manner.
He fancied he was keeping something back. He therefore tried
a bluff.

'*Accidentally* drowned,' he said grimly. 'Do you really state, Mr Buchan, that you had no suspicion that the man—er—drowned at Ballachulish was your old South African friend?'

Buchan hesitated again. Then he began to speak with some show of warmth.

'I really don't know, Inspector, what you mean by talking in this way. What right have you to come here and ask me these questions?'

Ross shook his head.

'Now, none of that, if you please, Mr Buchan. Your hesitation has given you away. What if I tell you that we know that that supposed accident at Ballachulish was no accident at all, that the whole business was part of a carefully planned murder, that you are known to have had an appointment with Crawley, and that your own movements that night are unaccounted for. Don't mistake me,' the Inspector held up his hand as the other would have spoken, 'I am not making any accusation. I am here for information, and I have told you enough to let you see it will pay you to give it me. Now, you've practically admitted you knew the Ballachulish man was your old acquaintance. You might tell me how you knew. Or rather'—Ross leaned forward in his chair and his voice took on a harsher tone—'tell me the one thing that really matters; tell me what you did for the twenty-five hours from 2.00 p.m. last Friday week until 3.00 p.m. on Saturday.'

Buchan's expression had changed. He was now staring at his visitor with an amazement stamped on his features, which changed as the other watched to a rapidly growing uneasiness.

'Good heavens!' he cried at last, 'you don't really mean to tell me that Crawley was murdered and that you are accusing me of murdering him? The papers said it was an accident.'

'I tell you there was no accident about it. Now, Mr Buchan, I hope you will see your way to answer my question. I don't wish to take any steps against you, but if you refuse I shall be forced to. Where were you that night?'

The man was very much taken aback. He did not at first answer, but sat gazing moodily at the Inspector. Finally he moistened his lips and said in a lower tone:

'Suppose I don't answer you?'

'In that case, sir, I shall be compelled to put you under police surveillance until I find out the answer for myself.'

Again there was silence. Buchan's face gradually paled, and something very like horror had dawned on it. He sat staring straight before him and whistling a little tune between his teeth.

'I suppose you won't tell me what the evidence against me is?'

'I would rather you answered my question first. Come, sir,' Ross spoke not unkindly, 'if you are innocent you have nothing to be afraid of.'

Buchan made a gesture of despair.

'But that's just it, Inspector, I fear I have something to be afraid of. I can tell you in a moment the extraordinary adventure I had that night, but the question is, will you believe me? I can see for myself that my story is not very probable and I can't possibly prove it. What you tell me makes the whole business an even greater mystery, and I couldn't at the time make head nor tail of it.'

Inspector Ross was greatly interested. 'He's doing it well,' he thought, 'but he's guilty for all that. He'll have a quite water-tight yarn ready to spin by the time he gets started,' but all he said was, 'Tell me anyway, sir; if your story's true, we'll prove it easy enough.'

'Well, I'll tell you; I can see I've no option. I don't suppose my word will count for much, but I give it to you at any rate that every word I say is the truth.'

Ross nodded as he answered:

'Thank you, Mr Buchan, I'm glad to have your assurance.'

'What I have to tell you is about this Crawley. You have asked me if I met him in South Africa. In Middeldorp, as I have already said, I knew him as manager of Hope Bros., the

large provision store in Mees Street. We were not exactly intimate, something more than mere acquaintances perhaps, but
not much. I don't know whether you are aware that about a
year or more before I left he got into trouble, was accused,
wrongfully, as I believe, of committing a murder. At the first
trial the jury disagreed, but at the second he was found "Not
Guilty" and discharged. He then left the town and disappeared
completely.

'You have also asked me if I knew Crawley had returned to
England. Well, I didn't, not until Wednesday week last. But
before I come to that, I must tell you how I came to return
myself.'

He had spoken with some difficulty at first, as if under the
influence of emotion, but now the words were coming more
freely.

'Nearly a year ago,' he went on, 'I had a letter from my uncle,
Mr Hector Buchan of this city, saying that the matron of this
school was retiring and that a business manager was going to
be appointed to do her work as well as to look after the accounts.
My uncle is on the Board of Governors, and he said that if I
applied he would give me a leg up. I did so, got the billet, and
moved here ten months ago.

'Since then everything has gone on normally until this business started on Wednesday week. On Wednesday week by the
last post I got a letter that surprised me greatly. You can read
it for yourself.' He took from his pocket a square, slate-coloured
envelope and passed it across.

It was marked 'Personal,' and was addressed in a strong
masculine hand to

Mr Alexander Buchan,
Business Manager,
St Andrew's College,
Kirkintilloch,
near Glasgow.

It bore a Newcastle postmark, and the date of 8.00 a.m. on the previous Wednesday week.

Inspector Ross's interest did not wane. He drew some closely-written sheets from the envelope, glanced at the signature, found it was 'Stewart Crawley,' and began to read.

'DEAR BUCHAN,—You will be surprised to get this letter, for I suppose after what happened at Middeldorp, you never expected to hear from me again. Well, after that business I couldn't stick the town, so I cleared out and went and staked a claim at the new diggings. There, after some time, I struck gold, not a great deal, but enough to keep me from starving. I knocked about a bit, then drifted to England, and have taken a small house not far from Newcastle.

'In the train to the coast I met Holt. I don't know if you remember him, but he was a bank official in Middeldorp. He told me you had left the town and taken on your present job. That is how I learned your address.

'On my way home, I sailed in the same boat as a man whom I shall call X. As a pure fluke it came out that he had some property with money in it. It's an island, but except that it's off the west coast of Scotland, I won't tell you where it is, and the money's in a deposit that's there and that no one knows anything about. He showed me a bit of the stuff he's had made into a walking stick handle because it looked sort of ornamental, but neither he nor the people that made it up had the least idea of what it was. Well, to make a long story short, he and I are going to work the stuff secretly, ourselves, but to our disgust we find we must have a third man. I know nobody over here and neither does he—he lives abroad—so I write to ask if you'd care to join in.

'Naturally, I can't give you any details now, as the essence of the thing is secrecy. But I would like to meet you and talk it over, and if you want to go on, and give the necessary guarantees, to introduce you to X. He has hired a seagoing motor launch, and my idea is that if we come to terms we could go right on to the island and prospect. But we don't want to be seen starting, so X has arranged to put in at a deserted place on the shore of Loch Linnhe on Friday night next. We would meet on shore, and if all was well join him on the launch. So if you want to come in, be at the eighth mile-post from Fort William on the Ballachulish road at 10.30 p.m. on Friday night. I will join you then or as soon after as possible.

'I should make it clear that the job would be a whole-time one, so don't come if you are not willing to give up the school. We would share alike, and you might get anything out of it from £5,000 to £50,000.

'You would have to leave Glasgow by the 3.46 train on Friday, and could get back (if you wished) at 1.40 on Saturday.

'Please don't talk about this, and don't bother to reply. If you don't turn up I'll know the proposal doesn't appeal to you, and look elsewhere.

'Yours truly,
'STEWART CRAWLEY.'

As Inspector Ross read this strange epistle, he snorted with annoyance. The thing was getting deeper and deeper and more and more involved. The case up to the present had seemed at least fairly straightforward, and he had hoped that his luck in finding Buchan would have led him to a speedy conclusion. But instead of that, here was a fresh and exasperating complication.

On the other hand, was he for the first time beginning to get a glimpse of something like motive in the tangle? If Crawley and Mr X were after a fortune, was someone else after the same? Ross, whistling gently under his breath, registered the idea as one to be looked into at a more convenient season, then turned back to Buchan.

'And you went?'

'Well, what do you think? Of course I went. I knew Crawley, and I knew that if he said he had a good thing on, well, he just had. I never knew Crawley to be anything but straight. I went, and I hugged myself for the chance of getting in with him.'

'You didn't doubt that he had really written the letter?'

Buchan looked up sharply as he answered, 'Not I; nor don't now. I know his hand too well for that.'

'Well?'

'Well, that's all there is of it. I left Glasgow at 3.46 and got to Fort William shortly after eight. I walked quietly out of the town on the road that runs south along Loch Linnhe. No one saw me so far as I know. I had eight miles to go and a little over two hours to do it in, just nice time. Fortunately, it was a fine night and there was a bit of moon, else I don't believe I'd ever have found the mile-post. There was no one there when I got up, so I waited—you remember the letter said Crawley might be late. Well, I waited and waited and walked backwards and forwards, but there was never a sign of anyone. At last, when it was nearly one, I was so tired I could stick it no longer. There was no hotel there to go to, and anyway I don't think I would have knocked them up at that hour if there had been. I had noticed some hayricks half a mile back, and I went to them and found a sheltered place to lie down. I had some food and then fell asleep. When I woke it was getting light. My train left Fort William at 9.18, and I saw I had just time to catch it. I finished my sandwiches, caught the train with five minutes to spare, and was back in Glasgow by a quarter to two, very tired and very much annoyed about the whole thing.'

'What station did you start from and return to in Glasgow?'

'Queen Street.'

'And how did you go from here to and from the station?'

'I went in by train on Friday, and taxied back on Saturday.'

'Continue, please.'

'There's no more to tell. I worried about the thing all evening 'til I saw the paper. Then I learned the explanation.'

For a moment Ross did not understand.

'The explanation?' he queried eagerly.

'Yes; poor Crawley's death. He had been coming to keep his appointment and evidently didn't know the road, and had been misled by his map into thinking there was a bridge where there was only a ferry. You see, the ferry is on the road to where I was waiting for him and only about five miles away. And now I shall never know who X was and where the deposit lies.'

Inspector Ross remained silent for several minutes, buried in thought. Then he handed the letter back to Buchan.

'You might make a copy of that for me, please,' he begged.

Buchan took a sheet of paper and began to write, but he had not covered more than half a page when Ross stepped round and looked over his shoulder.

'Thank you,' he said, 'that will be enough.'

He picked up the sheet, and, taking from his pocket the decoy letter which had lured Crawley to the empty house, he carefully compared the two. Satisfied with his scrutiny, he laid the latter down on the table before Buchan.

'Now, Mr Buchan,' he said sternly, 'if your story is true, will you please explain how you came to write this letter.'

As the man's eyes fell on the page he started, and an expression of profound amazement grew on his features. He picked up the sheets, turned them over like a man in a dream, and glanced at the signature. Then he raised his eyes and stared uncomprehendingly at his visitor.

'Good heavens, Inspector! What does this mean?' he cried helplessly.

'That is what I am asking you.'

Buchan with an effort shook off his stupor, and to Ross there sounded a ring of truth in his voice as he answered earnestly:

'I don't know anything about it. I give you my word of honour,

Inspector, I never saw it before. I no more wrote it than you did. What does it say? Let me read it.'

His expression of astonishment did not wane as he ran his eye over the closely-written pages. When he had finished he turned back to his visitor.

'As God is my witness, Inspector,' he declared solemnly, 'I know no more about it than you do. I never wrote it. I never saw it before.'

Inspector Ross did not know what to make of the whole business. That the two letters were connected he could hardly doubt. The choice of the Fort William road had clearly been designed to work in with the 'accident' at Ballachulish. If Buchan talked, or if the letter came to light, the accident theory would be strengthened.

It might be that, in spite of his denial, Buchan was the author of both letters, and in this case the first was obviously to lure Crawley to his death, and the second to provide Buchan himself with a credible alibi. On the other hand, Buchan might be innocent, and if so, the second letter was evidently an attempt by the murderer to throw suspicion on to Buchan and so off himself.

Ross felt very much annoyed. At the moment he was up against it in two ways. In the case as a whole, he had to admit himself at sea, and as to his treatment of Buchan he was equally in the dark. The first of these could wait, but he must make up his mind about Buchan at once.

As a matter of opinion, he was inclined to believe the man the innocent victim of a plot, but he could not afford to act on opinion. After some consideration he decided he would as far as possible lull the other's fears to rest, take his leave with a show of good fellowship, and trust to that and to Murdoch's shadowing to prevent the bird flying. He turned to his victim.

'Mr Buchan, sir,' he said, 'I'm doubting you've been hoaxed. And it's easy to see why. A scapegoat was wanted. Attention was drawn to you by a forged letter, then you were made to disappear on mysterious business during the time the murder was committed, so that you would be suspected. I tell you, sir, it's well for you you didn't do what you were asked and destroy that letter. And it's well for you you told me your story straight out as you did, else when I left here you would have come with me. You'll let me have the letter, I suppose?' Ross got up slowly from his chair. 'Well, sir, I'll bid you goodnight, and I'll let you know how I get on.'

He left the school, found Murdoch hanging about the gate, and instructed him to continue shadowing the manager, and drove thoughtfully back into Glasgow.

CHAPTER XVIII

ENLIGHTENMENT AND MYSTIFICATION

THE more Inspector Ross thought over his experiences of the day, the more difficult he found it to make up his mind about Buchan. At one time the man's guilt seemed obvious and his story an ingenious invention to account for his absence at the time of the murder; at another, Ross recalled the straightforward way in which he had spoken, and swayed to the opinion that he was the innocent victim of an elaborate plot.

There was, of course, one obvious line of inquiry which might lead to the solution of his doubts, though Ross was not sanguine of its doing so. With the idea of attempting to obtain confirmation of the story, he had asked Buchan for the details of his journey through the Glasgow area. Buchan had mentioned in reply that he had taken a taxi from Queen Street Station to Kirkintilloch. Ross wondered if he could find that taxi?

He got a Bradshaw and looked up the trains. The 8.40 a.m. from Oban, that by which the murderer had travelled, reached Buchanan Street Station at 1.15 p.m.; that from Fort William, by which Buchan said he had returned, was due at Queen Street high level at 1.34.

If it turned out that Buchan had taken a taxi shortly after 1.34 at Queen Street it would prove nothing, as he might have walked over there from Buchanan Street after arriving from Oban. But if he had made a slip and taken his vehicle from Buchanan Street *before* 1.34 it would be conclusive evidence of his guilt.

Ross recognised that it was most unlikely that so methodical a schemer had made such a slip, but he recalled how frequently an otherwise well thought out plan was wrecked by some trifling oversight or carelessness. The idea was far-fetched certainly, but in the absence of any other, he determined to follow it up.

He reached this conclusion the more readily because he could at the same time investigate another and more promising clue. Whether the tall, stout man with the black moustache was or was not Buchan, he had arrived at Buchanan Street at 1.34. Where had he gone? He might have taken a taxi. Inquiries on the point were clearly necessary.

In the morning, therefore, he began work. Borrowing a street directory, he made a complete list of all the taxi cab-offices and car owners of the city. These he arranged in location order, so that he could go round them with the minimum loss of time.

His method at each was the same. On arrival he asked to see the manager, told him he was a detective inspector engaged on the investigation of a case of murder, and asked his help. Had he or any of his staff done business about a fortnight previously with a tall, stout, round-cheeked man with a long, dark moustache, or had any of his drivers taken such a person, or any other man, from the city to Kirkintilloch between one and two o'clock on the same date?

The work was tedious, and in the nature of the case could hardly prove immediately productive. In most instances the men from whom he wanted the information were out, and he had to leave, content with the manager's promise to make inquiries from them on their return. He worked away, therefore, expecting no immediate result, until the afternoon was far advanced and he had reached the seventeenth name on his list. Another one or two, he thought, and he would knock off for the night.

Tired and a trifle irritable, he turned into the door of the eighteenth garage. It was a comparatively small place in a side street off Hope Street. The owner-manager was in his private office, a box about eight feet square, and thither Ross was shown. He was sorry to trouble Mr McAlastair, but he would be grateful for his kind help. He was a detective inspector . . . Had Mr McAlastair or any of his staff . . .

Mr McAlastair looked at him questioningly out of a pair of very keen, light-blue eyes, and then to his intense surprise answered:

'Ay, I mind the man ye mean. Dressed in a khaki-coloured waterproof and a brown cap and glasses? Funny looking chap; that's why I noticed him. He was in—Here, Charlie'—he called to a short, thick-set man in overalls whose head was hidden beneath the bonnet of a large racing car—'do ye mind that long fellow with the old Darracq? What day was he in? Was it last Friday was a week?'

The thick-set man withdrew his head.

'Na, it was Saturday—Saturday aboot dinner time,' he answered, as, wiping his hands on a sponge cloth, he slowly approached. Inspector Ross turned to him.

'I want a bit of information about that chap—strictly on the q.t.,' he said, trying to keep the eagerness out of his voice. 'I'm a 'tec, you understand, and he's wanted for murder. You'll not lose any if you tell me what you know.'

The thick-set man changed a plug of tobacco to his other cheek.

'Gosh,' he observed succinctly.

'I want to fix the time he got here,' Ross went on. 'Can you do it?'

'Ay, I can do it fine. It would be just'—he paused to transfer the plug back to the original cheek—'just five-and-twenty meen-utes past one Saturday was a week.'

Five-and-twenty minutes past one! Ten minutes after the Oban train got in. At last there was something working out as it should.

'How do you fix that?' Ross demanded anxiously.

'Easy enough. I go for my dinner at half twelve, an' back quarter-past one. I'm mostly on the tick, as the boss kens, but that day I was ten minutes late, for I went to leave a message for the missus in a shop. It was twenty-five past when I got here, an' the man just walked in the door before me.'

'And you had him driven out to Kirkintilloch, I suppose?'

Mr McAlastair shook his head.

'I hadna him driven anywhere,' he declared. 'He just came for his car and paid for the stabling and drove off in it, and that's all there's of it.'

Ross found himself brought up sharp in his self-congratulations.

'What's that you say?' he exclaimed in dismayed surprise. 'Paid for the stabling of his car? I don't follow.'

'It's no so deeficult that I can see. He drove in here—what day was it, Charlie, he left the car?'

The thick-set man expectorated skilfully.

'It was in the morning,' he said slowly, 'aboot half seven or thereabouts in the morning. It would be the Tuesday before, or maybe the Wednesday.'

The manager turned over the leaves of his ledger until he found a certain entry.

'That's right,' he agreed. 'He drove in here early on the Wednesday before, and said he wanted to leave his car for a few days. He said he wanted it filled up and ready for one o'clock on the next Saturday. An' then on Saturday he came in as you've heard, an' paid for it an' took it out.'

Inspector Ross's brain was in a whirl. This news was quite different from what he had expected. It did not seem to work in with Buchan's movements, and he began to wonder if for the second time he was on the wrong track, and if Buchan, like Swayne, was innocent. Bewildered, he demanded weakly, 'And you've no idea where he went to?'

It was a fatuous question, but to his own surprise it produced the information he was in need of.

'Not I,' the manager answered, uncompromisingly. 'How could I know when he didna tell me? But the car'—hesitatingly and as an afterthought he pronounced the priceless words—'the car was numbered for Newcastle.'

'What?' Inspector Ross roared, as the possible significance of this fact dawned on him. Newcastle! And it had arrived there early on the Wednesday morning and left on the Saturday at midday! And Swayne had left home on Tuesday night and returned on Saturday night. And Swayne for several other reasons he had suspected! Could it be? Was this the solution after all?

Then he remembered the alibi. Swayne had spent the Thursday night, the night before the crime, in London. It was utterly out of the question, therefore, that he could have reached Crianlarich in time. He *must* be innocent. And yet—this new information was very suspicious and intriguing. He did not know what to think.

But it was necessary that he should get full details from these men while he was there. He questioned them exhaustively, but the only further facts he gained were about the car. It appeared that it was a 1920 Darracq, with Dunlop tyres and various other distinguishing fitments. It had seen heavy service and had not been too well looked after—'a hack car, if ye ask me.' The owner's name was endorsed on the licence, but both men were blessed if they could remember it. It was Newcastle, anyhow, of that they were sure.

Ross left the shop in a chaotic state of mind. He was utterly mystified by the turn affairs had taken. At first thought the name Newcastle had suggested Swayne, but Swayne's alibi was watertight, and he felt he could not possibly be involved. The guilty man must therefore be someone else connected with Newcastle, someone of whom he had as yet heard nothing. If this were so it would indeed be a coincidence; an almost incredible coincidence . . .

At all events, Ross's course was clear. He must go back to Newcastle and trace the Darracq. The car once found, there should be little difficulty in getting hold of the man.

He wondered if he might dismiss Buchan from his mind. Did this news clear the school manager? He thought so, but he was not quite satisfied.

But a solution of this part of his problem was nearer than he had imagined. When he reached his hotel he found a message awaiting him. The manager of one of the other garages he had visited had telephoned, asking him to step round. The place was only a couple of hundred yards away, and Ross went at once.

'I have some news for you,' the manager greeted him. 'I've got the man who lifted that fare of yours. He came in half an hour ago. He's still here and you can see him for yourself.'

He gave some directions through his desk telephone, and a few seconds later an elderly, wizened man, in the leather coat and peaked cap of a taxi driver, was ushered into the room.

'Here, Andy,' the manager directed, 'tell this gentleman about that fare you lifted for Kirkintilloch last Saturday week.'

'Weel,' the man answered, fingering his cap nervously, 'I was passing slowly doon George Street lookin' for a fare, an' when I got to Queen Street Station this chap hailed me. I pulled over to the kerb an' he got in an' said, "St Andrew's College, Kirkintilloch." I drove there an' he got out an' I drove back here.'

Though this seemed conclusive, Ross cross-questioned the man narrowly, and finally was convinced beyond any possibility of doubt that Alexander Buchan had really made the journey he said.

'That taxi stunt didn't work out the way I expected,' he thought as he returned slowly to his hotel, 'but it did a darned sight better. Buchan's out of it, and the clue is Newcastle. So to Newcastle I must go.'

He left St Enoch's at 9.5 that evening, and by 3.00 next morning was between the sheets in his old room in the Hotel Metropole in Newcastle.

The next morning saw him repeating the tactics he had followed in Glasgow. From a directory he made a list of the public garages of the town, then, having arranged them in order of location, he started in on the search for the old Darracq.

He had luck sooner than in Glasgow. On his fourth call he struck oil. At a small place in a back street near the Central Station he came on what he wanted.

About 5.30 p.m. on Tuesday week, the manager stated, he had received a telephone call from someone calling himself 'Mr George Hopkins.' This gentleman said he wished to hire a reliable car for three or four days, which he would drive himself. As it was probably against the manager's practice to conduct such a deal, he proposed to deposit in cash with the manager the full price of the car, as a guarantee of its return in good condition. He would call for it that night about eleven o'clock, when it was to be ready and stocked with petrol for a 200-mile run. It would be returned about 7.30 or 8.00 p.m. on the following Saturday.

The man turned up at the hour named, and the deal was put through on the terms mentioned. He was fairly tall and very stout, with round cheeks, a long, dark moustache and glasses, and was dressed in a khaki waterproof and a dark brown cap. He had given the address of 18 The Crescent, Hopperton. On the Saturday evening shortly before eight he had returned the car, paid the bill, received back his deposit, and left.

'Hopperton's a new suburb on the south-west side of the city,' the manager concluded. 'I didn't know the man, but I'd know him if I saw him again. What's he wanted for, if it's a fair question?'

'Murder,' Ross answered shortly. 'It's a bad business.' Then with a change of manner, 'Well, sir, I'm very greatly obliged to you for your information. I'll let you know if anything comes of it.'

An examination of the directory at the restaurant to which Ross went for lunch showed that not only was there no George Hopkins living in the district of Hopperton, but that 'The Crescent' was also a figment of the unknown's fertile imagination.

Ross was greatly impressed by the hours at which the car

had been taken out and returned. Swayne had reached the Central Station on that Tuesday night at about 10.30 p.m., and the car had been called for by the stout stranger at eleven. On Saturday the stranger had returned the car about 8.00 p.m., and Swayne had been picked up at the Central Station about 8.30. 'Surely,' thought the perplexed Inspector, 'this is more than a coincidence!'

It was true that from the station to the garage was only a five minutes' walk. But if the stranger were made up, a few minutes would be required in which to assume or remove the disguise. Half an hour, Ross considered, was a reasonable time to allow for such a contingency.

Could Swayne after all be the guilty man? Were it not for the alibi Ross would have had no doubt, but the alibi staggered him. The alibi had seemed overwhelmingly complete, but now he began to wonder was it really as convincing as he had imagined. Was there no flaw, no trick? The hoax played on Buchan was ingenious, as was also the Ballachulish 'accident.' Could the man who had invented these not have worked out a fake alibi?

Ross racked his brains to think of some way by which he might test the point. And then the telephone message engaging the car occurred to him. That message was received at the garage at 5.30 p.m. on the Tuesday before the crime. Where was Sir Anthony at that hour?

He turned to the notes he had made of his conversation with the butler. Sir Anthony had gone out shortly before four and returned about 6.30 p.m. If he had telephoned, from where would it have been?

He would be anxious to keep the subject of his message secret, therefore would he not be more likely to ring up from a public call office where he could speak without being over-heard, than to use a neighbour's instrument? The idea seemed worth following up. It would, at least, be worth while finding out what, if any, call offices were near to Langholm Hall.

With the aid of his large-scale map and a telephone directory he soon obtained the requisite information. There were two. That in Norwick, the local village, was not more than half a mile from the estate; the other was at Hedley, a little over three miles away. With the exception of these, there was none within eight miles of Langholm Hall.

Ross looked at his watch. It was just half-past three, not too late to carry the investigation a step further that night.

He rang for a car, and ten minutes later he was whirling through the streets of Newcastle, bound for the little village of Norwick. The run was over the same road that he had already traversed on the day on which he had paid his visit to Sir Anthony, but on this occasion there was no bright sun to cheer the way. It was cold and grey, and rain threatened. Ross shivered as he drew his rug more tightly round him, and he was not sorry when the village came in sight.

'Put me down here and wait for me, will you, driver?' he ordered when they reached the outskirts.

He walked into the little town, and inquiring his way to the call office, entered. To his satisfaction he found that the instrument was not a penny-in-the-slot machine, so he had to make no excuse for calling the attendant. She proved to be a stout, motherly woman, quite ready to gossip to the Inspector as long as he cared to remain.

'I want to make a call,' he explained. 'Newcastle 357.'

While he was waiting for the answer he engaged her in conversation.

'By the way,' he said, 'I wonder could you give me a bit of information, or do your rules prohibit it? I have a bet on with Sir Anthony Swayne. Do you remember his telephoning from here about half-past five one afternoon about a fortnight ago?'

The woman shook her head.

'No,' she answered, 'Sir Anthony's not often in here. I'm sure it's a month or more since the last time I've seen him.'

'Ah, then I'm afraid you can't help me about my bet. I suppose he couldn't have come without your knowing? You have no assistant?'

'There's no one in the office but myself, sir. I'm quite sure he wasn't here.'

Ross saw that he had drawn blank, but it was in the nature of the man that he waited for his call, discoursing her the while, then finding that the hypothetical person for whom he asked was not in, he rang off.

He returned to his car and told the driver to go on to Hedley, the call office three miles from Langholm Hall. Here he pursued the same manoeuvres, but with a very different result. When he told the girl in charge about his bet and asked did she remember Sir Anthony Swayne telephoning from there at the time in question, she at once replied that she did. He had come in quickly, made his call, and gone off as soon as he could.

Ross grunted.

'H'm. Looks as if I have lost my bet. You couldn't tell me the day that was, I suppose?'

'Why yes, if it's important I could,' the girl answered. 'I should recognise the entry in my books.'

'Well you see, it's like this,' Ross explained. 'Sir Anthony, who's rather a friend of mine, was to arrange a car to bring another friend of mine, an architect, out to Langholm Hall about some building he wanted done. The car never turned up, and I bet Sir Anthony he had bungled the date. He said he came here and rang up the garage in Newcastle telling them to send the car on the following day, but when I pressed him he couldn't remember on what day he had done so. If it was last Wednesday week I've lost my bet, if it wasn't I've won. So you see, I'd like to know.'

The girl laughed as she drew a book from a receptacle beneath the counter and began turning over the pages. Presently her finger stopped at an item.

'You've won,' she said. 'It was at 5.37 on Tuesday.'

'By Jove! That's luck,' Ross cried heartily. 'And to clinch the matter absolutely, was it Newcastle he rang up?'

'Newcastle 1437,' she answered.

'That's right, that's the number!' Ross was like a schoolboy in his delight.

He took off his hat with a sweep, and left the office.

He could hardly control his impatience until they reached Newcastle and he was able to look up No. 1437 in a telephone directory. And then he could have shouted with triumph. It was the garage from which 'Mr George Hopkins' had hired his car!

It seemed then to Inspector Ross that Sir John Anthony Swayne, Bart., had driven to the Central Station in Newcastle on that Tuesday evening with the avowed intention of travelling by the night express to London. He had not done so. Instead, he had walked out of the station again, disguised himself, hired a car and driven to Glasgow. There on Wednesday morning he had stabled the car and disappeared, presumably after having posted the decoy letter to Crawley. He was next heard of at the Hotel Splendide in London, where he had arrived on that same Wednesday evening about 9.00. It was evident, therefore, that he had travelled up to town by the day service. A glance at a Bradshaw showed there was a train from St Enoch at 9.5 a.m. which reached St Pancras at 9.05 p.m. That would just work in.

There was then the difficulty of Swayne's stay in London. The evidence seemed to show that he was there on Wednesday night, Thursday and Thursday night. However, passing that over for the moment, Swayne had arrived at Crianlarich at 7.58 on the Friday evening, had gone to the lonely house, attempted to murder Crawley, and set the house on fire. Then taking Crawley's car, he had run it to Ballachulish and there staged the accident. Thence he had walked to Oban, travelled by rail to Glasgow, reclaimed the hired car, driven it back to Newcastle, removed his disguise, returned to the station, and left it again in his own car, ostensibly having just arrived from London.

Inspector Ross picked up the Bradshaw again and once more made a thorough investigation of the trains from London to the North. But he merely confirmed his previous conclusion. If Swayne was in London on Friday morning, he certainly was not in Crianlarich on Friday night.

He wondered if he could not have travelled in some other way than by train, a fast car from London, for example? But this he soon found was impossible. The distance was well over 400 miles, and running for eleven hours without a stop would have meant an average speed of nearly forty miles an hour—an utter impossibility over so long a stretch.

The thought of an aeroplane also occurred to him, only to be even more rapidly dismissed. There *wasn't* an aeroplane— that is, other than those known about by the police. The staff on the track of the tall, round-cheeked man would have seen to that.

The more Ross thought over the whole position, the more satisfied he became that he must return to London and once again go into the question of the alibi. If he could find a flaw in it, his case would be complete.

He telephoned to the station for a sleeping berth on the same train by which he had travelled before, the 10.30 p.m. from the Central, and that night travelled once more up to town.

CHAPTER XIX

LIGHT OUT OF DARKNESS

THOUGH Inspector Ross had been up half the previous night, he could not settle down in his berth in the sleeping-car. The problem of the alibi had gripped his mind, and as the train sped on through the darkness he turned and tossed in exasperation that he could not reconcile the apparently contradictory evidence. The testimony on each side was too strong. When he thought of what he had learned in Newcastle and Glasgow he felt convinced Swayne was guilty. When he remembered what he had heard and seen in London, he was equally assured of his innocence. In no way could he see how both sets of evidence could be true, and yet nowhere could he find the flaw.

Presently his thoughts switched over to another matter. From Mr and Miss Hope, as well as from Crawley, he had learned details of the earlier tragedy in South Africa, and by putting two and two together he had a pretty fair idea of what had taken place. Now, wearied of his immediate problem, he had begun in a desultory way to compare the Groote Park murder with this on which he was engaged.

He soon saw that there was considerable similarity between the two, and becoming interested, he began to follow out the points in detail. When he had finished he was amazed to find the method in each case was practically identical.

In each case the murder was committed by luring the victim to a prearranged and lonely spot, and there felling him with a sandbag. In each case the problem of getting rid of the body and diverting suspicion was met by staging a fatal accident at some distance from the scene of the crime. A further precaution was taken. Lest this accident should fail of its purpose, a scape-goat had been provided. Suspicion was thrown on an innocent man, and by the same trick. A forged letter took the scapegoat, at the time of the murder, to some place where it was unlikely he would be seen, and the circumstances of the journey were arranged to prevent the establishment of an alibi. Lastly, the two forged letters were written by persons who were aware of the scapegoat's most private affairs.

Inspector Ross was very much impressed. Surely so strange a series of parallels could hardly be a coincidence. There must be more in it than that.

But one explanation seemed possible, and the more Ross thought over it, the more convinced he became that it was the right one. The two murders were the work of one man, or, at least, both were inspired by the same brain. He did not believe that different people could hit on two such similar plots.

But if his two theories were correct, first, that Swayne was the man he wanted, and second, that the same man was guilty of each crime, it followed that Swayne must have committed the Groote Park murder. Was this possible?

He remembered that Mr Hope had told him that Vandam had first suspected Swayne. But Swayne had cleared himself by an alibi—still another parallel, Ross noted, between the two cases. If now it could be shown that Swayne's hotel alibi was faked, it would become practically certain that the Middeldorp alibi was false also.

He was thrilled by the thought. In this case he would not merely bring his own case to a triumphant conclusion; he would solve the South African one as well. He would beat Vandam on his own ground!

Next day, therefore, he entered the Hotel Splendide with the fixed determination to apply such searching tests to the hotel alibi that it would infallibly break down unless it was genuine. He felt that if he were to be robbed of all that potential glory, it would not be for want of doing his best.

He began with Miss Bushe at the office. Once again he heard her story and examined the documents she had to show. He questioned her closely, but without being able in the slightest degree to shake her evidence.

He then interviewed the hall porters and lift boys. Several of these had seen Sir Anthony, but their testimony did not help him much, as none of them were certain as to dates.

The chambermaid, whom he next saw, repeated her story about seeing Swayne on the Thursday night, and on the Friday morning finding the door of room No. 130 first locked, then open. She also was clear as to her facts, but could add nothing to her former statement.

Inspector Ross was growing more and more despondent. It looked as if he had been wrong, and that the alibi was sound enough. He did not see what more he could do. The testimony in Swayne's favour was growing very near to proof.

Almost despairing, he turned towards the coffee-room to re-examine Giuseppe, the waiter who had brought Swayne his bill. As he called him aside he noticed, or thought he noticed, a sudden flash in the man's eyes, and Ross, who was an adept in such matters, believed it was due to apprehension. Catching at the straw, he wondered if the waiter could possibly know anything, and he determined to put up a bluff.

'Well, Giuseppe,' he said in a low, but harsh voice, 'it's about that man I spoke to you of before. He's wanted for murder, so no information about him can be safely withheld. You understand?' He frowned menacingly into the man's face.

Giuseppe answered, 'Certainly, sair,' but Ross sensed a feeling of unease which left him dissatisfied with the reply.

'Now this man,' he went on, 'Do you still stick to it that he breakfasted here on that Friday morning?'

'He was here two days, sair. I think it was Friday I get him the bill.'

'Did he talk to you at all?'

'A leetle. He say he was ill and that he sleep late.'

'How late? What time did he breakfast?'

'About ten, sair, I think, or more early. I do not remember.'

'What time is breakfast usually served?'

'From seven to ten, sair.'

'If it is after ten there is an extra charge?'

'Yes, sair.'

Ross swung round on him.

'Then you must know!' he almost shouted. 'You got the man's bill. There was no extra charge for a late breakfast on it. Do you mean to tell me he had breakfast late and you said nothing about it?'

Giuseppe had gone white. There was now no doubt that he was seriously frightened. For a moment he did not reply, then he stammered, 'I do not remember, sair.'

Ross was becoming increasingly suspicious. There was nothing in the carelessness of an incorrect breakfast charge to account for such uneasiness. Suddenly it occurred to him that the waiter would be unable to make such a mistake. If he went late to the office with the account, the clerk would make inquiries about the breakfast and put in the extra charge.

That no such charge appeared seemed to show that the meal had been taken before ten o'clock. But the chambermaid had stated that at that hour Swayne was still in his room! There was a screw loose here, and from this Giuseppe's manner Ross believed he knew of it. But he felt that if there was anything to be learned, his only chance was to continue his bluff. He therefore took a bold line.

'Come with me to the office,' he said grimly. 'I must know more of this.'

He led the way in an ominous silence which had the effect of still further intimidating his victim.

'Now,' he said, when they had been accommodated with a private room, 'let me hear it all. Remember that anyone who keeps back information in a murder case is liable to be arrested as an accessory. I'm going to have the truth from you, and you may either tell it to me here or you may come and tell it to me at Bow Street, whichever you like.'

The man looked around him with frightened eyes.

'Sair,' he stammered, 'I not think any harm. He ask me to oblige him. I think it all right to do what he say.'

Ross, surprised and delighted, saw he was going to get something at last.

'Let me warn you your only chance is to make a clean breast of it. If you tell me the truth I'll do what I can to help you.'

The Inspector's manner was menacing, and the Italian broke down before it.

'Sair,' he cried earnestly, 'I will tell you all. But you will not get me into trouble? You will not, sair?'

'Not if you're quite straight with me, but if you're not—well, you may look out for yourself.'

'Thank you, sair. I will tell. On Thursday morning this gentleman, this Sir Swayne, he come in here for breakfast. I attend him. When we were alone, he call me over. He ask me in soft voice if I would like to earn five pounds. I say yes. He say that he is going to be married, and that the law makes him to live so many days in London before he can marry—I not understand. You, sair, may understand.'

'Yes, yes,' Ross answered impatiently. 'If he wanted to be married here he would have to reside in the parish for fourteen days previously.'

'Yes, sair, that was what he said. He said that that Thursday night would finish his fourteen days, but that he had to go over to Paris that day. To satisfy the law he must make appear he do not leave the hotel that night. He say it is only a form, not really a thing that matter. He say he give me five pounds to help him arrange a plan.'

The waiter paused, looking anxiously at Ross. The latter, striving to conceal his satisfaction, answered:

'Well? What then?'

'He tell me, sair, that he will go to Paris that night, but he will not give up his room, No. 130. He want me on the next morning, Friday morning, to go to the office and ask for the bill for No. 130, and to say there was breakfast to be added for that morning. That would be for two nights and two breakfasts and we think it will be about two pounds. He say he had already paid five, so there will be three of change, which he tell me to keep. He give me two other pounds to make the five.'

'And you got the bill?'

'Yes, sair, the bill and the money, but there was more than that to do. A very troublesome business, sair. On the Thursday night before he leave he give me the key of his room, number 130, and after I get the bill on the next morning I must go up and unlock the door and leave the key inside. It was hard to do it, sair, without being seen by the maids.'

'But you did it?'

'Sair, I did it. I admit it, but I thought it was as he said, no harm.'

Ross shrugged his shoulders.

'It's not so serious after all,' he said. 'If I find you've told me the whole truth, I'll forget it. But be very thankful you had me to deal with. Other officers mightn't have let you off so easily. Now don't repeat what you've told me to anyone. That'll do.'

Inspector Ross could hardly refrain from chuckling aloud in his delight at his discoveries. He now saw clearly enough what Swayne had done. He had undoubtedly left on Thursday night for Scotland, and to make an alibi for himself in London, he had invented this tale about his wedding and bribed this not very high type waiter to act as his dupe. The scheme itself was a good one, presenting a convincing alibi when you didn't understand how it was worked, and yet being perfectly simple when you did. Ross went over the steps again to make them clear in his own mind.

Swayne, travelling up by the day express from Glasgow, had reached London on the Wednesday evening and gone to the Splendide. There he had registered, and had taken care to impress his personality on the clerk by a little conversation. Having omitted to bring luggage, he had made a deposit of five pounds, so that the change would become a guarantee that the waiter would carry out his part of the fraud. Swayne had remained in London on that Wednesday night and the next day, Thursday. On Thursday evening he had established his alibi, by calling the attention both of the clerk and the chambermaid to himself by a conversation about a chill. That chill was valuable in another direction. He utilised it to ensure that his bedroom would not be entered in the morning. Why? *Because he was not there.* In his imagination, Ross saw him softly opening the door and peering out until he found the corridors deserted, saw him avoiding the lift and using a side door, then hurrying to the station and taking one of the night trains to the north. And in the morning Ross imagined Giuseppe completing the alibi by his visit to the office for the bill, and his unlocking of the bedroom door.

Well satisfied with his day's work, Inspector Ross got on board the evening express from King's Cross. An idea for the finishing up of the case had occurred to him, and before going to sleep he set himself to think out the details of his plan. The more he did so the more pleased he became with it, and he looked forward eagerly to the interview he hoped to have next morning with his Chief.

On reaching Edinburgh, he drove to headquarters, and soon had told his story. The Chief was much impressed by the report. He congratulated his subordinate on his achievements in a way which made that industrious delver after truth glow with satisfaction.

'You've brought credit on the Department, Ross,' he told him. 'This will be a big case, and, thanks to you, the police will come out of it well. You now would like a warrant for this Swayne's arrest, I suppose?'

'I wanted to consult you about that, sir,' Ross answered. 'I had an idea that we might get even more evidence against Swayne. I think there's a way we might make him confess.'

The Chief looked his question.

'You see, sir, he doesn't know his little game didn't come off. He thinks Crawley is dead—burned in that house. We kept his rescue quiet, and we also kept our suspicions about the Ballachulish affair quiet. Swayne thinks everyone is satisfied Crawley was drowned there. So what would you think if we were to get him here under some pretext, and then suddenly confront him with Crawley. I wouldn't mind betting he gives himself away.'

'Not a bad idea, Ross; not at all a bad idea. It would certainly be a shock if the man he believed he murdered two or three weeks before suddenly walked into the room. I agree with you. I don't believe there's a man in the entire world could avoid convicting himself under such circumstances. Arrange it, by all means.'

The Chief, who took a keen delight in a dramatic situation, smiled in anticipation.

'When will this fellow Crawley be able to come up?' he asked.

'I should think as soon as we can get Swayne here,' Ross answered. 'I have had a letter saying he is able to be up, and wanting to be relieved from remaining in hiding.'

'Good, then; the sooner you fix it up the better. Is there anything else?'

'There is another thing, sir.' Ross spoke somewhat deprecatingly. 'It's hardly in a way my business, but I thought I should like to mention it to you. It's about that murder in South Africa two and a half years ago that Crawley was tried for. Would you have time to listen?'

'Certainly. Go ahead, Ross, and let me know what's troubling you. Light your pipe if you care to.' The Chief drew his own from his pocket.

'Thank you, sir, I will. I was comparing the two cases in my mind, that South African murder and this one that we're on here, and it struck me they were mighty like each other.'

The Chief glanced up with sudden interest in his eyes.

'I noticed the same thing,' he said. 'Method practically identical in each case. Yes?'

'Yes, sir. Not only was the murder done in the same way, by sandbagging, but there was a made-up accident each time, and a scapegoat arranged in case suspicion arose. It seemed to me, sir, that all that couldn't just happen by chance. If it wasn't the same man did both of them, it was the same man thought them out. What would you think of that, sir?'

'Seems sound enough.' The Chief drew slowly at his pipe. 'Yes, I think you're probably right. Ah, yes, I see what you mean. You think Swayne did the South African one too?'

'Well, sir, wouldn't it seem likely?'

'It would seem darned likely; likely enough to bet on anyway. By Jove! yes.' He sat up with a look as nearly approaching excitement as a Chief of Police in the presence of his subordinate could exhibit. 'Very good, indeed, Ross. I believe that's the solution of the whole thing. It would turn the South African men a bit green if we pulled their case off here. But what about Swayne's alibi?'

'That's just it, sir. That applied in this case also. But a man that could work out that hotel stunt would have certainly fixed up a good alibi in South Africa.'

The Chief nodded.

'Pity those papers haven't arrived yet from Middeldorp. We've only what Crawley and those Hopes told you to go on, and there may be more that they don't know.'

'There may, but I don't fancy there's much. That Griffenhagen, the solicitor that defended Crawley, seems to have been pretty well in with both sides. He told Crawley after the first trial that Vandam, that was the Inspector in charge of the case, had told him confidentially what he had done about it. He told him about Swayne's alibi anyway.'

'I remember it, and I'm free to confess that I can't at the moment recall anything more conclusive in the way of a defence. Can you?'

'No, sir, I quite admit that. But then, you see, these fellows didn't know what we know. If I hadn't been sure in my own mind that Swayne was guilty, I would have been taken in over the hotel business. They hadn't any reason to believe Swayne guilty, so they took the alibi at its face value. It's my belief that alibi's cooked.'

'See how?'

'No, sir, I do not. But I believe it all the same.'

Silence reigned in the little office for several minutes, as both men sat lost in thought over their problem. Ross's face wore an expression of stern determination, while the Chief's foot tapped steadily on the floor, a trick he had when thinking deeply. From the pipe of each a thin trail of smoke ascended, gyrating in eddies as it slowly dissipated.

Presently the Chief moved.

'Well,' he said, 'think it over. Meantime, better arrange for that interview.

When Inspector Ross, back in his own office, began to consider how he was to lure Sir Anthony Swayne to police headquarters, he found he was up against a more difficult proposition than he had anticipated. The baronet could, of course, be arrested and brought there by force, but Ross felt that the shock of suddenly seeing Crawley alive and in the flesh would be reduced, to some extent at least, if Swayne knew he was suspected. The more unexpected the meeting, the more probability of a complete give away. He would prefer, therefore, that Swayne should call of his own accord, expecting to be received on some quite different business.

For more than an hour he thought over the problem, and then at last he thought he saw a way of making him not only willing, but anxious, to come.

Getting through to Newcastle on the telephone, he called

up Swayne. The baronet was at home, and in a few minutes was at the instrument.

'This,' said Ross, speaking in an assumed tone, 'is police headquarters in Edinburgh; Inspector Ross speaking. We understand from the solicitors of the late Mr Stewart Crawley, the gentleman who recently took the Hill Farm, not far from your residence, that you and he were acquainted with one another in South Africa. May I ask if that is so?'

'That is so,' came Swayne's voice.

'Then, sir, I am sorry to trouble you, but we want your help. A body has just been washed ashore in Loch Linnhe, and we think it may be that of the late Mr Crawley. Unfortunately, the deceased's man and housekeeper are on leave pending the settling up of the estate, and we can find no one but yourself to identify the remains. We must therefore ask you to attend the inquest, which will be held on the day after tomorrow at Ballachulish.'

'I'll certainly go, Inspector. At what hour will it be held?'

'It's not settled yet, Sir Anthony, but I'll phone you of it later. But it may not be necessary for you to go so far. We have had the remains photographed, and the prints will be with us in the morning. I would suggest that you call with us tomorrow and see the prints. If you can say definitely that the body is not that of Mr Crawley, that will end the matter so far as you are concerned. If you cannot say so, I'm afraid you will have to go on to Ballachulish.'

Inspector Ross was pleased with his little stratagem, for he felt sure Swayne would jump at the chance of finally proving Crawley had been drowned. And he was justified. Swayne replied that he would be at headquarters at 2.00 o'clock on the following afternoon.

Ross then made a second call, this time to Callander, and soon he had arranged that Stewart Crawley should turn up at headquarters at 1.00 p.m. next day.

To his bitter regret, he decided it would not be possible to be present himself at the interview. He had already made Sir Anthony's acquaintance as Mr Cairns, of the firm of Cairns & McFarlane, solicitors, and to appear in his rightful capacity would be to give away his hoped-for coup. It was, therefore, the Chief himself who suavely greeted Swayne when the latter was shown into his room.

'Ah, Sir Anthony,' he said, rising and bowing, 'we are extremely sorry to have put you to this inconvenience. Won't you sit down?'

The room had been prepared for the meeting. Swayne's chair was placed in front of the Chief's desk and with its back to the door. At each side of the visitor was a sergeant, one writing notes at a desk, the other laboriously clicking at a typewriter. Just beside Swayne was an Inspector whom the Chief introduced.

'This is Inspector McDougal. He was at Fort William when the accident took place, and I wired him to go on to Ballachulish to see what had happened, as I could not understand the report of the local men. That is all, I think. Now we may get to business.'

At this moment there was a knock at the door.

'Come in,' called the Chief, then swiftly turning to Swayne added, 'A friend of yours, surely, Sir Anthony?'

Swayne, suddenly realising a hostile change in the atmosphere of the room, swung round, to see Stewart Crawley, pale and cadaverous, framed in the opening of the door.

For a moment there was a breathless silence in the room. Swayne's jaw dropped, his face went greenish white, and his eyes started from their sockets, while an expression of deadly horror and fear formed itself on his features. The gaze of the other four occupants of the room was fixed on his face as he stood unable to move, paralysed by the shock.

Presently the Chief's eyes strayed to Crawley's face and became riveted there. If Swayne's features expressed surprise, Crawley's betokened overwhelming, incredulous amazement.

He stared at Swayne even more fixedly than Swayne stared at him. Each seemed to regard the other as a visitor from the tomb.

Suddenly Crawley gave a cry.

'Why,' he gasped, 'it's—'

With a snarl of rage like that of a savage dog, Swayne interrupted him. Suddenly recovering the power of movement, he snatched a small automatic pistol from his pocket, fired pointblank at Crawley, and then turned the weapon upon himself. The four officers with one accord sprang on him. There was a short, sharp struggle and he stood dishevelled, panting, disarmed, handcuffed.

They turned to Crawley, who, pale and trembling, had collapsed into a chair, and was holding up in a dazed way a hand from which the blood slowly trickled.

'Doctor,' the Chief growled. Then to Crawley, 'It's well, Mr Crawley, it's only your arm. You're nothing the worse otherwise, I hope?'

Crawley took no notice of him. Pointing his uninjured hand at the scowling prisoner, he murmured, 'It's not Swayne, it's Albert Smith!' and rolled off the chair in a faint.

CHAPTER XX

THE news that the Sir John Anthony Swayne who had reigned at Langholm Hall for the past two and a half years was not Sir John Anthony Swayne at all, but a usurper who had carried through one of the most audacious cases of personation known in criminal history, and that the real Sir Anthony was lying in a South African cemetery, caused a sensation throughout Great Britain, and, indeed, the whole civilised world, which will be remembered by all who read these words. To the newspapers it proved a veritable godsend, to the public a theme for animated discussion during more than the allotted nine days, to Stewart Crawley and Marion Hope it foreshadowed the fulfilment of their hopes, and to the lawyers it furnished a knotty problem as to the Swayne succession.

But to the police it meant more than any of these things. To them it proved a key which resolved that maze of mysteries through which they had been floundering. When tested with this key, the strange doings in Middeldorp became clear as day. Supplied with it, Inspector Vandam took up once more his old case, and in a short time was able to lay before his superiors a report covering the whole of Albert Smith's activities in the city. Before the trial other facts came out which enabled the details of the whole series of crimes to be established. Summarised, these details are given below.

The trouble may be said to have begun something like forty years earlier, when Reginald Seagrave Swayne, the father of John Anthony, was smitten with the charms of Lucy Marks, a pretty parlourmaid at one of the houses in the neighbourhood of Langholm Hall. The infatuation soon passed—too soon for the poor girl, for when her baby was born, Reginald was seeing the world in the bars and teahouses of the East. He had, however, left her some money, and she struggled on without acquainting old Sir Aylmer of the truth. When Reginald returned home she had left the district, and he never again heard either of her or of his son.

In due course he married the actress and, being disinherited by his father, went to South Africa. John Anthony's birth and history have already been recounted, but it was not until the antecedents of Smith were gone into that it was discovered that he was not named Albert Smith at all, but was none other than the son of Reginald and Lucy Marks. Lucy, it appeared, had not lost sight of her former lover, and had brought up the boy with a bitter hatred of his father and of the whole house of Swayne, implanting in his mind the idea that by all the laws of justice and right he should be the inheritor of his grandfather's wealth. On her death, he followed Anthony to Middeldorp, and applied for a position in the Hope Bros. firm.

After some months he disclosed his identity to Anthony, at first making a pretence of good-fellowship. Anthony, though horrified at the revelation, received him as a friend and showed him many kindnesses. But soon Smith—as we may continue to call him—began to show his real character, and used Anthony Swayne's fear of publicity as a lever with which to subject him to all kinds of petty tyrannies.

When Smith heard that Swayne had been sent for by his grandfather, the jealousy which he had always felt burst all bounds, and he swore to himself that he, and not his half-brother, should be the one to go. The idea of murder and personation at once occurred to him, and he set himself to work out the details, until he flattered himself he had constructed a plot which must infallibly deceive the cleverest detective that could be put on to it.

First he devised a scheme to lure Swayne to the potting shed. This he himself afterwards admitted, took the form of a letter purporting to come from Miss Hope asking Swayne to meet her there at 9.00 p.m. to undertake a certain private commission for her in England. Smith would not say what that was supposed to be, but judging from the remainder of his plans, it would be plausible enough to bring Swayne without raising his suspicions.

Meanwhile Smith, having dressed himself in a certain suit of clothes, packed an almost identical suit in his suitcase, and left his rooms at 8.10 p.m., taking the case with him. To account for its presence, he put in sleeping things and told his landlady that he was going to the Pendlebury suburb, and might stay the night. He carried the suitcase to the Scala Cinema. There he bought two tickets, and his conversation with the porter about the alleged friend was devised to account for this purchase. He entered the building at 8.30, passed through it, and left by one of the exits leading directly on to the street. Still carrying the suitcase, he reached the potting shed, shut the door, and by the light of an electric torch swept it and laid the newspapers. Then, armed with his sandbag, he waited.

Swayne came up to meet Miss Hope at 9.00 p.m., and Smith, crouching in the shadows, crept up behind him and knocked him senseless. He dragged the inanimate form into the shed, closed the door, turned on his light, and stripped the body. He re-dressed it in his own clothes which he had brought in the suitcase, transferred to the pockets the articles from those in the suit he was wearing, and packed Swayne's clothes in the suitcase. With difficulty he carried the body down on to the railway, and placed it where it would be struck by the next train. But before leaving it he had a gruesome task to perform. Lest it might be found before being run over, those tell-tale features must be removed. Hence the hammer, and hence the choice of the tunnel, for to destroy the features light was necessary. The hideous deed done, he returned to the shed, burned the papers, and scattered the swept-up earth. And there he made his mistake. Upset by the ghastly business on which he had been engaged, he had overlooked the notebook. In the hands of a more skilful man than Inspector Vandam, that note-book would have hanged him. If Smith had made a proper search in the shed, it is unlikely that suspicion would ever have been aroused.

He left the shed and crossed the railway to the town, hiding the hammer and the sandbag under a stone which he thought would never again be raised. Reaching the cinema, he watched until the porter had disappeared on some errand, and slipped in on the second ticket which he had bought. Once more passing through the auditorium, he left by the bar exit. In the bar he established his alibi by his conversation with the barmaid, calling her attention specially to the time. Then leaving, he went to a public lavatory and changed into Swayne's clothes. He left the suitcase with his own garments in a dark entry and hurried to Swayne's hotel, fixing the time of his arrival by a discussion with the waiter.

In order to divert suspicion, should such be aroused, he included in his plans three separate and distinct safeguards, anyone of which, he believed, would alone be sufficient to clear him. The first was the episode of the diamonds. The whole of this involved story proved to be an invention, and Smith had shown his evil skill by duping not only Moses Goldstein, but Jane Louden as well. There had never been any diamonds nor any betting, nor had Smith ever had the slightest intention of marrying the girl. The single stone he had used to carry out the fraud he had hired for two nights from a shady down-town dealer, at a cost of twenty pounds, giving as security a receipt which would have rendered him liable to a prosecution for theft had the stone disappeared. He believed this story of the diamonds would account for his supposed murder, and also that Goldstein might be accused of the crime.

But should this safeguard fail, he devised a second, this time intended to involve Crawley. He deliberately provoked a quarrel on the night of Mr Hope's dinner, forged the note fixing the appointment in the potting shed, and by sending Crawley the letter about the supposed intrigue between himself and Marion, prevented the former from establishing an alibi at the time of the murder.

Finally, lest any suspicion as to his real identity might arise, he worked out a third scheme. Before leaving Middeldorp he bought a camera, and on the excuse of his half-brother's approaching departure, he privately took and developed some photographs of him. On reaching England, he commissioned a professional photographer in London to touch the negatives up and make him a few unmounted prints. Later he had a portrait of himself done by Wheeler & Cox of Newcastle. To remove one of these from its mount, and substitute that of Swayne was a simple matter, and the excuse of sending some useless information to the police enabled him to get his faked print into official hands in Middeldorp.

The publicity resulting from the arrest of Smith brought all these matters automatically to light. The dealer from whom he had hired the diamond came forward with his story, thus giving Vandam a sufficient hint of the truth to enable him to reconstruct what had been done. The return of the faked print to Messrs. Wheeler & Cox of Newcastle showed the fraud that had been carried out, and judicious advertisements brought to light the London firm which had unconsciously assisted in it.

When, two years later, Smith heard that someone named Crawley had taken the Hill Farm, he had at once found out that it was his old acquaintance, and seeing discovery must ensue, he had worked out a plan to murder him also. Sandy Buchan he was watching for the same reason, and his plan was to attempt to destroy both his enemies at the same time.

A fortnight after the trial, Albert Smith paid the supreme penalty for his crimes. Such was the just ending of one of the most cold-blooded monsters of the century.

Just one last view. At the rail of a great liner stand, arm in arm, Mr and Mrs Stewart Crawley, bound from Tilbury to Middeldorp, to take over from Mr John Hope the ownership of the great provision store in Mees Street.

May happiness and prosperity go with them!

THE END

THE DETECTIVE STORY CLUB

FOR DETECTIVE CONNOISSEURS

recommends

"The Man with the Gun."

Philip MacDonald

Author of Rynox, etc.

MURDER GONE MAD

MR. MacDonald, who has shown himself in *The Noose* and *The Rasp* to be a master of the crime novel of pure detection, has here told a story of a motiveless crime, or at least a crime prompted only by blood lust. The sure, clear thinking of the individual detective is useless and only wide, cleverly organised investigation can hope to succeed.

A long knife with a brilliant but perverted brain directing it is terrorising Holmdale; innocent people are being done to death under the very eyes of the law. Inspector Pyke of Scotland Yard, whom MacDonald readers will remember in previous cases, is put on the track of the butcher. He has nothing to go on but the evidence of the bodies themselves and the butcher's own bravado. After every murder a businesslike letter arrives announcing that another "removal has been carried out." But Pyke "gets there" with a certainty the very slowness of which will give the reader many breathless moments. In the novelty of its treatment, the humour of its dialogue, and the truth of its characterisation, *Murder Gone Mad* is equal to the best Mr. MacDonald has written.

LOOK FOR THE MAN WITH THE GUN

THE DETECTIVE STORY CLUB

FOR DETECTIVE CONNOISSEURS

recommends

"The Man with the Gun."

The Murder of Roger Ackroyd
By AGATHA CHRISTIE

THE MURDER OF ROGER ACKROYD is one of Mrs. Christie's most brilliant detective novels. As a play, under the title of *Alibi*, it enjoyed a long and successful run with Charles Laughton as the popular detective, Hercule Poirot. The novel has now been filmed, and its clever plot, skilful characterisation, and sparkling dialogue will make every one who sees the film want to read the book. M. Poirot, the hero of many brilliant pieces of detective deduction, comes out of his temporary retirement like a giant refreshed, to undertake the investigation of a peculiarly brutal and mysterious murder. Geniuses like Sherlock Holmes often find a use for faithful mediocrities like Dr. Watson, and by a coincidence it is the local doctor who follows Poirot round and himself tells the story. Furthermore, what seldom happens in these cases, he is instrumental in giving Poirot one of the most valuable clues to the mystery.

LOOK FOR THE MAN WITH THE GUN

THE DETECTIVE STORY CLUB

FOR DETECTIVE CONNOISSEURS

recommends

"The Man with the Gun."

THE PERFECT CRIME

THE FILM STORY OF

ISRAEL ZANGWILL'S famous detective thriller, THE BIG BOW MYSTERY

A MAN is murdered for no apparent reason. He has no enemies, and there seemed to be no motive for any one murdering him. No clues remained, and the instrument with which the murder was committed could not be traced. The door of the room in which the body was discovered was locked and bolted on the inside, both windows were latched, and there was no trace of any intruder. The greatest detectives in the land were puzzled. Here indeed was the perfect crime, the work of a master mind. Can you solve the problem which baffled Scotland Yard for so long, until at last the missing link in the chain of evidence was revealed?

LOOK OUT
FOR FURTHER SELECTIONS FROM THE DETECTIVE STORY CLUB—READY SHORTLY

LOOK FOR THE MAN WITH THE GUN